PRAISE FROM LAW ENFORCEMENT
on *Eleven* (Brandon Fisher FBI series)

"I spent thirty-eight years with a major police department in Missouri, fifteen of which were in the homicide section. I also had numerous dealings with the FBI throughout my career, mostly bank robbery, interstate shipment thefts, and a few kidnappings. *Eleven* kept my interest piqued throughout… Loved it."
–Richard Bartram, Sergeant (retired), St. Louis Metropolitan Police Department, St. Louis, MO

"I am a forty-year veteran of police work. All local, no Fed. *Eleven* was a great read. All the descriptors and nomenclature were spot on."
–Joe Danna, Police Officer, Katy Independent School District Police Department, Katy, TX

"Very good! I worked as a police officer for eleven years and with the Federal Bureau of Prisons for twenty-two. I have also dealt with the FBI."
–Richard Smith, Facilities Development Manager (retired), Federal Bureau of Prisons, Central Office, Washington, DC

continued...

"A great police procedural! ... Full of twists and turns. The characters are well-developed and a mix of interesting personalities. ... Holds your interest to the end!"
–**Mark Davis, FBI Special Agent (retired),** Washington, DC

ALSO BY CAROLYN ARNOLD

Brandon Fisher FBI Series
Eleven
Silent Graves
The Defenseless
Blue Baby
Violated

Detective Madison Knight Series
Ties That Bind
Justified
Sacrifice
Found Innocent
Just Cause
Deadly Impulse
In the Line of Duty
Power Struggle
Life Sentence

McKinley Mysteries
The Day Job is Murder
Vacation is Murder
Money is Murder
Politics is Murder
Family is Murder
Shopping is Murder
Christmas is Murder
Valentine's Day is Murder
Coffee is Murder
Skiing is Murder
Halloween is Murder

Matthew Connor Adventure Series
City of Gold

Assassination of a Dignitary

CAROLYN ARNOLD

REMNANTS

HIBBERT&STILES
PUBLISHING INC.

Hibbert & Stiles Publishing Inc.
www.hspubinc.com

Publisher's Cataloging-In-Publication Data
(Prepared by The Donohue Group, Inc.)

Names: Arnold, Carolyn.
Title: Remnants / Carolyn Arnold.
Description: 2017 Hibbert & Stiles Publishing Inc.
    trade edition. | [London, Ontario] : Hibbert & Stiles
    Publishing Inc., [2017] | Series: Brandon Fisher FBI
    series ; book 6
Identifiers: ISBN 978-1-988353-62-3 (paperback 4.25x7)
Subjects: LCSH: Criminal profilers--Georgia--Fiction.
    | United States. Federal Bureau of Investigation-
    -Fiction. | Serial murders--Georgia--Fiction. |
    Dismemberment--Fiction. | LCGFT: Detective and
    mystery fiction. | Psychological fiction.
Classification: LCC PS3601.R66 R46 2017b | DDC
    813/.6--dc23

REMNANTS

PROLOGUE

The time had come to select his next victim. He had to choose carefully and perfectly—he wouldn't get a second chance. The mall was teeming with life, and that made for a lot of eyeballs, a lot of potential witnesses. But he supposed it also helped him be more inconspicuous. People were hustling through the shopping center, interested solely in their own agendas. They wouldn't be paying him—or what he was doing—much attention.

He was standing at the edge of the food court next to the hallway leading to the restrooms eating a gyro. The lidded and oversized garbage bin on wheels that was behind him would ensure that anyone who did notice him would just think he was a mall janitor on his lunch break.

The pitchy voice of a girl about eight hit his ears. "Daddy, I want ice cream."

Trailing not far behind her were a man and woman holding hands. The woman was fit and blond, but his attention was on the man beside her. He was in his twenties, easily six feet tall with a solid, athletic build. He'd be strong and put up a fight. Yes, this was the one. And talk about ideal placement—he was across from the Dairy Queen.

He wiped his palms on his coveralls and took a few deep breaths. What he was about to do wasn't because of who he was, but rather, because he had to do it.

And he had to hurry. The family was coming toward him.

"It's almost lunchtime," the woman said, letting go of the man's hand.

"Daaaaaaddyyyyy." A whiny petition.

The man looked to the woman with a smile that showcased his white teeth. "We could have ice cream for lunch?"

The little girl began to bounce. "Yeah!"

"Really, Eric?" The woman wasn't as impressed as the girl, but under the man's gaze she caved and smiled. "All right, but just today..."

"Thank you, Mommy!" The girl wrapped her arms around the woman's legs but quickly let go, prancing ahead of her parents and toward the DQ counter.

"Brianna, we wash our hands first." The woman glanced at him as she walked by and offered a reserved smile. Had she detected his interest in them?

Breathe. She thinks you work here, remember?
Smile back.
Remain calm.

Look away and act uninterested.

"Oooh," the girl moaned but returned to her mother anyway.

"We'll just be a minute," the woman said.

"Hey, doesn't Daddy have to wash his hands?" the girl asked.

Sometimes things just work out...

The woman smiled at the man. "Eric?"

"Yes, he does," he playfully answered in the third person.

Mother and daughter headed to the restroom, the man not far behind.

It was time to get to work.

He took the last bite of his sandwich, crumpled the wrapper, and tossed it into the bin. He casually moved behind it and pushed it down the hall into the men's room.

He put up a sign that said it was closed for cleaning and entered, positioning himself next to the door. From there, he could see his target at one of the urinals and another man washing his hands at the sink. Otherwise, it was quiet.

Just as if it was meant to be...

The stranger left the restroom without a passing glance. This left him alone with his target.

He twisted the lock on the door and then moved behind the man, who paid him no mind. He took the needle out of his pocket and plunged it into the man's neck.

The man snapped a hand over where he'd been poked. "Hey!"

It would take a few seconds for the drug to fully kick in. He just had to stay out of the man's way and block the exit in the meantime.

"What did you…" The man was away from the urinal now, coming toward him on unsteady legs. Both his hands went to his forehead and then it was lights-out. He collapsed on the floor.

He hurried to the bin, wheeled it over to the man's body, and lifted him just enough to dump him inside. Once the man was in there, he lowered the lid, unlocked the restroom, collected his sign, and left.

His heart was thumping in his ears as he wheeled the bin out a back service door. Some people were milling around, but they didn't seem curious about him. He went to his van and opened the back door. He put the ramp in place and simply wheeled the bin inside.

When he was finished, he closed the doors and headed for the driver's seat. He wanted to hit the gas and tear out of the lot. The adrenaline surging through his system was screaming, *You got away with it again*, but he didn't like to get too cocky.

Still, he did take some pride in the fact that he'd gotten what he'd come for—and it had been so, so easy.

CHAPTER

1

VALENTINE'S DAY WOULD HAVE TO wait until next year, and I couldn't say I was disappointed—or surprised. Working as an agent in the FBI's Behavioral Analysis Unit makes planning anything impossible. This time, being swept out of town for an investigation was saving me from a day that was otherwise full of expectations and pressures. And even though my relationship with Becky was casual, it had been going on for several months now and she would be expecting a romantic evening.

But all that was hundreds of miles behind me now...

When I stepped off the government jet, the warm Savannah air welcomed me and made me think of my childhood in Sarasota, Florida. No cold winters there, either, unlike Virginia, where it could dip below zero this time of year, occasionally bringing that white stuff along with it.

My boss, Supervisory Special Agent Jack Harper, walked in front of me. This was his first time heading into the field after an unsub had almost killed him this past summer. He'd barely scraped by, but he was far too stubborn of a bastard to die. Having come so close to death, though, he had to be looking at life differently. I knew when I had just *thought* I was going to die during a previous investigation, it had taken me a long time to shake it.

He had more gray hairs than I'd remembered, and the lines on his face were cut deeper. His eyes seemed darker these days, too. More contemplative. He had been cleared for field work, but I still questioned how he could have fully bounced back in six short months.

I looked over my shoulder at the other two members of our team, Zach Miles and Paige Dawson. Zach was a certifiable genius, and although he was older than my thirty-one years, he had the sense of humor and maturity level of a college student. He'd found endless amusement in calling me "Pending" for the entire two years of my probationary period. Another reason I was happy to be a full-fledged agent now.

Paige was another story. She and I had a rather complicated history, and whether I wanted to admit to it or not, I loved her. But we had to make a choice—our jobs or our relationship. Since we'd both worked far too hard to throw our careers away, the decision to remain friends was, in effect, made for us.

We silently weaved through the airport and picked up a couple of rental SUVs. Jack and I took one, as we usually did, and Paige and Zach were paired together. We were going straight to meet with Lieutenant Charlie Pike, who commanded the homicide unit of Savannah PD, and his detective Rodney Hawkins, at Blue Heron Plantation where human remains had been found in the Little Ogeechee River. According to our debriefing, an arm and a leg were found there a week ago, and yesterday, another arm showed up. Savannah PD had already run tests confirming that we were looking at three different victims, and that was why we'd been called in.

The drive went quickly, and when the plantation's iron gates swung open, I spotted a female officer guarding the entrance. She lifted her sunglasses to the top of her head as Jack rolled to a stop next to her and opened his window.

Jack pulled out his credentials. "Supervisory Special Agent Jack Harper of the FBI. I'm here with my team."

The officer's hazelnut eyes took in Jack's badge, then she looked behind us to Paige and Zach in the other SUV. She lowered her sunglasses. "Lieutenant Pike is expecting you. He's just down there." She pointed to a path that came off a parking lot and seemed to disappear amid cattails.

We parked the vehicles and wasted no time getting to where she had directed us. The echoing calls of red-winged blackbirds and the whistling cries of blue herons carried on a gentle breeze, but the presence of investigators wearing white Tyvek suits drove home our purpose here and it had nothing to do with relaxing in nature.

As we approached, a black man of about fifty was talking animatedly into a phone. He was easily six foot four, thin and fit, and he had a commanding presence, even from a distance.

A younger male officer in a navy-blue uniform stood in front of him and gestured in our direction.

The black man turned to face us, his phone still to his ear. "Gotta go." He tucked his cell into his shirt pocket and came over to us while the officer went in the opposite direction. "I take it you're the FBI."

"SSA Jack Harper, and this is my team." Jack gestured to each of us.

The lieutenant took turns shaking our hands and getting our names. He finished with me, and I was surprised by how firm his grip was.

"Brandon Fisher," I said. "Good to meet you."

There was a loud rustling in the tall grass then, followed by a splash.

"Probably just an alligator," Pike said.

Yeah, just an alligator…

As if on cue, twenty feet down the bank, someone began wrangling one of the reptiles, the animal's tail and head swiping through the air as it tried to regain its freedom. No such luck, though, as its captor worked to get it away from the investigators. I took a few steps back. There was no harm in being extra cautious.

"I'm glad all of you could make it as quickly as you did. I'm Lieutenant Pike, but most people call me Charlie."

Maybe it was his age or his rank, but I knew I'd continue to think of him as Pike.

"Unfortunately," he went on, "Detective Hawkins won't be joining us today or for the remainder of the case. He's dealing with a family matter."

"I hope everything will be all right," Paige said, showing her trademark compassion.

Pike shook his head. "They were expecting and just found out that they lost the baby."

His words had my past sweeping over me. I knew exactly how that devastation felt. My ex-wife, Deb, had gotten pregnant once, but her body had rejected the fetus. She'd never really been the same after that, truth be told. And by the time she had seemed to return to a version of her normal self, she'd asked for a divorce.

Jack's body was rigid. "Where was the arm found yesterday?" As always, his focus was solely on the case. While he was a person who sheltered his emotions quite well, he usually could muster some empathy.

"Ah, yes, right out there." Pike pointed toward a boat in the water, about halfway out from the riverbank. A diver surfaced next to it. "The arm was lodged in some mud and sticking out above the surface."

To be out that far, either the limb had been dumped from a boat, had come down the river and settled here, or our unsub had a good throwing arm. If we could determine which, it would give us some helpful insight into our unsub.

The investigation by Savannah PD had dismissed the idea of the murders taking place on plantation property, though. But if our unsub had chosen here as the dump site, it would tell us how organized he was, whether he assumed risk or preferred isolation.

"Are the gates normally left open for the public?" I asked. "It seems rather remote back here, but is there much traffic?"

Pike wasn't wearing sunglasses, and he squinted in the bright sunshine. "It's not an overly busy place, and they close at night."

"But could a person come down the river to the plantation on a boat at night after hours?" I asked.

Pike curled his lips and bobbed his head. "Yeah, I suppose that's possible."

"I want the parts of the river going through the property under surveillance. Twenty-four seven," Jack directed, drawing Pike's gaze to him.

"I'll make sure that happens."

"And make sure the officers are hidden so if our unsub is brazen enough to return—"

Pike nodded. "Not our first rodeo."

"And make sure the search for more remains continues during daylight hours."

"Those are already their orders." Pike put his hands on his hips. "The community has gotten wind of yesterday's finding, and on top of last week's discovery, let's just say people are panicking.

Somehow a local news station found out that the FBI was being brought in. Don't ask me how."

While I probably should have, I didn't really care. My senses were too busy taking in the crime scene: marshland, relative seclusion, an arm and leg discovered last week, an arm yesterday. Aside from the human remains that had been found here, the property had a serene feeling to it, a sense of peace. There was a tangible quality to the air, though—or maybe it was the presence of law enforcement and crime scene investigators—that made it impossible to deny that death had touched the place.

"What else can you tell us about the limbs that were recovered?" Paige asked.

The lieutenant cleared his throat. "Well, both arms didn't have hands, and the leg didn't have a foot. We found incision marks indicating the hands and foot had been intentionally cut off."

"Our killer could have taken them for trophies or to make identification impossible," I suggested.

Pike gave a small nod and continued. "And while we know the hands and foot were removed, it's not as clear how the appendages separated from the torso. It would be something we'd need the medical examiner to clarify."

Jack's brow furrowed, and I could tell his mind was racing through the possibilities.

"But," Pike continued, "all the limbs have one thing in common: muscle tissue remained, even though the skin had been removed."

"It is possible that the skin was also taken as a

trophy," Zach speculated.

"We could be looking for a hunter or a sexual sadist," Jack said.

Hunters were typically identified by the type of weapon they used—a hunting knife, rifle, or crossbow, for example—and they tended to dispose of their victims' bodies in remote, isolated areas. A sexual sadist, on the other hand, got off on the torture and pain. But we'd need to gather more facts before we could build any sort of profile on our unsub. Even knowing more about the victims themselves would help. Was the killer choosing people he or she was acquainted with? Were the victims of a certain gender, age group, occupation? The list went on and on. From there, we could more easily speculate on our killer's motive and what they had to gain.

"Any IDs on the victims yet?" I asked.

Pike shook his head. "Not yet, but they're working on it. I'm not sure when we'll know."

I looked at Jack. I didn't know all the steps involved with processing DNA, but it could take weeks, if not months, to go through the system. Things could be sped up if the government was willing to foot the bill for a private laboratory, which was costly and would still take days. Oftentimes this was approved for cases involving serial murder, but primarily when we had seemingly solid evidence that we believed would lead us to the killer.

Jack gave a small shake of his head, as if he'd read my mind and dismissed the private laboratory.

"Anyone reported missing from the area recently?" Zach asked.

"No." Pike's single word was heavy with discouragement.

"It could be that the victims aren't being missed by anyone." Zach's realistic yet sad summation was also a possibility.

"The ones from last week were all Caucasian males in their mid- to late twenties," Pike offered next.

"What about the arm from yesterday?" Jack asked.

"It was male. I called in a friend and colleague to get us more information. She's an anthropologist, and she'll take a look at it as she had the other remains, but she won't get to it until much later today."

"She?" Paige queried.

"Shirley Moody. She's one of the best in the field but from out of town."

Jack nodded his acknowledgment. "What can you tell us about the guy who found the arm yesterday?"

"Name's Jonathan Tucker. He works at the plantation, and we took his statement, of course," Pike began. "His record is clean, and he seems like a down-to-earth guy. He's got two young girls and his wife died a couple years back. He seemed really shaken up by all this."

"What about Wesley Graham?" Jack asked.

"The man who found the remains last week? Nice guy. He's single and proud of it. Never been married.

No record, either. But he didn't seem too upset by the whole situation."

So far we weren't getting much more out of Pike than we had his detective's reports. Graham didn't work for the plantation, and the file noted that his reason for coming to the plantation was to de-stress.

"This site attracts tourists and locals," Pike said. "People like to surround themselves in nature. Personally, I could live without mosquitoes." He swatted near his face as if to emphasize his point. "I know you'll probably want to pay Tucker and Graham visits yourselves, but—" Pike made a show of extending his arm and bending it to consult his watch "—right now, I've got you an appointment with the owner of the plantation. We should probably get moving toward the main house."

"Lieutenant!" A female investigator shouted as she waded through the water toward the riverbank in a hurry. She was holding a clear plastic evidence bag.

"We found a cell phone," she called out as she reached us.

Pike looked at the investigator skeptically. "Where?"

Her eyes dipped to the ground, but she regrouped herself quickly. "It was near where the arm was found."

"And it took a day to find it?" Pike raised his eyebrows.

She squared her shoulders but shrank somewhat under the lieutenant's gaze. "It was in a tangle of weeds, but it could have just come to rest there in recent currents."

It seemed Pike was a hard one to please, and he reminded me of the way I used to view Jack—an unforgiving perfectionist. And while Pike might not be impressed, I was pleased. That phone could lead us to a killer.

CHAPTER

2

ACCORDING TO THE PLAQUE ON the lawn, the two-story main house had been built in the late eighteen hundreds. It was white with a beautiful facade that had columns the height of the building. A second-floor balcony was positioned over the entrance.

Pike knocked on the front door, and a woman answered.

"We're here to speak with Shane Park," he said.

She nodded and let us inside.

Just ahead and to the left of the entry stood a grand staircase, all oak banisters and spindles. A narrow carpet ran down the middle of the steps in a dark, Victorian pattern. To the immediate left and right of the entrance were sitting rooms decorated with floral wallpaper and antique furniture.

"This isn't the original main house, which would have been constructed pre-Civil War," Pike said as if he were catering to tourists. "Some people say it's haunted, though, if you believe in such things."

I wished he hadn't pointed that out, not that this

was the first time I'd heard of plantations having their fair share of ghost stories. The hairs on my arms rose, and I swear a shadow moved along the wall.

Paige put her hand on my shoulder, and I jumped.

Pike and Zach both laughed while Jack just shook his head.

I glared at Paige. Why had she touched me in the first place? Had she been *trying* to scare me?

"I've been here before and haven't ever seen anything out of the ordinary," Pike assured me. "But, now, we do have the remains in the river." Pike and Jack shared a smile.

As long as they were amused…

The stairs creaked for no apparent reason, and I glanced at the others. Had they heard it?

Pike pointed toward the upstairs landing where a man dressed in a suit was coming down.

Old house, old floorboards. Not *a ghost.*

I took a deep breath.

"Good day, officers," the man said as he stepped off the last stair.

"Shane, these people are with the FBI." Pike went on to introduce us all by name.

"I'm Shane Park, the owner of this fine plantation. Please, come this way." He turned toward the door on his left and gestured inside the room. "Sit wherever you would like."

In the case file we'd received, there was a full background on Shane Park and the locals had cleared him of suspicion.

I stepped into the room, and a chill crept down my spine. It felt like I was being watched.

Pike remained in the doorway, leaning against the frame.

"Lieutenant Pike said that you close the gates to the public at night," Jack began, "but is there any way a person could come through on the river?"

I couldn't help but take some pride in the fact that Jack had started off with my point.

"I suppose it would be possible."

"Your guests ever spend the night?" Paige ventured next.

Staying overnight in a haunted house wasn't exactly on my bucket list, but I knew some people were fascinated by things going bump in the night.

"Yes, of course. And ever since the word's been getting out about the remains, we've been booked solid. Usually February is a little slower and it doesn't pick up again until March, but we're already booked through August."

So much for murder hurting tourism…

"And what about your guests? Do they have access to the grounds all night?" Paige asked.

Shane crossed his legs and nodded. "Absolutely."

"We'll need full access to your reservation book." Jack's tone left no room for negotiation.

"I'd be happy to cooperate."

We didn't have a timeline on the remains yet, or so much as a window for when they came to be in the river, so it was impossible to know how far back we'd need to go in Shane's records, but given the condition of the remains and the fact that there had been muscle tissue present, I couldn't imagine that they had been in the river long. And that made the men who'd found the remains highly suspect.

"How long has Jonathan Tucker worked for you?" I asked.

Shane eyed me with curiosity. "He's been here for ten years. Wonderful man. Honest worker."

This man's word wasn't going to release my suspicion yet, though. "Did he have access to the grounds and the river after hours?"

"No, he—" Shane's face paled. "Wait, you don't think he— No, he wouldn't do this."

I held eye contact with him for a few seconds, and he seemed genuinely convinced that Tucker wasn't involved.

As if reading my mind, Pike added, "Backgrounds were pulled on all plantation employees."

"I am aware of that." I let my words sit out there, with no need to explain myself. What was on paper didn't always tell the whole truth.

"Do you get returning customers?" Paige cut through the mild tension in the air with her soft-spoken question.

"We do," Shane replied.

She kept the questions rolling. "What about in the last few months?"

"Not that I recall, but you can check the reservation book."

"Let's take our focus off guests of the main house for a minute," Jack chimed in. "Did you notice anyone else around in the last couple months who seemed strange or suspicious to you?"

"Besides tourists?" He laughed. "You've seen them, right? Always with their cameras and their phones, taking selfies every minute. But if you are asking if I can recall anyone who really struck me as a killer? No."

"Killers can look like your average Joe," Jack stated drily. "They can fit right in, be chatty, overly friendly. Do you remember anyone like that?"

"The first people who come to mind are a mother and her grown son who were here a couple weeks ago."

"Tell us about them," Zach said.

"I don't know their names, but they told me they were from Michigan."

"Did they come more than once?" Paige asked.

Shane nodded. "The guy, anyhow. He looked familiar to me, and I might have seen him since then."

Her eyes widened. "When?"

"I think he was here a few days ago."

"What were they like?" I asked.

"Pleasant." He shrugged. "The mother loved having her picture taken."

"Her son didn't?" I guessed based on his wording.

"Not at all. Actually…" Shane rang a bell that was on a side table next to him. Shortly afterward, the woman who had answered the door came into the room.

"Yes, Mr. Park?" she said.

"Jayna, I need the photograph from the board. Remember the woman from about two weeks ago who came with her son?"

"Certainly, Mr. Park." With that, Jayna was off.

"What else did you observe about the man?" I asked.

Shane's mouth fell in a straight line as he seemed to give the question some thought. "He was quiet, but attentive to his mother."

Jayna returned then, photo in hand, which she extended toward Shane. "Here you go, Mr. Park."

"Please give it to him." Shane tilted his head toward Jack.

Jack glanced at the image and passed it around the room. It came to me last. A gray-haired woman of about sixty was smiling at the camera with the river to her back. And while she didn't look like a killer or as if she was caught up in a conspiracy to cover her son's crimes, it was far too early to rule anyone out.

In all likelihood, the victims weren't from Savannah, and these two had come from Michigan. They could easily have transported the remains from there.

"A few more questions before we leave," Jack said. "Before last week, have you had any crimes committed on your property that you didn't report to police? Anything you can think of at all—small offenses, even?"

"Uh, let me—"

"Sir?" Jayna was standing in the doorway.

Shane's gaze went to her, then skimmed over me and landed on Jack. "We had a problem with a previous employee."

"What sort of problem?" Jack's gaze homed in on Shane.

The man flushed. "I found out that he was coming onto the property after hours, and…" He glanced at Jayna as if he was looking for the strength to verbalize what he had to say. "He was using an outbuilding for…"

"He said he was cleaning and gutting fish in there," Jayna picked up for Shane. "But there seemed to be a lot of blood for fish."

"And you never reported this to the police?" Jack was not impressed, and I didn't blame him.

Shane took a deep, staggered breath. "I gave him the benefit of the doubt."

"His name?" Jack asked.

"Jesse Holt."

Jack got to his feet. "We'll need to take a look inside the building."

"We did that last week," Pike started, "but we didn't find anything."

"He hasn't worked here for two years," Shane added.

"Neither matters." Jack was already on his way to the front door, the rest of us trailing behind.

CHAPTER

3

I'M NOT SURE WHAT I expected us to find in the shed. Concrete proof that a killer had murdered and mutilated his victims here? More remains yet to be dumped into the river? Lieutenant Pike had said that the place had been clean when his people had checked it last week, but it could have been a matter of timing.

Shane led us to the parking lot. "The building's on the far end of the property. It's best we drive there."

The four of us and Pike loaded into one SUV, and Jack followed Shane as he weaved along a gravel road that cut through fields and ran parallel to the river. A walkway lined the edge of the river here, and my guess was that we were a couple of miles from the main house by now. How big *was* this place?

Shane pulled to the side of the gravel road, got out, and walked back to us.

Jack put his window down.

"We'll have to walk from here," Shane said.

We all got out and continued to follow Shane, this

time down a wooden walkway that led us through tall grass.

This building's isolation and proximity to the river, which was only about fifty yards to its right, would have been beneficial to the unsub, but one thing working against Jesse Holt, if he was our unsub, was that he had been caught here before and now risked being found out for something much worse than gutting fish—if that was really what he had been doing.

None of the windows in the building were broken, and there was a padlock on the door that was intact.

"That's a good sign, isn't it?" Shane asked, but he didn't sound convinced.

And the truth was, it didn't mean anything other than if the unsub was using the shed, he or she had a key.

No one replied to him, and Shane unlocked the door and stepped back.

Jack held up a hand to him. "You stay out here."

"You don't have to tell me that." Shane crossed his arms, avoiding eye contact and looking anywhere but the shed.

I stepped inside. The space was rather empty save a long worktable against one of the walls with cabinets mounted above it. There was nothing on the table.

I gloved up and opened the first door, holding my breath as I gripped the handle. Nothing. I repeated the process for all four doors.

"If our unsub was ever here, he did a good job of covering up," I concluded.

"We'll still have a forensic team come out and take some swabs." Jack pulled out a cigarette and his lighter, and stepped toward the door.

"We had that done the first time," Pike said, "and nothing came back."

"Is that why this building wasn't so much as mentioned in the reports we got?" Jack stared at the lieutenant, who didn't bother responding, and he went outside.

Paige, Zach, and I followed him. Pike was the last one out.

Shane looked up at us, hope filling his features. "So?"

"It looks clean, but we're going to have forensics come in anyway," Jack stated matter-of-factly and lit up his cigarette. He took a deep inhale and exhaled a cloud of smoke.

Shane's head pivoted to face Pike. "That was already done."

"We'll be doing it again." Pike squared his shoulders.

Jack continued. "Is this the only outbuilding on the property?"

"Yes," Shane responded.

"We'll need the former employee's information. Address, phone number," Jack stipulated.

"Absolutely. I asked Jayna to pull it together before we left the main house."

Jack took a step in the direction of the SUV when Pike spoke. "Since we're already out here, let me show you where the arm and leg from last week were found."

"If you don't need me, I'm going to head back to the house," Shane said.

"We'll see you for that information before we leave." Jack's cigarette bobbed in his lips as he spoke.

Shane nodded and left.

"Come this way." Pike led us alongside the river about a hundred yards.

A pinch on the back of my neck had me slapping myself, and Pike turned around with a smile. "Like I said, I could do without the mosquitoes."

When we came to a section where the tall grass thinned out and revealed the water's edge, Pike stopped and pointed toward the river. It would be accessible by foot—not that any of us were going out there in our dress shoes and slacks, as the ground looked spongy.

"The leg was lying there, and—" he gestured down the bank "—the arm was out there, partially in the water."

My mind went back to the report. Shoe prints had been found in the mud but had tied back to Wesley Graham, the man who had found the arm and leg.

"Well." Pike clapped his hands. "It's probably time for our appointment with the chief medical examiner."

I looked to Jack. He usually kept investigations closed to those outside of our team, but this time, he didn't seem to object to Pike coming along.

I shrugged. If he didn't have a problem with it, neither did I.

CHAPTER

4

GIVEN WHERE THE REMAINS HAD been found, the forensics were being handled by the Coastal Lab of the Georgia Bureau of Investigation. While the institution offered various areas of expertise, it also housed the chief medical examiner we were going to meet. Usually a coroner was charged with determining cause and manner of death, but since this case was a high-profile one, that responsibility had shifted onto different shoulders.

A man in scrubs met us with a friendly smile. He was easily in his fifties and balding.

"This is Chief Medical Examiner Garrett Campbell." Pike made the introduction for him, but we provided our own names and shook his hand.

"Come on in," Garrett said. "We can get started if you're ready."

The bones from an arm and leg were laid out on a steel gurney. Knowing that the arm found yesterday was with an anthropologist, these were the ones from last week's victims, which had already been stripped of their muscle tissue. Next to the gurney, a wheeled tray held a fat folder.

Garrett pressed his lips together. "I can just share what I've found first, or if you have any questions, we can begin with those."

"We have a lot of questions," Jack said. "But let's start with a time of death. Any luck with that?"

Garrett shook his head. "Unfortunately, finding just a single body part makes determining TOD extremely difficult, if not impossible."

Jack frowned. "I had a feeling you might say that."

"Do you know if the skin was removed before or after death?" I asked.

Garrett looked at me. "Given the state of the remains, it is another one of those things that is hard to determine."

"All right, what *can* you tell us?" Jack's tone was unforgiving now.

Garrett proceeded with respect and caution. "The bone marrow was intact in both cases, and we were able to test it to see if there was any evidence of drugs in the victims' systems. The results from these remains—" Garrett gestured to the bones "—were negative."

So our unsub had managed to subdue their victims without weakening them with drugs—at least not ones that showed up in a general tox screen. Running with the assumption that drugs were not used, we could be looking at a strong unsub—one that could overpower men in their twenties—but it was also possible that a means of manipulation was used.

"As you've likely read in my initial report, the hand and foot were intentionally cut off." Garrett pointed to the end of the arm where the hand had been severed. "You can see the nicks in the bone there."

We took turns moving closer to look, and I couldn't help but sink into a moment of reflection. This was what happened to us when we died. We were catalogued, poked, and prodded, and strangers studied our remains.

Garrett continued. "Since the markings in the bone seem rather clean, I do feel comfortable concluding that the victims weren't aware of the mutilation."

"They were already dead?" Paige clarified.

"I believe so. Now, these nicks also help us determine the shape of the instrument used and the blade type. Molding has confirmed that the blade is relatively smooth and slightly curved. It's apparent the killer would have used a sawing motion to remove the hands and foot." Garrett picked up the folder, pulled out a sheet of paper, and held it up for us to see. It was an image of a tear-shaped blade. "Our lab has come back with this."

"Not a standard-shaped knife," I noted.

Garrett shook his head.

"Was Forensics able to pull anything from the nicks that could indicate what the blade was made of?" Zach inquired.

"Unfortunately, we weren't that lucky. However,

take a look at this." Garrett exchanged the photo for another one. It was an arm with the muscle tissue still attached. "This is the arm that was found last week. The one from yesterday looked similar. Look at the wrist area. With the state of decomposition, I had almost missed it, but if you look closely, you'll see areas of hematoma." He handed the photo to Jack, who was standing next to him, and pointed to the area.

"It would have taken a lot for the bruising to reach the muscle tissue," I said aloud, surmising.

Garrett looked at me. "For it to show to this extent, yes." He took out another photo. "The leg also shows sign of subdermal bleeding, just above where the foot was cut off."

"The victims were restrained," Zach said.

Garrett nodded. "It seems that way."

"It's possible, then, that they were drugged initially and held for a period of time," I posited.

"Entirely," Garrett agreed.

That dismissed the need for our unsub to be physically stronger than the victims.

"Have you figured out how the limbs became separated from the torso?" Paige asked.

"My strongest hypothesis is that the victims were stretched out, and their limbs were disjointed from the torso. Then as the remains decomposed, the tissue broke down and detached."

The killers we hunted never ceased to surpass their predecessors. "So they held on to the dead bodies for a while?"

"How long would depend on a number of things. Namely the rate of decomposition, which can speed up because of heat, immersion in water, burial, the presence of bacteria, predators… What I can say is that every body part found so far is at a different stage of decay."

"So the unsub kept the bodies and decided to start dumping the parts one or two at a time," Paige said.

My stomach clenched.

"If that's the case, though, they took a great risk hanging on to the bodies for the time they did," Zach stated. "Someone could have found them out."

Paige was nodding. "Unless there was no one else around to find out."

"The killer's a loner," I concluded.

"Or a team of unsubs who stick together and don't have an outside circle," Paige said, handing Garret back the photos. "Going back to the restraints… Were you able to tell what was used?"

"Given the amount of damage to the muscle tissue, I'd say it was something hard and rigid. Metal perhaps."

"Handcuffs?" I asked.

Garrett shook his head. "I'd estimate a wider cuff of approximately one and a half to two inches."

"Sounds like some kind of metal bracelet," Zach suggested.

"Possibly. Now, everything I've shared with you on the remains from last week is mirrored in the arm found yesterday, less the toxicology results that we're waiting on. And the age of the victim," Garrett stated.

Jack pulled out a business card and gave it to Garrett. "Keep us informed of any new findings."

He slipped it into a pocket. "I will."

Out in the parking lot, we gathered with Pike, who I'd almost forgotten was there since he hadn't said anything beyond Garrett's introduction.

"What are you thinking?" Pike asked Jack.

"We still don't know how the remains got into the river, but it seems they were dumped there," Jack began, "and they couldn't have been in there too long given the rate of decomp."

"Agreed. Also, if they'd been in there for a length of time, alligators would have eaten them," Pike said.

"That means we're looking at anyone who had access to the plantation, from tourists to employees," I said.

"To trespassers," Paige added.

And that just shot the suspect pool wide open.

"Yeah," I said. "Those too."

"You cleared all current plantation employees," Jack said, looking at Pike. "Did you look at Jesse Holt?"

"There was no need to before, given he's an ex-employee."

Jack nodded. "If you could pull his complete background for us…?"

"Sure."

"But first—" Jack took in his team "—we're going to pay visits to Tucker and Graham, get a feel for them ourselves."

Paige's earlier comment about a team of unsubs with no outside circle came back to me. "What if we're looking for more than one killer? Maybe it wasn't a matter of drugging or the unsub being stronger than the victims, it could have simply been a matter of manpower." I turned to Pike. "Do these two men know each other?"

"I…" Pike rubbed his jaw and glanced at Jack. "I don't know."

"I think he's got a point," Jack said. "We've got to figure that out. Paige and Zach, you talk to Graham. Brandon and I will pay Tucker a visit."

"I'll get you their addresses right now." Pike sauntered off to his sedan and came back with two pieces of paper. He handed one to Jack and one to Paige. "Neither of them are too far from here. Say, fifteen minutes."

"All right…" Jack consulted his phone. "It's about five now. We'll meet back at the precinct after we've finished and see where we're at. Aim for about sixty thirty. And, Pike, if you could have the background ready on Jesse Holt when we get there, that'd be great."

"Will do."

With that, we all parted ways.

And so the hunt for a serial killer begins.

CHAPTER

5

JONATHAN TUCKER LIVED IN A modest home on a tree-lined street in Carver Village, a Savannah neighborhood.

Jack parked in Tucker's driveway, and we got out. The laughter of children was coming from the backyard, along with the smell of barbecuing hot dogs—an aroma northern states associated with summer, not the month of February—and we headed toward the back.

A man peeked around the side of the house and walked toward us, pointing a pair of tongs in our direction. He brought the smell of beer with him, and there were mustard stains on his shirt. "Who are you?"

Aside from his unshaven face, he closely resembled the DMV photo we had for Tucker.

"You're Jonathan Tucker." Jack stated it as fact.

"What's it to you?"

Jack held up his credentials. "My name is Jack, and this is Brandon."

Rarely did Jack introduce us by our first names, but there were times he did it to set someone at ease. Since we didn't know if Tucker was involved, and until we had a gauge on how we felt about that, it was better for him to think of us as his allies.

"Whoa, the FBI is on this now?" Tucker asked. "Though I guess that shouldn't surprise me, especially with another arm being found."

"Daddy!" The shrill scream came from a little girl in the backyard, and Tucker went running in her direction. Jack and I followed, and when we rounded the house, flames were coming off the grill, at least a foot high.

How the man had managed that while cooking hot dogs was beyond me.

Tucker grabbed a near-empty beer bottle from his patio railing. He tossed the liquid onto the fire, but it did nothing to douse the flames. I wedged in front of Tucker and cranked the propane tank off. The fire kept going. I turned the valves off, too, and disconnected the tank from the barbecue and moved it several feet away.

The fire kept raging.

Two girls were hugging each other, watching in horror, both sets of eyes wide. The younger of the two was crying. Tucker was just standing there staring at the flames.

I scanned the back of the house for a garden hose and found one dangling from a reel not far from where the barbecue was, but Jack had made it there first. He turned it on full force and aimed the water at the fire.

There was a lot of smoke, but when that cleared, what remained on the grill were the black, shriveled husks of what were once juicy hot dogs. They gave *charbroiled* a whole different meaning.

The younger girl ran to Tucker and flung her arms around his legs. "Daddy."

"It's all right, Bethany." Tucker fanned his daughter's blond hair, and then she seemed to notice Jack and me for the first time.

Jack had a scowl etched on his face, likely not thrilled by this little detour. Barbecuing really should come with the same warning as operating a vehicle or boat did: *Don't mix with alcohol.*

Bethany pointed at us. "Who are they?"

"They're here to talk to me for a bit. Go back and play. I'll order up a pizza as soon as we're done here." Tucker attempted to downplay the fire situation, but his gaze was on the spoiled food and his soaking-wet barbecue.

Bethany ran off, barefoot, toward a swing set. The older girl remained, eyeing us with curiosity and disdain. My guess was that she blamed us for her ruined lunch.

"Go with your sister, Cora," Tucker said to the girl.

She grimaced but obeyed her father.

After she walked away, Tucker turned back to Jack and me, his eyes flashing irritation. Over his change in lunch plans, his spilled beer, or the need to relive what he'd discovered, I wasn't certain.

"I'm not sure what more I can tell you." He lowered his voice and added a rather detached, "I found an arm."

For someone Pike had described as being upset over the find, Tucker wasn't showing much evidence of that to us yet.

"You work at Blue Heron Plantation, yes? What do you do there?" Jack asked.

"I'm paid to ensure the marsh is clean. I pick up any litter or debris in the water. Yesterday, I got more than I'd bargained—" Tucker bit down on his bottom lip, emotion now coming to the forefront.

He seemed suspicious to me, despite his noticeable discomfort. If this guy was in charge of the marsh, why hadn't he found the remains last week? It could mean a couple of things—he and Graham were working together and had planned on staging the discoveries at certain times or Tucker wasn't very thorough in doing his job. But the remains last week were found closer to shore, so they could have gone unnoticed.

"Are you responsible for the riverbanks, as well?" I asked.

Tucker shook his head. "Primarily the river itself. I'm out on a boat. But if I see something on the bank that needs taking care of, I'll do it. You've probably seen the place, though? There's a lot of tall grass and in most places, I can't see through to the shore."

"Your statement says you thought it was a stick at first?" I recalled this tidbit from the case file.

Tucker nodded. "It wasn't until I got closer…that

I realized what it was."

While I was starting to witness his upset, it wasn't enough to convince me of the man's innocence. While Tucker's living arrangements—a modest house and two young daughters—would make it nearly impossible to murder and mutilate men without being discovered, it didn't mean that he hadn't teamed up with someone, like Graham, and carried out these acts elsewhere.

I pulled out my phone and brought up a picture of Wesley Graham. "Do you know this man?"

Tucker took the phone from me and looked at the photo for a few seconds. "No," he said as he handed it back.

"What about the name Wesley Graham?" Jack interjected.

"That sounds familiar." Tucker's brow furrowed. "But I'm not sure why…"

If he thought we were going to feed him that answer, he'd be waiting forever.

Tucker's eyes lit up. "Ah, he was the one who found the body parts last week."

"And do you know him?" Jack asked, repeating my initial question.

"Never met him before in my life."

Based on Tucker's assuredness, body language, and facial expression, he seemed to be telling the truth. "Did you notice anyone around the plantation in the last month or two who seemed strange or off in some way?"

"Nah, not really. I mean, we get some interesting

tourists coming through, but no one stuck out as a killer to me." *Killer* was said at a lower volume than the rest of his words, and he gave a quick glance over at his girls.

"What about any locals? Do any visit often, or is there anyone in particular who stands out to you?" I pressed.

"Every town has their oddballs. Here is no different. There's one man who comes most mornings during the week. I don't know his name, though. He's always dressed in a suit. I think he goes to the plantation before heading to work."

"What does he look like?" Jack asked.

Tucker ran a hand over his mouth, and he squinted as if he were trying to pry a memory loose.

"You said he's there most days…" Why was it taking such mental effort for him to conjure up an image of the guy if that was the case?

Tucker met my eyes. "I'm usually still half-asleep when he's there."

"What time is that?" Jack asked.

"Usually between six and seven."

"You remember that he dresses in a suit… Brown hair? Blond? A white man?" Hopefully something I said would jog Tucker's memory.

"Actually, he has short brown hair, and he's always clean shaven. I think he drives a red Prius, come to think of it. I've seen him pull into the lot a few times."

A man who frequents Blue Heron Plantation. A seeming draw by our unsub to depose of body parts there.

"Are his visits a new thing or has he been going there for weeks, months, years?" I asked.

"I'd say years."

I was probably taking a long shot with my next question. "Do you know his name?"

Tucker shook his head.

"Did you ever speak to him?" I continued.

"Nothing more than 'hey' or 'morning.'"

What did that say about society when two people run into each other over a course of multiple years and didn't get past a basic greeting?

"Did he have any sort of accent?" Jack asked.

"He didn't sound like he was from the South."

I nodded. Now we were getting somewhere. "Did he sound American?"

"Yeah, but from a northern state."

I continued to press our luck. "When did you last seen him?"

Tucker squinted in thought again. "Yesterday, before shift."

"And what time was that?" Jack inquired.

"Six thirty."

Jack handed his card to Tucker. "Call if you remember anything else."

Tucker nodded, and we headed back to the rental. As soon as we were in the SUV, Jack called Pike. "I need you to run a quick search for anyone who owns a red Prius in the area."

CHAPTER

6

PAIGE WAS ALL FOR HUNTING sadistic serial killers, but it would have been nice if the investigation could have waited one more day, just until Valentine's Day was behind them. Instead, she'd had to explain to the man she'd been seeing for eight months now that she was suddenly out of town. It was hard enough to make a long-distance relationship work without the added flux of her job. Adding to the list of complications was that he'd planned to fly into Virginia to visit her today from where he lived in Grand Forks, North Dakota.

She'd texted him when they were still in Quantico—taking the coward's way out—but hadn't heard back from him. Maybe he'd just been too busy to check his messages, or maybe he had and he wasn't going to talk to her again. What if he had been headed to the airport? What if he'd already…

"Zach, can you just pull over for a minute?"

Zach looked at her from the driver's seat. "Right here?"

"Sure."

"Okay." He pulled to the side of the road and put the hazard lights on.

"I'll just be a minute," she said before hopping out of the vehicle. Shit, she really should have called him sooner, not just assumed he'd get her message in time. But she'd boarded the government jet and had gotten swept up in the investigation.

Ring. Ring.

"Hey," he answered. His unimpressed tone told her he'd seen her message and his caller ID before picking up.

"It's Paige," she said anyway.

"I know. What's up?"

"You got my message, I take it."

"I did."

"I'm sorry, Sam."

The line remained silent and it was stirring up her anger. She tried to douse it with reasoning: maybe he hadn't been able to get a refund or exchange his ticket. "I didn't have advance notice or you know I would have—"

"Called sooner? Yeah, I'd hope so. Listen, Paige, I've gotta go."

"You know what the job's like," she pleaded.

Sam Barber was a detective and knew that neither of their jobs was a strict nine-to-five.

He sighed. "I know. I just wish you would have called instead of texting."

"We were headed right out of town." Paige caught Zach looking out at her. "I've gotta go, too. Talk later?"

"Sure." He hung up before she could say good-bye.

Heat bloomed in her cheeks. She would be forty-four this year, and she'd spent all her life single, unattached, and happy. There was a lot less drama that way. Why had she ever thought a relationship could give her more? Sadly, she knew the answer: she'd had a taste of what one could have been like with Brandon. But Sam wasn't Brandon, and Brandon... Well, he wasn't an option.

The back window lowered. "You coming?" Zach asked.

She pressed on a smile and got back in the SUV. "Yeah."

Zach merged onto the road again and headed to Wesley Graham's house. Pike had given them Graham's work information and his home address. They'd tried the hotel where he worked first and were told he'd booked the week off months ago. Hopefully, this was a staycation and they'd find him at home.

A Honda was in the driveway, and Zach parked behind it. "Looks like we might have gotten lucky."

"That is promising," Paige agreed.

Zach pointed to the open front window. "And so is that."

The door was wide open by the time they reached it. A thirtysomething man smirked and said, "Let me guess, you're the FBI." He held up his hands. "And no, I'm not a mind reader. I saw that the FBI was being called in on the news last night."

"Wesley Graham?" Paige asked while holding up her creds.

"The one and only." He smiled at her, and she felt oily from his leering gaze.

The lieutenant's words came to mind. *Single and proud of it.*

Well, if he made a woman feel this cheap with just a look, his bachelorhood wasn't much of a surprise.

"Come in." Graham stepped back into the house, holding the door for them to enter.

Paige looked around. The living room was to her immediate left, and an eating area and the kitchen were on the right. The place smelled of recently fried eggs and onions, but the stovetop and counters were clear and clean. Except for a game console in the middle of the living room floor, a stack of Blu-ray movies, and a glass partially filled with a dark liquid on his coffee table, the house was exceptionally tidy. And while Graham lived in a residential neighborhood, he was single, and if his staycation was any indication of his social life, he might not have many friends. That would certainly make it easier to murder and mutilate men. Then again, he might have a lot of friends who were all working this week.

"Do you have somewhere you'd prefer we sit?" She guessed he'd want to be next to that drink.

"Just head into the living room. Park it wherever you like." Another smirk—laid-back, casual. Predatory.

Paige had stood by the marsh, surrounded by bugs, coated in humidity, but now was when she needed a shower.

She and Zach sat in chairs that faced the couch, and Graham resumed his position next to his drink and picked up his glass. He had it to his lips but lowered it without taking a sip. "Oh, how rude of me. Would either of you like something to drink?"

"No, thank you," she said.

Zach shook his head.

"Suit yourselves." Graham gulped back a few mouthfuls and set the glass back on the table.

"We're here to talk to you about the remains that you found last week," Paige said. "Can you run us through what happened?"

"Ah, sure. I found the leg first, then the arm. They were rather close to each other."

"Do you remember anyone being around when you found the remains?"

"There was a family with two young kids, and I hurried over and told the parents what I'd found and to stay back. They didn't listen, and they looked at me as if I were insane or a killer. I thought the woman was going to scream, but instead, she hightailed it outta there. I'd never seen a woman push a stroller so fast. The man was running behind her with a toddler on his shoulders."

"After they left, what did you do?" Paige asked.

"I called nine-one-one."

His composure was calm. Paige could imagine him finding the limbs and going about everything in an organized fashion. Adrenaline could account for focus in the moment, but that had long worn off, and Graham wasn't giving any indication that he was truly affected by what he'd found.

"Have you seen dead bodies before?" she asked.

He shrugged. "At funerals. Why?"

"You just seem very calm about everything." Paige glanced at Zach, and he was watching Graham intently, likely doing his own assessment of the man. She turned back to Graham. "Most people wouldn't handle this so well."

"I watch crime dramas on TV. Maybe I've become desensitized? I don't know, but what I *did* know was I had found body parts and I had to report them."

"Why were you at Blue Heron Plantation?" Zach inquired.

Graham looked at him. "I'm paid well, but my job is stressful. I just needed a break."

Zach nodded. "Do you often go to the plantation to de-stress?"

"Not a lot, but from time to time. I chose quite the day last week." Graham looked at Paige, then to Zach, and back to Paige. "The news said more remains were found and they belong to a third person. Is there a serial killer in the area?"

"It's an open investigation," Paige said.

"That's code for yes."

"That's code for we're not telling you anything," she fired back.

"All right. Fine. What else would you like to know? I think I've about covered everything. Do you know who I found? Who was found yesterday?"

Paige angled her head.

"Right. 'It's an open investigation,'" Graham parroted.

"Do you know a man named Jonathan Tucker?" Zach asked.

"Nope. Should I?"

Paige brought up his picture on her phone and held it for Graham to see.

"Is that Jonathan?" he asked.

"Yes," Paige said.

"He looks familiar."

"Do you know where you've seen him?"

"I think he works at the plantation. I don't know him, though."

"All right, well, that's all for now." Paige got up, handed Graham her card, and headed for the door.

Back in the SUV, Paige turned to Zach. "He really doesn't give the impression of being shaken up by all this. Beyond that, it's too soon to conclude anything about him."

"Except for he obviously had eyes for you." Zach was smiling as he punched the precinct address into the GPS and put the vehicle in reverse.

She rolled her eyes. "Tell me something I didn't notice. I was going to make *you* leave your card."

"As you're always telling me, we're not in the field to pick people up," Zach teased.

She narrowed her eyes at him. "You know that's not why I left my info."

"Uh-huh, and it seems to me that for all your

preaching, you are dating someone you met during an investigation."

"A detective," she clarified. "That's not the same as a potential suspect."

"How are you and Sam by the way?"

"Doing fine." A big, fat lie.

"Wow, that sounds exciting."

"It's not perfect. I'm not going to lie about that." Why did she say that? She could have just let the conversation die.

"But you did…just a moment ago."

"Yeah, I guess I did." Guilt over the initial deception snaked through her. "I don't think I'm cut out for a relationship."

"Hey, long-distance relationships are never easy."

She turned to him. "I didn't know you had experience in that regard."

"There's a lot you don't know about me."

She smiled. "True enough."

Silence fell between them for a few seconds before Zach said, "If anyone can make it work, though, it's you."

Paige laughed. "Now you're just being patronizing."

"I'm trying to be positive."

"Yeah, okay." Zach might have just been saying what she wanted to hear, but she was thankful for his effort to build her confidence. Though instead of focusing on Sam and relationships, she'd focus on what she was good at—hunting down killers.

CHAPTER

7

JACK AND I BEAT PAIGE and Zach back to the precinct by a few minutes. It was about six thirty by the time we got situated in the room that Lieutenant Pike had set aside for us.

A conference table sat in the middle of the room, taking up most of the floor space while whiteboards lined three walls, and pictures of wanted persons covered two of the boards. The last one seemed dedicated to our investigation. At least a third of it was covered with photographs of the three limbs. The dates of the discoveries were written on the board beneath them.

We all took seats and filled one another in on our conversations with Tucker and Graham.

"I find it interesting that this man who frequents the plantation has a northern accent," Zach stated thoughtfully. "It seems, at least based on what we have gathered so far, that our unsub—or unsubs—has a draw to the property. Usually that indicates a history, a connection, of some sort."

"Family could be in the area. Maybe they were born here but grew up in a northern state," Paige reasoned. "They could have moved back to the area."

"Or could just be visiting," I tossed out there, and then shook my head. "I just wonder how this theory connects with this man in the suit that Tucker sees most weekdays. He said the guy has been going to the plantation for years." My mind went to the older mother and her grown son. If only we knew who they were. But maybe there was a way of working backward to find out. "At this point, we have no real way of identifying the victims, but what if—and this is a big one—the mother and son from Michigan are behind this? We should see if any missing people from that area connect in any way to the remains found here."

"Brandon," Paige began, "we don't have any sense of a timeline, though. We only know the remains from last week belonged to two twentysomething white males."

"No, the kid has a point," Jack said.

Kid was a nickname Jack would pull out for me periodically. I usually cringed when he used it, but this time I was willing to overlook it since I'd impressed him.

"Nadia could do a search," Jack continued.

Nadia Webber was our go-to analyst who worked out of Quantico. To me, she was a true miracle worker who produced something seemingly out of thin air. I knew she had the aid of warrants and technology, but she also had an analytical mind that made her perfect for her job.

"Instead of going about it from the standpoint of the victims and missing persons, though, I'd be interested to know if there are any similar cases in Michigan. It's conceivable that the unsub— assuming it's this man—disposed of body parts in his home area, as well."

Paige's eyes widened. "I just had a thought. If both mother and son were from Michigan, they had to have stayed somewhere locally. We might be able to track them down that way."

"It's also possible that they lied about where they're from," Zach stated sourly, overriding anything that Paige had said. He shrugged when I looked at him.

"Let's explore Brandon's suggestion," Jack decided.

"So if we're going to look into this, where does that leave us with Tucker and Graham? Jesse Holt? The man with the Prius?" Zach asked.

Jack tapped his shirt pocket, clearly in nicotine withdrawal already, but instead of pulling out his cigarette pack, he went to his suit jacket pocket and pulled out his cell phone. He dialed on speaker, and Nadia picked up on the second ring. He provided her some background on the situation and said, "I need you to dig deep into the history of Jonathan Tucker and Wesley Graham. See if you can find a connection between them somehow, somewhere their paths might have crossed outside Blue Heron Plantation. Also, see if either of them have other properties under their names."

"Will do."

Jack continued. "We also need to know if there have been any reports of severed remains remotely resembling what has been found in Savannah in the state of Michigan."

"Boss?" she asked.

Jack explained our theory.

"Do you want me to pull the background on Jesse Holt, too?"

"No need. The lieutenant is getting that for us. You could see what properties he owns, though. I'll call you first thing in the morning to see where you're at."

"On it."

Jack clicked off, and Pike came in holding a tray loaded with a pot of coffee, paper cups, packets of sugar, and containers of creamer. He placed it on the table.

"Usually, you can find all this in the bullpen, but I thought you might like it real handy." Pike took a seat at the table and grabbed a coffee that had already been made up.

Zach took a cup, dropped in a couple of sugar cubes, and poured himself some coffee. "Anyone else want any?"

"Sure," Jack replied.

"No, thanks," I said.

"Black for me." This from Paige.

Zach handed a coffee to Jack and another to Paige.

Pike waited until we were situated. "I've got the information you wanted on Jesse Holt." He handed the report across the table toward Jack, who shuffled it down to Zach, our resident speed-reader.

Jack sipped his coffee while Paige regarded Pike with interest. "When we spoke with Graham, he mentioned a young family being there when he found the arm and leg," she said.

Pike nodded. "Yep, told us, too. But no luck in tracking them down."

Zach lowered the report and held up a photo of Holt. His brown hair reached his shoulders and he had brown eyes. After we all took a look, he said, "Nothing too exciting here. He's twenty-seven, single. He's spent time in foster care. No criminal record, though. He's works at the cement factory in town where he's been for a couple years now."

Jack nodded and looked at Pike. "How did the investigators make out at the shed?"

"Initial results show no evidence of blood or bodily fluids—human or otherwise."

"We'll still pay him a visit," Jack said. "And the Prius?"

"The search is being run by a detective of mine as we speak," Pike replied.

Jack nodded. "The phone pulled from the river?"

"Should have the results momentarily."

It felt like Jack had placed Pike in the hot seat.

Then Jack changed direction, picking up on Zach's earlier suggestion. "I'd like to know why the remains are being found in the river on plantation property. We need to figure out if this matters to our unsub, and, if so, why," Jack said.

"We've ruled out previous crimes on the property,"

Zach said. "Shane said there weren't any. So if the place does carry a meaning to our unsub, it's hard to say what that would be. But I'd think the unsub does have a history there."

"Wait a minute…" I was thinking my hypothesis through as I spoke. "We know those visitors came from Michigan, then a man who often goes to the plantation has an accent from a northern state. What if they are the same person and he moved here from Michigan, but his mother still lives there."

Paige was smiling. "Look at you."

I wasn't celebrating just yet. "Yeah, it's great in theory, but it doesn't get us closer to ID'ing him."

No one offered words of reassurance.

Jack's mouth set in a firm line, and he addressed his team. "Let's keep brainstorming."

"It's possible our killer is placing the remains so they can be found," Zach suggested. "They could be drawing attention to their work, trying to call us out."

"If that is the case," I began, "wouldn't the remains be placed somewhere they'd be more easily found?"

"Easier than a riverbank or sticking out of mud?" Paige countered skeptically.

"Fine." I held up my hands. "Why did our unsub cut off the hands and foot? Was it for a trophy or for making identification impossible?"

Jack's expression was sour when he faced me. "Hands and feet make rather large trophies, but we can't rule it out. Same with the skin."

A shadow filled the doorway, and a man was

standing there.

Pike lifted his head. "This is Detective Roger Rowlands."

"Hey." He flashed a perfunctory smile. "I've got the list of red Prius owners and the results on the phone pulled from the river." He paused as he looked at Pike. "There's one name in common. I've got the phone company working on the records."

"What's the name?" Jack asked impatiently.

"Stanley Gilbert."

And just like that, any suspicion directed at the man in the suit with the Prius lessened. If Stanley was our killer, I doubt he'd drop his phone in the same river where he dumped his victims. Then again, maybe the phone hadn't been intentionally left behind.

Pike's face fell, his shoulders sagging.

"You know him," I said. Given the lieutenant's body language, it wasn't a question.

Pike lengthened his neck. "Stanley Gilbert is my personal banker."

"And…?"

"Can you excuse us, Roger?"

"Sure." Roger tapped the doorframe on his way out.

"Stanley's wife called last night and said that he hadn't come home from work."

Jack's neck snapped in Pike's direction. "You said that no one in the area had been reported missing recently."

"Yes, I did, and he wasn't…not officially. Heck, I'd

forgotten all about it. And the remains were from twentysomething males."

"The arm and leg from last week were. We don't know about the arm from yesterday," Jack spat. His focus was steely and directed at Pike.

"He hadn't been gone twenty-four hours when she'd called. And Stanley's not exactly the type to make enemies."

For a missing person report to be filed before twenty-four hours had passed, there had to be suspected evidence of foul play.

A pulse tapped in Jack's cheek, and I was happy I wasn't in Pike's shoes right now. "And what type is that?"

"A nice way of putting it? The man doesn't have a backbone or at least not that I've seen. To make enemies you normally need to take a stand on something." Pike paused but Jack's glare was still on him. "His wife is a miserable coot with a burr up her butt about anything and everything. She wears the pants in the relationship, let me tell you."

"But you failed to mention her call." Jack was seething.

"As I said, I didn't see him factoring in at all."

"Based on what? The age of the victims from last week? The arm found yesterday could be Stanley's." Derision licked Jack's eyes.

"How do you know it is?" Pike asked. "Maybe the guy just finally grew a backbone and ran away. And I, for one, wouldn't blame him if he had."

"We need full disclosure, Lieutenant, to do our

jobs properly. Do you understand?"

Pike looked away from Jack.

"We're going to need his wife's information." Jack's tone had cooled slightly.

"Her name's Darla Gilbert. I'll get you everything you'll need." Pike went to stand up.

"Get a nationwide BOLO out on his car ASAP," Jack directed.

"Nationwide?"

"It's been over twenty-four hours," Jack said. "Whoever has Stanley's car could easily be out of the state by now. We need to tie this up." He looked at Paige and Zach. "You two pay a visit to Jesse Holt. Brandon and I are going to talk with Stanley's wife."

CHAPTER

8

IF IT WAS STANLEY GILBERT'S arm being examined by an anthropologist while Jack and I headed to talk to his wife, it was possible that the killer had simply acted on an opportunity. Stanley was often at Blue Heron Plantation, and if our unsub had the affinity to the property we expected, it could make sense. Stanley would present a low-level risk. He was there during daylight hours, but it was early in the morning, meaning there were likely very few people around. Based on Pike's summation of the guy, he didn't sound like the type who could physically defend himself.

Then there was the matter of what finding his phone represented. If the unsub had dumped Stanley's arm, why his phone as well? They hadn't left personal belongings with the other remains—at least not that had been found.

Jack tapped his cigarette on the frame of the opened SUV window as he drove. Most of the smoke was directed outside, but the odor wasn't discriminatory. I might as well have been puffing away myself.

Soon we reached the Gilberts' driveway, which was pocketed between two rows of live oaks, their curvy branches draped in Spanish moss. Sadly, the newer construction of the house dispelled some of its southern charm. Two stories and beige siding stood out among the otherwise picturesque setting. The house was set in from the road and backed against the Little Ogeechee River. A luxury SUV was parked in front of the garage.

At the front door, I rang the bell and then knocked.

"Hold your arse," a woman barked from inside.

If this was Darla, I understood Pike's assessment of her being a "miserable coot."

The door cracked open, and a tiny slip of a woman—all of five feet tall, if that—appeared. Her hair was black and swept into a loose bun. Her hooked nose and pointed chin gave her a somewhat comical appearance. I'd bet she'd make a pretty good witch for Halloween.

"Who are you?" An obtuse question on her part as Jack and I were holding up our FBI credentials. Her brown eyes slid from Jack to me, and I felt my skin tingle under her gaze. She might be crammed into a small package, but she wasn't someone you'd want to mess with. Like a Chihuahua with fangs.

"Supervisory Special Agent Jack Harper, and this is Special Agent Brandon Fisher."

"So?" She pressed her lips into a fine line.

"We're here about your husband, Stanley. Can we come in?" Jack articulated it as a question, but his demeanor said refusing wasn't an option. He took a step toward the door. Darla stood her ground for a moment, but looked up at Jack, whose more than six-foot frame towered over a woman of her size.

Inside, the home smelled of vanilla, and she gestured us toward a living room where Jack and I sat on a couch.

She remained standing, hands on her hips. "Did you find his body?"

Wow, this woman was something else…

"Is there a body to find?" Jack countered, leveling his gaze on her.

She crossed her arms. "I have no idea. It's not like I killed him."

"Who says anyone did?" I ventured.

I was cut down by a nasty glare.

"It's the only reason he wouldn't be here," she said.

I was surprised she could speak with her jaw clenched so tightly.

"We understand that you called the lieutenant last night and reported your husband missing," Jack said.

"Ah, yes. I assumed that's why you're here. I'm also guessing you found him," she said impatiently.

"Why don't you take a seat?" Again, Jack wasn't really asking.

Darla consented and perched on the edge of a sofa cushion as if she was ready to jump up at a moment's notice.

Jack let the silence ride for a few seconds. "We found your husband's phone at Blue Heron Plantation. Do you have any idea why it would be there?"

Darla's eyes narrowed. "None. He'd have no reason to be there."

"Are you sure?" I asked, risking another cruel stare down.

Darla's head snapped to face me. "Yes, I am sure. My husband has a job to go to."

"Maybe he goes out there before work," I suggested. It earned me a beady glare.

"Stanley starts work at seven. He always leaves here about six to get an early start on the day. He says it looks good to his boss. And he's *always* home by six thirty."

"Where does he work?" It took careful thought to think of Stanley in the present tense, seeing as he was either AWOL or dead.

"A bank in Savannah." She raised an eyebrow. "But you're the FBI. You should know all this."

This woman seemed incapable of talking without sarcasm. I wouldn't blame Stanley if he *had* run off. There might not be any more to his seeming disappearance than that he'd left Darla. He could have just tossed his phone into the river to sever the connection to his wife, and it wasn't related to the investigation at all.

But we were a long way from jumping to any conclusions. And while we were currently leaning toward Stanley being a victim, we had to keep our minds open to all the possibilities. One thing seemed certain, though: Stanley had been living a double life. There was no way he worked at a bank from seven until six, and Tucker had said the Prius was at the plantation *most* weekdays, so where did he go the other mornings, and where did he spend his time after the day job actually ended? Something was keeping him busy, but was it a mistress or murder and mutilation?

"Did Stanley give you any reason to suspect that there might be another woman?" I asked.

Darla's face scrunched up so tightly it had me thinking of something my mom would say to me as a child: *Watch it or your face will stay that way.*

Darla crossed her arms. "He would never cheat on me. I'd cut him off."

"Cut him off?" I asked, my voice strained.

"Yeah, my family has money."

That explained the nice house and the luxury SUV. Stanley must have chosen to drive a Prius for environmental reasons.

"If you have money, then why did Stanley work?" I realized I'd slipped into past tense but just let it go.

"He liked to." She shrugged. "I let him because it gave him some independence."

She *let* him. How nice of her.

If I were Stanley, I'd have run away a long time ago. Though I'd hope I was smart enough not to get involved in the first place.

"How was Stanley the last time you saw him?" Jack asked, taking over. "Did he seem like himself or was he upset in any way?"

Darla rolled her eyes. "He seemed normal."

"Which for him was…?" I fished for an elaboration.

"He did whatever I asked of him, but yesterday he seemed to be mumbling more than usual when I asked him to come straight home after work. And I texted him twice not long after he left the house and never got a response."

That potentially narrowed the window of Stanley's supposed disappearance. "Was that unusual?" I asked.

"Yes."

"What were the messages about?"

Darla slid her eyes to Jack, then back to me. "About him coming straight home."

"The same conversation you had before he left for work. So a response wasn't really necessary," I pointed out.

Darla glared. "Stanley knows I hate my messages to be ignored."

"Could we look at the messages you sent?" I asked.

Darla got up and returned to us less than a minute later. She unlocked her phone and handed it to me. I opened the messaging application and found the conversation she had with Stanley. I had to scroll up to get to the texts she would have sent in the morning, as more recent ones—riddled with swear words—filled up the feed. I glanced at Darla. "It seems you sent him a lot of messages."

"He's my husband, and I have a right to know where he is. I left him voice mails, too."

I didn't say anything and counted the messages backward from the most recent. Seventeen messages since the first one sent at 6:42 AM yesterday.

Messages prior to yesterday supported what Darla had said about Stanley always replying. He usually responded within a couple of minutes, keeping to simple, mostly one-word replies.

I passed the phone to Jack for him to take a look. If Stanley left the house at six and didn't reply to messages sent just past six thirty, he'd either been abducted within that timeframe or made a run for it. But then again, all we could really speculate was that his phone likely ended up in the river between yesterday morning and yesterday afternoon when Tucker found the arm. There'd be no way for him to access the property and toss his phone with a police presence there.

It was possible that he hadn't left the house with his phone, though. He could have tossed it before yesterday, and Darla might not have known.

"Do you know if he had his phone on him when he left the house yesterday morning?" I asked.

"I make him show it to me before he leaves. A phone doesn't do much good if it's not on a person."

I glanced at Jack, who was reading the messages I'd just gone through.

"If you're thinking Stanley left me, there's no way. He doesn't have enough guts." Darla's words were big but came out tiny. Her conviction in her husband's loyalty was slipping, as shown by both her tone and her inclination to fill the silence. "I can't believe the FBI is here. The lieutenant told me to give it time, that I had to wait twenty-four hours."

There was a glimmer of desperation in her voice, as if she were giving real consideration to Stanley having left her. But the possibility that Stanley hadn't left of his own choice was something we needed to make her aware of. There were at least a couple of ways to look at the situation: tell her and have it not be her husband, or don't tell her and have it be him. There was no winning.

I opted for a variation of the former since reports of the remains were already hitting the news. "You may have heard that human remains were found in the Little Ogeechee River at the Blue Heron Plantation…"

She swallowed loudly. "Yes…"

I had to proceed delicately. "Your husband's phone was recovered in the river in that same area."

Darla's eyes widened, and then she seemed to go catatonic.

"Mrs. Gilbert?" I prodded.

"Don't you 'Mrs. Gilbert' me. He left me." Darla was seething.

"We don't know that," Jack said. "All we know right now is that his phone was found." Somehow he was always the epitome of calm.

I had more to add, though. "The remains that were found haven't been identified. It's also possible that—"

"So he might be dead?" She sounded hopeful.

My job was to understand people, but sometimes… Well, sometimes, they were too much of an enigma to figure out. "It's a possibility."

"Who would want to kill Stanley, though?" Darla's eyes went reflective, although I didn't detect any grief.

I wasn't going to point out that serial killers didn't need to have a personal vendetta against their victims. Usually they didn't. "Could you provide us with his toothbrush or his comb?"

"You're looking for his DNA?" she asked.

"Yes." The anthropologist could rule Stanley out as a victim long before the DNA was processed, but it would be good to have on file if it became necessary for official identification.

"Sure." Darla left the room again and returned with a comb and a handful of hair. "Stanley shed like a dog. I got this from the wastebasket in the bathroom."

Did she really expect me to just take his hair like this? "Do you have a plastic bag or something you could put this in?"

"Oh, sure." Apparently, the thought hadn't occurred to her.

While she was out of the room, I turned to Jack. He met my gaze, and I sensed he wasn't feeling much love for Darla, either. Then it hit me. *Stanley shed like a dog.* It was uncommon—although not unheard of—for people to refer to their lost loved ones in the past tense so quickly. For some it took days, weeks, or even months before being able to do so. In Stanley's case, death hadn't been concluded and Darla was at it.

She returned with Stanley's hair and comb, now in a plastic sandwich bag. She handed it to me. "Here you go."

"One more thing," I started, proceeding slowly as I watched her facial expression and read her body language. "We'd like to look around your house, if that would be all right."

"Ah, sure. If you have a warrant." Darla laced her arms. "I do know my rights."

Jack was apparently a lot more skilled at phrasing a demand as a request.

"If that's how you want to handle this, that can be arranged," Jack said coolly and stood.

I kept my attention on Darla. She was biting her bottom lip—a sign of nervousness. The question was, what did Darla have to be nervous about?

CHAPTER

9

PAIGE DIDN'T WANT TO GIVE too much weight to the thought, but Jesse Holt could very well be their unsub. Shane Parks had given Holt the benefit of the doubt all those years ago, but what if Holt had been perfecting his MO on animals or murdering people in the plantation's outbuilding? There'd be no way of knowing at this point.

She glanced out the passenger window. "I'm not so sure I agree with Jack sending us to see Holt by ourselves." What she was really thinking she wouldn't verbalize: Jack didn't seem like his old self. Yes, he was focused, but there was something about him that was a little off. It was hard to place a finger on it. He wasn't handling the case the way he normally did—his eyes kept glazing over, and he'd expressed no sympathy when the lieutenant told them that Detective Hawkins had a family matter come up. He wasn't someone who wore his emotions on his sleeve, but she would've thought he'd have a bit more compassion. Especially after losing his mother not long ago.

"We're just going in friendly, getting a feel for this guy." Zach's words offered reassurance, but she wasn't buying it.

"If this guy is guilty, he's going to think we're on to him. And then who knows how far he'll go to protect his secret. We should have spoken up; it might have been better to bring backup."

Zach looked over at her and tilted his head. "Yeah, and that would have gotten us far."

She sighed. "You're right."

"Of course, I am. I'm a genius."

"And so modest." She smiled at him, but he'd gone back to watching the road.

A few minutes later, they were pulling in front of Holt's house, a small bungalow in a modest neighborhood. There was a decades-old Nissan in the drive, but the body appeared to be in good shape considering its age.

The front screen door slammed open, and a woman came running out. Holt was behind her, waving his arm in the air and yelling, "Get your fucking ass off my property."

Paige looked over at Zach. "Wow, good timing for us." Sarcasm dripped off every word as she jumped out of the SUV.

"You piece of shit!" the woman screamed. She had two armfuls of clothing and was trying to balance her load, but with her erratic movements, she wasn't doing a very good job. A pair of pants was the first thing to fall to the lawn. Next, a shirt.

Then underwear, shorts, pajamas, until her arms were empty and she was standing there crying.

"Hey," Paige said to her, "it's going to be all right." A stupid sentiment, really, when Paige had no idea what they'd walked in on, but then again, it couldn't get much worse from the look of it.

"Get out of here!" The man was at the door, and now he seemed to be directing his words to all three of them.

Zach hurried over to him while Paige did her best to split her attention between the woman and Zach. Emotions were running high, and domestic calls were among the most dangerous.

The woman dropped to the grass, openly bawling now. Any potential threat didn't seem to be with her, but rather Holt, who was waving his arms and talking loudly.

"Who are you?" he growled.

"The FBI," Zach responded.

Holt's voice raised in volume as he said, "Get off my property."

Paige put a hand on the woman's shoulder. "Stay right here. Okay?"

She nodded. "There's nowhere for me to go."

Paige looked at her and quickly assessed her. Her eyes weren't dilated, and she didn't smell of alcohol. She didn't appear to have been struck, but wounds could have been covered. "Did he hit you?"

"No."

"All right. What's your name?" she asked, though she really wanted to get to Zach.

"Stephanie."

"I'm Paige. I'll be right back."

"Whatever."

Paige hurried up to the door where Holt was still worked up. "We need you to calm down," she said.

"Don't you be telling me to calm down, ho."

It took a lot to summon up control and not immediately slap cuffs on the guy, but she was reined in by Zach's earlier words: *We're just going in friendly, getting a feel for this guy.*

"We just came here to talk." Paige glanced past Holt into the house. "It has nothing to do with anything that just happened."

Like hell it doesn't. His first impression, combined with their preconceived notions about him, weren't working in the man's favor. It would take a lot of rage to skin and cut up a body, and Holt definitely had a temper. While Stephanie had claimed he hadn't hit her, his attitude made Paige question whether she had told the truth.

Holt eyed her with steely intensity, but she held her ground.

"We just want to talk," she repeated.

Holt glanced at Zach. "Fine."

Zach took a step inside, and Holt yelled at Stephanie again. "Get off my property!"

"Go to hell!" Stephanie yelled back amid garbled sobs.

Holt went into his house, and Zach and Paige followed. She wasn't at ease with this guy and kept her hand near her service weapon so it was readily accessible. No doubt Zach would be doing the same.

"Oh, that woman." In his anger, Holt was heaving for breath.

They waited a few minutes for him to settle down, and just when Paige thought he'd cooled off, he walked toward the front door. "Is she still out there?"

Zach put his hand up, and Holt stopped.

"It doesn't matter," Zach stated calmly. "You're with us right now."

"And who are you again?"

"We're with the FBI," Zach said.

"No shit." Holt let his gaze go from Zach to Paige. "What do you want with me?"

"You used to work at Blue Heron Plantation?" Paige asked.

"Yeah, what's that matter? I've got a better job now."

"And what's that?" she asked, letting him tell her.

"I work at the cement factory." Holt clenched his teeth. "What's this about?"

"Why did you leave the plantation?" Zach asked.

"I told you. I got a better job."

"Is that the only reason?" Paige pressed.

"Ah, no, and I'm guessing you've heard the story. Although, it's probably been entirely twisted. Shane has a way of blowing things up."

Paige angled her head. "What do you think he told us?"

"The guy thinks I'm a psychopath. I was using a building on his property for gutting fish I caught in the river."

Paige scanned his eyes, looking for a flicker in his gaze, any tell that he was lying.

"Why were you gutting fish at night?" Zach asked, not a hint of suspicion in his voice. He was good at putting people at ease.

"It was quiet. I love peace and quiet. But I never get it." Holt waved his arm toward the front of the house, alluding to the woman on his front lawn.

"Wives can get a little much," Zach said, and it almost had Paige turning to face him. After all, what would Zach know about marriage? And Jesse Holt's file indicated that he was single.

"Nah, she's not my wife. She's a ho."

And there was that lovely word again...

"She's a girlfriend, then," Zach stated.

"Was. She slept with an old boyfriend and she expects me to just be all right with it. Unbelievable." Holt shook his head.

"How long have you been together?" Zach was running with the questions, and Holt finally seemed to be opening up.

"Long enough. About a year."

"Living together?"

"Kind of... Not officially. She's still got an apart—"

Police sirens interrupted his words. And they were coming closer...

It seemed that someone had called the cops.

CHAPTER

10

It wasn't long after we left Darla's that Jack called it a day. Darla must have been enough to push him over the edge, too. But it was after nine by the time we'd dropped off Stanley's hair to the lab and checked into the hotel that would be our home away from home until we solved this case.

We got a hold of Paige and Zach and they were having their own "fun" at Jesse Holt's. Maybe Darla was tamer than a domestic call, by comparison... Maybe.

"Check in and then meet me down in the restaurant in twenty," Jack told me.

I adjusted my bag's strap on my shoulder. "You got it."

There was something in both his tone and his eyes that told me the workday wasn't *really* over, but then again, it was hard to fully turn off an investigation. Short of lights-out, any waking hour was open for profiling.

I dropped off my bag in my room and came back

down to find Jack sitting alone at a table for four nursing a martini. Jack and I might spend a lot of time together during an investigation, but it was hard getting a personal conversation moving with him.

I slipped into the chair across from him. "No Paige and Zach yet?"

"Paige called. They'll be here soon."

I bobbed my head.

A smiling waitress came to the table. "Hello. Welcome."

A redundant greeting...

"Can I get you anything to drink?" she asked.

I glanced at Jack's martini, and for a moment, I was tempted to indulge but decided against it. "No thanks."

"All right, then. Just holler if you need me," she said.

I picked up the menu on the table in front of me. Jack's remained beside his arm, which was leaning on the table, seemingly untouched. Of course, it was entirely possible he'd looked at it before I had gotten there and already knew what he wanted.

At least the place offered healthy options. The last thing I needed was something deep-fried sitting in my gut.

"I see them, thanks." It was Paige's voice, and she was talking to the hostess while pointing our way.

The hostess led Paige and Zach to the table. Paige looked like she'd had better days. The red hair that normally fell in soft curls was frizzy around her forehead, and her tired eyes promised a story.

I laughed. "Had a live one?"

"Glad you think it's funny, Brandon." She narrowed her eyes at me as she sat down on my left. Zach took a seat, too.

"What are your thoughts on Jesse Holt?" Jack's tone was all business as he looked at Paige.

She glanced at Zach. "He has a temper. Local PD took him in for disturbing the peace."

"When you said there was a domestic issue I assumed he'd hit someone," I said.

"Nope." She flagged down a waitress and ordered a Reuben and a beer.

The rest of us ordered, too. And surprisingly, the conversation after that wasn't about the investigation.

By the time we were finished with our meals, we were ready to go our separate ways.

The waitress returned with the check. "Happy Valentine's Day," she said.

Oh shit! I had forgotten all about canceling my hotel and restaurant reservations. More importantly, I hadn't called Becky to let her know I'd gone out of town for a case.

I stood up, tossing my napkin on the table. "If that's everything, Jack, I'm going to head up to my room."

He dipped his head and lifted his hand. "Tomorrow morning, down here at seven."

Seven? Had I heard him right? That was sleeping in for Jack. Normally, he was up before the sun and had us up with him.

I nodded. "I'll be here."

I hurried in the direction of the elevators and was happy to find one was already on the ground floor. The doors opened the second I pressed the button to go up. I pulled out my cell phone. Missed calls. Voice mails. The caller ID for both showed Becky's name.

I silently cursed Jack because he was the reason I missed the calls in the first place. His rule about limiting personal calls when we were on a case had me setting up a call profile that shuffled personal numbers directly to voice mail. Becky was on that list, along with my parents. Having the calls routed saved me the grief that would come otherwise, especially if the phone started ringing in the middle of an interview or when we were following a lead. I changed the call profile setting now, though, seeing as I was in my hotel room and the work day was technically over.

I sat on the edge of the bed. I'd come up to my room with the intention of calling Becky, but it was rather late—already midnight.

A text message will be fine, I reasoned, but I wasn't sure if I should check the messages first or go in blind. I opted to listen to what she had to say and dialed my voice mail.

"You have three new messages. To hear your first—"

I pushed the appropriate button.

"Hey, this is Becky. You told me to keep tonight clear and I did, but I haven't heard from you. Give

me a call."

The message had been left at ten that morning. I would have been on the government jet at that time.

"Next new message…"

"It's me again. You must be busy, but I'd like to know what we're doing tonight." Her voice contained a trace of irritation.

That one had been left at three in the afternoon.

I clicked "delete" and listened to the final voice mail.

"Brandon, it's seven o'clock. Where are you? I've left two messages for you. I'm all for surprises, but I'd also really like it if you'd return my calls."

I hung up and paced the room, wondering if I should just call. But she had sounded pissed. If I texted, I might be able to put off the confrontation I was certain was going to happen. She might not even see my message until morning when I'd have personal calls forwarding again.

Yes, I'd text.

I'd just hit "send" and placed my phone on the nightstand when it rang.

The caller ID said it was Becky.

Uh-oh…

It was probably best to get right to an apology.

"Becky, I'm sorry," I answered. I'd never claimed to be the best boyfriend in the world. I hadn't been any good at being a husband, but regardless guilt snaked through me for disappearing on Becky on Valentine's Day.

"Where are you?" she asked, her voice tight.

She must have figured out that I was away on a case. "Savannah, Georgia. I'm not sure how long I'll be."

"Well, I'm pretty sure you won't be back in time to celebrate tonight," she fired back. "You know, seeing as the night is pretty much over."

"We got called away quickly. We left first thing this morning." As soon as that last sentence came out, I could have slapped myself. I'd chalk up the disclosure to my being exhausted.

"First thing this morning? And you couldn't find two minutes to give me a heads-up? Instead, you left me hanging. You didn't bother to return my calls."

I could feel the heat of her anger through the phone line, and with the speed at which she fired off her words, they may as well have been live ammo. But I wasn't going to take the hit.

"You know what I do for a living," I said through clenched teeth. "You also know that I can be on a jet at a moment's not—"

"That is not the point."

"It is, actually."

"You had all day to call."

"You can't expect me to push aside my job for you." I pinched my eyes shut. Speaking of live ammo, I'd just pulled the trigger myself. "I didn't mean—"

"Oh, no, I think you did." She sounded smug, distant, hurt. "This relationship isn't your top priority, a fact that you remind me of all the time. You're not ready for anything serious. You're not ready to commit. And I've been fine with that,

Brandon. God knows, I'm not ready for wedding bells, either, but after about eight months, I'd at least expect you to be someone I can rely on."

"You're not being fair," I said.

"I'm not being fair?" She was bordering on hysteria.

And I was speechless. I had, in fact, responded to her message. I'd explained what had happened and where I was. What else did she want from me?

"I think we should call this for what it is, Brandon."

"This *what*?" I snapped back, arrogant, hotheaded.

"Unbelievable. We're over." She hung up, the tone of the dead line drilling in my head.

I gripped my phone and stared at the wall. Now would be a good time to punch something.

Since I clearly wasn't going to sleep, maybe I'd just hit the hotel gym. If I was lucky they'd have some punching bags for me to jab at and roundhouse kick.

CHAPTER

11

THE CLOCK ON THE WALL said it was eight o'clock, and we were at the precinct. And I could barely keep my eyes open. I'm not sure why I had bothered trying to sleep last night. It wasn't the case keeping me up but how the conversation had ended with Becky, how our "arrangement" had ended. Maybe I cared about her more than I'd realized. Things between us had been simple and unassuming with no strings attached. But there was some reliability to it—or at least there had been.

I'd given up on sleep by five and hit the hotel gym again. They didn't have punching bags, but I got my heart rate up and rode a cardio high. Working out normally invigorated me almost immediately, but it hadn't had that effect today. I refused to give any real consideration to the fact that I might have a broken heart. Besides, if it had been broken, I'd know because I'd been there, done that. My ex-wife had decided to end our marriage over the phone, for God's sake. She hadn't even had the decency to tell me to my face that our marriage wasn't working for her anymore. There were still days the bitterness from that dissolution sank in, but I was working through it. It was what left me in no hurry to make any kind of commitment again. But maybe this wasn't about me; maybe it was the job. It seemed to be the common denominator in all my failed romances.

My wife had suffered emotional issues with losing the baby, but in the end, I really think it had been my job with the FBI that had sent her over the edge. My job had been the reason a psychotic serial killer had set their sights on her during the course of my first investigation.

Then there was Paige. Our relationship was at a stalemate; it was either us or our jobs.

Fast-forward to the present with Becky... The job had gotten in the way again. Or that was the gist of it. If there hadn't been a last-minute investigation out of state, we'd still be together. And maybe I should have just told her, but it's not like I'd intentionally kept it from her. I had gotten caught up in the case quickly; it hadn't been personal. And she was well aware of my fluid work schedule. Come to think of it, she hadn't given me the benefit of the doubt in any of her messages. She'd basically just attacked me as having abandoned her, as if there had been something I could have done about it.

A knot settled in the pit of my stomach. Maybe I didn't have a broken heart, but I was disappointed. At least there were some perks to bachelorhood. I wouldn't have to worry about Valentine's Day or romantic gestures, for one.

"Earth to Brandon."

I snapped out of my thoughts to see Paige waving her hand in front of my face, and I smiled.

What had I missed?

Jack had called someone on speaker and the line was ringing.

"Hey, everyone," Nadia answered, sounding wide-awake. "All right, I have a lot of info for you guys."

"We like to hear that," Paige chimed in with a smile.

Zach raised his cup as if he were toasting the air.

I just took a long draw on my coffee.

"I'll start with the men who found the remains—Tucker and Graham. You asked me to see if I could find another connection between them besides possibly running into each other at the plantation. Well, my searches into their finances didn't turn up anything in common. They don't even go to the same grocery store."

"What about properties registered to either one of them?" Jack asked.

"Only their houses."

Dead end there.

"Now Holt…" Nadia paused. "Records show he was arrested last night?"

Paige slid her gaze to me, and there was a slight curve to her lips. At least we knew if Holt was the killer, there wouldn't be any more murders with him behind bars. I smiled at her.

"That's right," Zach confirmed. "Paige and I got a front-row seat."

"I'd love to hear that story, but as I said, I have a lot to share. Holt's search didn't show any properties in his name. He's renting the house where he lives now, and I have the landlord's information if you want it."

"Just keep it handy," Jack said.

"Will do. Now, I looked for cases that were similar in Michigan and did find one from five years ago in Lansing. A woman's body was found in the Red Cedar River."

"An entire body?" I said. "That's different from what we have here."

"You didn't let me finish," Nadia said. "The body was severed into pieces, and everything but the hands and feet were found."

Jack sat up straighter and leaned on the table. "ID on the victim?"

"A prostitute by the name of Esther Pearson."

"Our unsub could have been working out his MO. Took someone who might not be missed," Zach reasoned.

"The victims we're trying to identify don't seem to have been reported missing by anyone," I reminded the others. "Coincidence? Maybe not. Maybe the unsub has been killing transients or young men who live or work on the streets."

Jack nodded. "Were there any suspects?"

"None. The case went cold."

"Send us the information so we have it," he

directed.

"Done."

I no sooner heard a mouse key click on Nadia's end than Jack's phone chimed with a new message.

"Do you want me to dig into people who moved from Michigan to Savannah, Georgia?" she asked.

"That's probably a good idea," Jack responded.

There was a knock on the door.

"Hold on, Nadia," Jack said to her, and then to the person at the door, "Come in."

Lieutenant Pike entered, and his jaw was as hard-set as his eyes. "More remains have just been pulled from the river."

"Nadia—"

"I heard." She disconnected, and we all hurried out of the room.

CHAPTER

12

KILLING WAS THE BEST SEDATIVE. Just knowing that the time was coming had allowed him to fall asleep the second his head had hit the pillow last night, and now the clock on his nightstand told him it was almost noon.

He got out of bed and opened the curtains, letting the sun spill in and blanket him in its warm glow. Closing his eyes, he bathed in its splendor. His breath was calm and deep as he got down onto his knees and spread his arms heavenward, giving thanks for not just another day but for the blessing of life. Not his, but what would be the beginning of another offering.

He remained there in a meditative state, letting his consciousness drift to the other realm, a place far too few visited or were even aware of. But it was in this stillness that he found his true self, his identity, and his purpose, where he became centered and focused on the seriousness of his mission.

He wrapped himself in a black robe and shuffled

downstairs and out the back door. He stood on the patio facing the riverbank with his eyes closed.

As the sun warmed his eyelids, he imagined himself being carried up toward the sky, merging with the flames, the source of life, and shedding his human form. He knew that he belonged somewhere else—a different plane of existence—but the physical required roots. So for now, he was grounded.

He remained standing there until the sun ducked behind a cloud, the shadows casting over him. He opened his eyes and knew. It was time.

His stride was full of purpose as he returned inside to where he kept the man in a dimly lit room. He closed the door behind him and headed for the preparation room.

The man was standing, restrained at the wrists and ankles, and held up by a clasp around his neck. His arms and legs were stretched out like rays of sunshine. The offering was free to talk, but his spirit had become broken with the passage of time and he rarely whispered a word.

The preparation room was about eight feet by ten feet and boxed off within a larger room where he made the sacrifice—a room within a room. The floors were poured concrete, and there were drainage holes—both practical investments. In the corner of the preparation room, there was a small table where he kept his supplies, including a knife. He'd grabbed it as he'd entered.

He ran the back of a hand along the offering's cheek. "Soon, it will be your time."

The offering trembled beneath his touch, and tears streaked down his cheeks. "No, please..." he pleaded, but his eyes disclosed a resignation to his fate.

The man sobbed heavily. "I...have...a...family."

"And you will be honored." He lifted the blade, jabbing the point toward the offering's lips. "Now open your mouth."

"No!" The offering thrashed, but the restraint around his neck didn't leave much room for mobility. The chains around his wrists and ankles clanged against the concrete as he tried to worm his body away from his captor and closer to the wall. As if that would stop him...

He grabbed the offering's jaw with one hand, tempted to squeeze hard enough to pop the bones out of joint, but he preferred to dole out torture in increments so that each infliction could be fully felt.

The offering was mumbling incoherently. He opened the man's mouth with sheer force and slid the knife inside.

The offering's eyes grew large and panicky, sweat beaded on his forehead and face, but none of that would stop the enviable.

He swiped the blade inside the offering's mouth, and blood poured out. He withdrew the fine morsel, taking for himself what he saw fit. Words were no longer necessary.

CHAPTER

13

PIKE TOLD US WHERE TO GO—nicely, of course—and the four of us split up in the two SUVs and followed his directions.

A man's torso and a human skull had been pulled from the river at the outer edge of Blue Heron Plantation, but the easiest way to get there would be by going through the property.

At the end of the road, next to the river, there was a cluster of local law-enforcement vehicles, including one belonging to Forensics.

I barely waited for Jack to stop our SUV before jumping out. For my enthusiasm, I received a mild glare as Jack snubbed out his cigarette in the ashtray—yes, he was smoking again.

Paige and Zach parked behind us and the four of us approached three male investigators who were standing around a tarp that would hold the remains.

The skull was simply bone, and it was intact except for the lower mandible. The face could still be reconstructed. The torso had skin, though, and it appeared to be blue, but the coloring didn't look like it was from natural decomposition.

I crouched down on my haunches beside it, stupidly banking on adrenaline to help me process the scene in front of me.

Flies were buzzing all around the area, and bugs crawled over the torso. It stank beyond belief. I held my breath, hoping the nausea would abate.

Taking a closer look at the torso, I realized my initial assumption about the blue coloring had been correct. There appeared to be a coating on the skin. A type of paint perhaps?

Beneath the blue, however, I could see that the skin was pale. We were looking at another Caucasian male. The sockets where the arms and legs would have been attached at one time were badly decayed. But, hopefully, the medical examiner could confirm or retract his previous thought about the limbs being torn at the joints.

There was something else, though: a horizontal slice going across the chest on the left side, a couple inches down from the nipple. I looked over a shoulder to my team. "I think his heart was removed." I could barely slide the statement from my throat.

"We think so, too," one of the investigators said. "An on-call ME's on his way. We'll know for sure soon enough."

"Where did you pull the remains from?" Jack asked.

I went back to standing.

The same investigator pointed off to the left of where the road met the river. "Just right there."

"Outside of the plantation property?" Jack put his hands on his waist and turned to Pike. "You had men watching over the river in this area last night?"

"I did."

"And they kept a low profile?"

Pike crossed his arms. "Absolutely. They were under strict orders to do so and to keep their distance."

"Now, if a boat or a person had come along—"

"If they'd been close to the perimeter of the property, my guys would have seen them," Pike stated.

Jack turned to his team. "Things have changed. Our unsub might not be as closely connected to the plantation as we had thought. We had Nadia look at similar cases in Michigan. It's time to have her look for similar crimes here in Savannah."

My eyes drifted to the skull. The skin had been removed from the arms and leg found previously, but there had been muscle tissue left over. Was the head only bone because of bacteria, or a predator, or was it just further along in its decomposition? And assuming it had something to do with the latter, what caused the different rates of decomp? All the remains were pulled from the river. It was likely the victims weren't killed at the same time, but there had to be more.

"Ah, guys…" Everyone looked at me. "Remember that case we worked near Dumfries?" It was a stupid way to start; there'd be no way any of them would forget. "I've just been thinking about rate of decomposition and trying to figure out where the remains might be coming from."

"The Dumfries victims were buried near water," Paige said.

"Uh-huh," I said. "Maybe we're looking at that here."

"You're thinking these victims were buried and then their remains were carried out to the river?" Pike's brow raised, skeptical.

"Exactly. It could explain the slower decomposition, as well, that led us to believe these victims were killed more recently."

"I'm also going to have Nadia take a look for missing twentysomething white males within twenty miles of Savannah going back, say, ten years." Jack had his phone to his ear by the time he was finished talking. "Nadia?"

"Have you had any heavy rain lately?" Zach asked Pike.

"Yeah." Pike glanced at one of the investigators. "What, two weeks ago?"

The investigator nodded.

"Around the time the first set of remains were found?"

"It rained for at least three days on end," Pike added.

"Savannah's already below sea level. Then combine a shallow grave with heavy rainfall…" I let my words trail off.

"You think the killer was stupid enough to risk burying his victims near the river?" Pike retorted.

The three of us were looking at him until our conversation from a few seconds ago seemed to strike.

"Ah, guess it's been done before," Pike said.

"If this is the case, it could potentially tell us something else about our killer or killers. They might not be concerned about the bodies being found," I added.

Pike's brows were raised again. "Keeping in line with that theory, why bury them at all, then?"

"The lieutenant has a point, Brandon," Paige treaded delicately. "I don't think our unsub wanted the bodies to be found."

Pike continued. "Then that means if they see the local news—"

"It might cause them to act," Zach concluded.

Pike faced Zach. "Why not keep a low profile?"

I had the answer to that one. "They've already been exposed. Self-defense instinct will kick in. They also might want to prove they have something over us—intelligence, power."

There was the crunching of tires, and a news van was pulling in. Before the van stopped, a cameraman jumped out along with a reporter.

"Get them out of here!" Pike barked to anyone who'd carry out his order.

An officer took care of it, and the newspeople were sent on their way.

I looked past the tarp to the river. There was a

boat out there, and investigators were wading in the water, combing for more remains.

Zach gestured to the river. "I could probably calculate the distance the appendages could have traveled by factoring in regular water flow and comparing it to the higher water levels. I'll just need access to a computer and few minutes."

Pike nodded and glanced at an investigator, who waved Zach over, saying, "This way!"

If Zach could pull this off, we just might be able to figure out where the limbs had come from.

CHAPTER

14

My GAZE WENT BACK TO the remains in front of us, and I refocused. What sort of killer were we looking for? Running on the assumption the bodies had previously been buried, we were likely searching for an unsub who preferred isolation for their murders.

I was running through our unsub's profile when Zach returned to the group. Not that I consulted my watch, but I didn't think he'd been gone five minutes. He looked at Pike. "Are there any areas within, say, ten miles that are either public or obscured property?"

"There are easily hundreds of houses along the river, and there's definitely not enough manpower to go from door to door," the lieutenant responded.

"What about having officers go down the river and look along the banks?" Jack asked.

Pike wiped his forehead with his arm. "Could be done, for sure. Not sure how much they'd see, but you never know. I'll have that arranged."

"Thank you."

My eyebrows rose in surprise. It was rare for Jack to verbalize his gratitude.

"Yep. There are some public areas I know off the top of my head, as well. We could have officers go in on foot to check those."

"Sounds good."

Pike pulled out his phone, but Jack held up his hand. "Before you call…"

Pike stopped, his finger poised over his cell phone.

Jack filled him in on the prostitute found in Red Cedar River. "Get some uniforms or detectives on the street, too, and have them ask around about missing vagrants and prostitutes."

Pike put his phone back to his ear, walked off a few feet, and started making arrangements.

I glanced at Zach, whose gaze was fixed on the tarp and the remains. He had that glazed-over look in his eyes he'd get when he was deep in thought. "What are you thinking, Zach?"

"Hmm?" He looked up at me. "Oh. Well, I don't think this guy's just adhering to a MO… I think he's conducting a ritual."

Based on the flicker in his eyes, this was going to be good. "Go ahead," I said.

"This is just a theory, and it might be a reach, but I am going by what's in front of me. We have two missing hands and a missing foot, both of which were cut off. It's an assumption—but also a likelihood—that the unsub does this to all his victims." Zach gestured to the torso. "Now, we have a missing heart. Add to this, the blue coloring of this torso." He paused, his gaze going to each of us. "Did any of you study the Mayans when you were in school?"

I was no history major but the mention of the Mayans brought human sacrifice immediately to mind. "They cut people's still-beating hearts out of their chests."

Oh, this wasn't good. If Zach was right, there'd be nothing textbook about this, not that most serial killers fit neatly into a predefined package. In fact, with each new case, I wondered how the next would top the last, but somehow they always came to us more gruesome and depraved than the previous.

"So our unsub's MO is a cultural ritual from thousands of years ago?" I asked.

Zach's eyes were deadpan when they met mine. "That's what I'm thinking." He swept his gaze over the others. "Now, the Mayans had various rituals, but with the heart-extraction ritual, a conquering warrior carried out the sacrifice of his enemy."

"If our unsub is mimicking this ritual, then it's likely our unsub is male," I reasoned.

"I'd lean that way, yes."

"What exactly happens in this ritual?" Jack asked.

Zach cleared his throat. "Well, the sacrifice would be stripped and painted blue, a color that is now referred to as Mayan blue. It's a durable dye that has been studied and analyzed extensively. Once blue, the sacrifice would be stretched over a round stone called a convex stone. This would make it so the sacrifice's chest would be extended for easier heart extraction."

"Could something like this pull joints apart?" Paige interjected.

Zach just nodded before continuing. "Then the nacom—that's the conquering warrior—would use a knife made from flint or obsidian to cut out the heart." Zach pointed to the remains, not that he needed to. The image was seared into my mind. "But that's not all. After that, the victim's heart would be given to a priest, who would smear the offered blood on idols' faces. Sometimes they'd throw the body down the stairs of the temple and then it would be skinned. The officiating priest would then remove his black ritual attire and dress himself in the skin. Sometimes the victim was eaten by other ritual attendees, including warriors and bystanders."

Zach relayed all this in a way that was completely devoid of emotion. I applauded his ability to detach because my stomach was beyond sour.

He looked at us each in turn again. "The victim's skin would then be worn while performing a dance—"

"A dance?" Paige interrupted.

"What was their reason for doing all this?" I asked.

"The ritual was often in honor of Huitzilopochtli, a Mayan deity associated with warfare, the sun, and human sacrifice."

Say that name five times fast…

"Wearing the skin was a way of symbolizing

rebirth," Zach added. He pressed his lips together, seeming proud of his recount of history.

Maybe I should pat myself on the back, too. The bile *was* staying down.

"How do the feet and hands tie into the ritual, Zach?" Paige asked.

"Ah, good question. Those body parts were the priest's trophies."

"In our case, it also makes identification next to impossible." Jack pulled out a cigarette.

Pike came back to our huddle, slipping his cell phone into a shirt pocket. "Did someone mention the Mayans?"

"I did," Zach said.

Pike's eyes lit up. "Some people believe there's a connection between Georgia and the Mayans."

"Yes, I was going to get to that." Zach smirked with confidence. "You seem up on your Mayan history, Lieutenant."

Pike waved a hand. "Oh, no, not really. Honest to God, my wife is more into all this than I am, but as it turns out, I'm a good listener when she talks about it."

"Go on," Jack said drily.

Zach stuck his hands in his pockets and tapped a foot on the ground. His gaze was flitting about as if he was anxiously awaiting his turn to talk.

"Well, there have been remains found in Georgia that show cranial elongation just like the Mayans would do."

"What else?" Jack's impatience was tangible.

"They also found stone structures that mimic ones in the Yucatán. But that's not the most interesting part." Pike pointed to the torso. "Some people believe that the Mayans got the materials to make their blue paint from the land here in Georgia."

CHAPTER

15

"OKAY, NOW BEFORE WE GET too carried away with the assumption that the blue paint on the torso is the same as this Mayan blue, let's focus on what we do know." Jack was pacing the room back at the precinct while Paige, Zach, and I were seated at the table. We'd been at the crime scene for hours before regrouping here, and the hands on the clock were moving fast.

"Even if the blue isn't the same, other elements in the unsub's MO match up with the ritual," I began. "What if we're looking for someone of Mexican heritage?"

"Or someone who has studied it," Paige pitched in.

"It could be a teacher or professor of Mayan culture," Zach opined.

Pike came into the room then. "I've got a lot for you."

"That's what we like to hear," Jack said.

"The search of the public areas near the river

came back clean. Same with the officers who took boats down the river. No sign of any graves. But there have been more remains pulled from the river since you left. Teams are still working down there."

I wondered how many victims we'd get up to.

Pike continued. "I've also heard from the anthropologist. The arm found on Monday belonged to a twentysomething white male, so we won't need Stanley Gilbert's DNA to rule him out."

"That's the same as the victims' remains found last week," I said. It didn't mean Stanley's remains weren't going to be found, but with another victim being confirmed as a male in his twenties, Stanley—who was almost forty-one—didn't fit the mold.

Zach cleared his throat. "What about the blue—"

"The paint will be tested, and as soon as I hear anything, you will," Pike interrupted.

Paige looked at Jack. "I'd say we've found our killer's type, and it's another indication that the unsub is a man. It would be hard for an average woman to overpower these victims." Paige lifted her coffee cup to her lips and paused with it suspended there. "Not that it's impossible… If our unsub is a woman, she could have used a weapon or be exceptionally strong. We know that there was no evidence of the victim being drugged, though."

"I think we're looking for a male unsub, too," Zach said. "In Mayan culture, women were important to society, but they didn't get involved with the heart-extraction sacrifice."

"I don't know how long the Mayans took with

their sacrifices, but we know that this torso was covered in a blue paint or dye. If they followed the ritual, they would have painted the entire body blue," I said. "And if this guy is working by himself— we have no reason to believe otherwise right now— that would take awhile. Probably enough time for any drugs to leave the victim's system." I agreed with Paige and Zach, but playing devil's advocate was part of the job.

"True," Zach said, but then changed the subject. "For the Mayans, only select individuals were offered for sacrifice. In the case of heart extraction, it was conquered warriors of high station. By extension, our unsub is likely being very selective about his victims. We can already tell that he sticks to the ritual…at least mostly." He took a sip from his coffee cup.

"What do you mean *mostly*?" I asked.

"Well, if he'd adhered to the ritual strictly, then the skin would have been removed from the torso, but it wasn't."

"Maybe he decides in the moment whether he's going to skin them or not," Paige suggested.

"If that's the case, he's not adhering strictly to the ritual," Zach stated.

"So he's either not completely educated on it or he's choosing to make exceptions," I added. No one said anything, so I continued. "He doesn't seem to be making exceptions when it comes to his criteria for picking his victims, though. All the remains so far were from twentysomething males. Did someone that age wrong the unsub or did something pivotal happen to him as a young adult?" I was just thinking out loud now.

"Not sure if we can take that leap, Brandon," Zach stated soberly. "If he is performing the ritual, the gender and age of the victims can't be used as a basis for profiling. The unsub would be picking young men in the prime of their lives because they were worthy adversaries, worthy sacrifices."

"The question is, how do these young men go missing without anyone noticing?" Paige asked. "Do we really think they're all homeless or estranged from family, without friends?"

Zach shook his head. "The more I think about it, I don't think so. Men like that wouldn't strike our unsub as worthy adversaries."

"And if there are no recent reports of missing people from Savannah, it's safe to say he's picking his 'adversaries' from another area," Paige said.

"That means the unsub is hunting elsewhere and bringing his sacrifices back to this area where he does his thing and then kills and disposes of the bodies," I summarized.

"And he's likely not selecting his victims from the same vicinity or the similarities would get flagged in the system," Zach noted.

Not targeting the same vicinity…

"Our unsub must have a means of travel, then. A long-distance truck driver who likes to bring his victims home, maybe?" I suggested.

"Hmm. I'll call Nadia to check on any individuals

in the area who drive rigs," Jack said. "I'll have her examine any drivers' routes, too, and see if any missing persons matching our victimology intersect."

"There's something else the anthropologist told me," Pike chimed in. "The arm found on Monday was broken in the past."

"Does she know how long ago the injury happened?" Jack asked. "That could help us find his identity."

Pike nodded. "Around ten years ago."

I did the math based on the age range of the victim. "He would have been between ten and nineteen."

Pike turned to leave the room but stopped and spun around. "Actually, one more thing. Garrett Campbell will be conducting the autopsy on the torso first thing tomorrow morning. I figure you'll want to be there." Pike spoke as if Jack was the only one in the room. "Feel free to bring your team."

"Wait," I called out to Pike.

He came back into the room and cocked his head.

Everyone else seemed so fixated on the fact that we had a victimology type, there was someone else who was slipping through the cracks. "Where does this leave Stanley Gilbert?"

They all looked at me.

"His phone was in the river and he's just seemingly vanished," I continued. "What if he *is* the killer? Pike mentioned he doesn't have a backbone. If he was that way all his life, he could have been bullied.

Often kids who are bullied grow up to become involved in serial crime, sometimes killers, just to assume some control over their lives."

"Statistically speaking," Paige said.

"Which we rely on heavily," I fired back, and then I addressed Pike. "I'd like a full background on Stanley."

"Be my guest." He gestured for me to follow him. He led me through a bunch of hallways and finally pointed to a desk with a computer. "Use this one."

I sat down, and he leaned over the desk and brought up the database. I typed in Stanley's name, and within seconds, his face was looking back at me. The address on file matched where Jack and I had spoken to his wife. I suddenly remembered how the property backed up against the river.

I shook my head. I'd need more to substantiate a warrant for the property.

"You all right here?" Pike asked me.

"Yeah, I'm fine."

Pike left.

I went back to the screen, and my eyes landed on Stanley's previous address: Lansing, Michigan.

A northern accent...

A closer look at the report told me the Gilberts had moved to Savannah five years ago, but I was wondering about something else. I picked up my phone and dialed Nadia. "I need a favor."

"Brandon?"

"That's me. Listen, I need to know if Stanley Gilbert and his wife, Darla, own any other property besides their home."

"One minute," she said. Keys were being clicked in the background, and I envisioned Nadia madly typing away. A few minutes later, she said, "Other than their house, there are no other deeds in either of their names."

"Thanks, Nadia."

"Sure, don't mention it." She hung up before I could say good-bye.

I tapped my fingers on the desk in front of me, then brought up the backgrounds for Stanley's parents—Cecil and Arlene—starting with the mother.

The address staring back at me was in Lansing, Michigan, and her face was one I'd seen before in Shane Park's photo. I printed everything off and brought it back to the room.

Jack had Nadia on speaker.

"I didn't find any criminal cases in Savannah similar enough to get my attention, Jack. Solved or unsolved," she said. "But Missing Persons came back with a hit from five years ago here in Savannah. His name was Colin West and he was twenty when he was reported missing by his parents. That information is coming to all of you now."

Our phones chimed.

"Good job, Nadia," Jack said before ending the call and looking at me. "What have you got?"

I shared everything that I had learned and passed around the paperwork.

"Could be a coincidence," Jack said.

I stared at him blankly. "You don't believe in coincidences."

"Okay, Brandon, let's say these things don't look good for the guy," Paige started. "He's not of Mexican heritage and he's not a truck driver. How can we connect him to Mayan culture? How would he transport the bodies?"

I didn't like the answer that immediately fired in my head, and I looked at Jack. "We've got to speak with Darla again."

"Agreed, and while we're doing that," Jack said, addressing Paige and Zach, "you two speak with the parents who reported their son missing five years ago."

CHAPTER

16

IT WAS ABOUT SEVEN AT night and it had been about twenty-four hours since Jack and I had visited Darla the first time. And, here, we were back again. Lucky us... But this time we'd approach things as if Stanley was our unsub.

She greeted us with, "Did you find him?" Sadly, I sensed she wasn't too concerned about Stanley's welfare but, rather, missing her lackey.

Jack stood with his back straight, his hands clasped in front of him. "We'd like to come in as we have a few more questions about your husband."

She stared at Jack for a few seconds, but then let us in. We returned to the living room where we had sat the day before.

"We don't believe your husband is one of our victims," Jack began. "In fact, your husband is now wanted for questioning in regards to the murders themselves."

Darla didn't so much as blink slower, shift her body, or give any indication that she'd heard what

Jack had said. Either she thought Stanley was capable of murder and mutilation, or she was hard of hearing. Maybe she was in shock, though it seemed a stretch for her.

"Did you hear me, Mrs. Gilbert?" Jack paused. "He's a suspect for the murders."

"I heard you. I'm not deaf." Heat licked her voice.

Jack pursed his lips. "You don't seem too surprised."

Darla shrugged. "Should I be? And yesterday you believed he might have been a victim." There was no emotion as she nonchalantly discussed her husband's potential murder.

Jack glanced at me, and I assumed I was to take the conversation from here.

Stanley likely had little need to travel as an investment banker, but there was a question that we needed to ask anyway. "Did your husband's job ever take him on the road?"

"Why would it?" she spat. "He had a desk job."

I took a few paced breaths to calm my redheaded temper. "No conferences or work events?"

"No."

"What about for pleasure? Did he go away for—"

"No. I'm telling you, this is the longest we've been apart—from Monday until tonight—since we got married seventeen years ago."

Stanley might be our unsub, but in a way, I felt sorry for the man. "He never took a vacation and went somewhere without you?"

Darla jabbed a pointed finger toward me but

addressed Jack. "His ears need to be checked."

Heat laced down the back of my neck, and I tried to calm myself down with the sentiments that she wasn't worth losing my temper over and that we'd soon be gone. "It's important that you cooperate with us," I said.

"I am, but I'm also telling you we weren't ever apart except for when he went for work or ran errands for me."

"What kind of errands?" I asked.

She rolled her eyes. "You know, groceries, other odds and ends that needed buying or doing."

We didn't have proof that Stanley traveled without his wife's knowledge, but he could have beefed up the time it took for him to run errands. "Did he ever take an extraordinary amount of time with any of these activities?"

Both Jack and Darla looked at me. I would've sworn that Jack seemed impressed by my question.

"Not that I can recall." Darla eyed me critically. "Why? Do you think he chopped up people between grocery runs?"

Yes, that's exactly what I'm wondering…

"You said that Stanley spent all his time with you"—looking at Darla, it was easy to see what could cause the guy to snap—"but did he have any friends?"

"How the hell would I know?"

I don't know… You were married to him for seventeen years!

We were going to have to speak to Stanley's boss

and coworkers. Hopefully, we'd be able to get some names from them.

"When did you meet Stanley?" Jack inserted himself back into the conversation.

"We met in college. I just saw something in him."

"Saw what exactly?" I inquired.

"Just…something."

"Why are you being so vague about what attracted you to the man who became your husband?" I ground out, no longer able to keep everything bottled in.

"If you must know, he was just nicer than the other guys."

Translation: she could manipulate and control him.

"I can't believe he might have left me," Darla said. "What makes him think he can make it without me?"

Jack bristled. She might think I was hard of hearing, but she was hard of *comprehending*. Her husband could be a killer and she was choosing to wallow in self-pity?

"What did Stanley major in?" I asked.

Darla rolled her eyes again. "History, can you believe it? Do you really think that a lot of places hire historians? He ended up going to night school for banking, business, and investments."

"He didn't really have to work, though, if we get right down to it, did he?" I remembered the conversation from yesterday when she'd revealed that she had money.

"I let him."

Right, I'd forgotten that part.

I took a few deep breaths to cool my temper once more. "Do you know what he loved most about history? A certain culture?"

"I don't know. Stanley wasn't too much of a yapper, but he used to talk to me about going to Mexico. But there's no way I'm going there. You kidding me? Montezuma's revenge? No thanks. I don't want anything to do with that."

Pulling from a very, very deep place inside me now, I said, "Thousands of tourists go there every year and are just fine."

"Those are the ones you hear about."

Another deep breath. "Did he say why he wanted to go to Mexico?"

She waved a hand. "The people, their culture."

"Anything specifically?"

She shrugged. "He wanted to see Chichén Itzá."

A Mayan pyramid...

"You really think my Stanley is behind the murders?" Darla asked.

Jack and I remained quiet.

Darla's mouth gaped open—the first sign that our accusation had made any impact. "There's no way. He's too weak and timid. People walk all over him."

Neither Jack nor I would say this out loud, but she'd just provided a reason that supported Stanley being the killer. The unsub we sought claimed power over his victims and could very well be someone who didn't have it in his daily life.

"You said he stuck close to home," I said.

"No, I said he was usually *at* home."

"Was there anywhere he liked to visit, though? It's apparent he liked going to Blue Heron Plantation sometimes."

"Which I just found out about. From you." Darla shook her head. "I'm starting to wonder if I knew that man at all. He was the same-old for all the years I've been married to him. He'd go to work, come home; he'd do anything I asked of him. And now this? He's run off and he's a murder suspect? Why is he doing this to me?"

It was impossible to conjure empathy for her. I attempted to keep the conversation moving forward. "Why did you move from Michigan?"

"Why?" She appeared more shaken by that question than the thought of her husband being suspected of serial murder.

I kept my eyes on her. "Why is that an intrusive question?"

She took a deep breath. "It's not really. It's just a tough one." She played with the hem of her shirt. "My parents left this place to me when they died. I'd loved it ever since I first visited them here."

"One more question for now," I began. "Was your mother-in-law here for a visit recently?"

Darla's belly laugh brought tears to her eyes. "Mrs. Gilbert?"

She held up a finger. Not an index one to indicate for us to wait a minute but, rather, her middle one.

The treadmill at the hotel was in for another

pounding tonight.

"What is so funny?" Jack's tone was gruff.

Darla lowered her hand. "It's not really funny, I guess."

"Well, it sure as hell seemed like it was," Jack snapped.

"You'd just have to know our relationship. It's, well…it's not good. We can't stand each other."

Now that was bizarre. Stanley's mother was without a doubt the one Shane Parks had shown us. But whether they liked each other or not, why wouldn't Darla know she'd been in town?

CHAPTER

17

PAIGE AND ZACH WERE HEADED to speak with Norman and Gloria West whose son Colin had went missing five years ago. The couple still lived in Savannah.

As Zach drove, Paige was watching his profile. "You know, we talked about my love life yesterday, but we didn't get to yours."

"Oh yeah?" Zach glanced over. "I hadn't noticed."

"So…?"

"So, what?"

"Give me something." Paige might be a skilled profiler and investigator, but when it came to Zach, he kept his secrets well hidden. All she truly knew about him was that he enjoyed doing renovations on his home. She'd never been over there.

"My life isn't that exciting," he said. "Sorry to disappoint."

Ha! Now there was a tell in his eye, that glimmer that told her that whatever he'd just said was the opposite of the truth. She smirked at him. "Who is she?"

He kept his eyes on the road.

"Come on. What's her name?" Paige shifted in her seat and angled against the door so she could face him.

"Why does everyone need a love life?" he asked.

"I can tell you're avoiding here."

He glanced over at her. "Fine. Her name is Sheri."

"Ooh." She smiled at him, certain she looked like she was busted doing something evil. "How long have you been seeing her?"

Zach fell silent and turned into the driveway for the Wests.

"Zach?" she asked.

He turned the car off and unclipped his belt. "We have a job to do." He passed her a smile and got out.

What a brat.

She followed him to the front door. "You're really not going to tell me?"

He knocked. "Not right—"

The door opened, and Gloria West was standing at the threshold. They'd called ahead, so she just stepped back to let Paige and Zach inside.

"They're here, Norman," Gloria called to her husband as she closed the door.

Gloria was a slight woman in her fifties with pale-blue eyes and deep frown lines. A brief look at their backgrounds indicated that she and Norman didn't have any other children besides Colin.

A man came into the entry. Like his wife, Norman had deep wrinkles, his concentrated mostly in the brow.

Paige could only imagine how horrible their last five years had been. Waiting for a call that never came, knowing but not ever wanting to accept that their son was most likely dead.

"Is there somewhere we can sit?" Paige asked.

"Uh-huh," Gloria said, turning to lead them toward the dining room by the look of it. "Here, take a seat wherever you like." She implied the table, which had a lace tablecloth and two placemats atop it. Gloria picked up the mats and stuffed them into the drawer of a sideboard covered with framed photographs of an overweight young man, probably Colin. "Do either of you want an iced tea? Water? Coffee?"

Paige held up a hand and smiled politely. "No, thank you."

"I'm fine," Zach replied.

"I'm just going to grab a glass of water for myself, then," she said.

They took seats on either side of the table, leaving the heads for Norman and Gloria.

Norman walked around and sat down. Seconds later, Gloria returned with her water. She slipped into her chair and held on to her glass with both hands. The water clearly wasn't so much something Gloria had needed because she was thirsty, but a psychological aid to calm her.

Gloria pointed to the row of framed photos on the sideboard. "He was a handsome man, wasn't he? He had his whole life ahead of him."

"Sweetheart," Norman said softly from the other

end of the table.

"I know, I know." Gloria looked at Zach and then Paige. "I promised him I wouldn't get carried away talking about the past, but it's so incredibly hard. Do either of you have children?" Her gaze was on Paige.

"No, I don't," she answered.

"You don't know what you're missing. They are a blessing. And we were blessed with one. He was a miracle. And then—" her chin quivered "—he was just taken away from us."

"Gloria," another loving verbal poke from her husband.

"Yes, Norman." Gloria palmed her cheeks although no tears had fallen.

Paige imagined that she must have run out of tears over the past five years.

"What interest does the FBI have in Colin?" Norman asked the question, but he seemed to do so hesitantly, as if he expected them to say they had found his body. He wanted to know but didn't at the same time. A body meant any hope that had kept them moving forward would be extinguished.

Alternately, Gloria's eyes were wide with hope, but the spark was dim. "Did you find him?"

"Have you heard why we're in town, Mrs. West?" Zach asked.

Gloria's gaze drifted to her husband, and she blinked slowly. "We have."

"The remains of several people have been found," he went on, "but we haven't identified them yet."

"We're hoping there might be something you

could tell us to help our investigation," Paige jumped in before the Wests could respond to Zach.

"Well, I'm not sure what," Norman said. "We filed the missing person report. The cops investigated for a little while but nothing came of it."

"They told us to accept that our son was dead. Can you believe it? Accept it?" Gloria's cheeks reddened.

"Was Colin living with you at the time he went missing?" Paige asked.

"No, he was renting a place in town with Jesse Holt."

Paige's ears perked up. "Jesse Holt?"

"I take it you know him," Norman stamped out.

Paige glanced at Zach and then looked back at Norman. She nodded. "We do."

"Oh, he's bad news," Gloria lamented.

Zach leaned on the table. "Why's that?"

"He experimented with drugs," Gloria answered. "Tried to get my Colin involved, too."

Paige noticed how she had claimed Colin as her own, but it didn't seem to make any impact on Norman. The couple was an exception to the statistics of what normally happened when a child went missing and was presumed dead. They gave the impression that they were there for each other, weathering the storm together. Most marriages fell apart. Paige had to wonder, though, if the foundation would crack if they found Colin. Given how long ago he'd gone missing, though, if his remains were found, they'd likely just be bone now and the identification process would likely take awhile, especially if they had to wait on DNA.

"Colin never did drugs, though?" Paige asked.

Gloria was quick to shake her head, but Norman pursed his lips.

"You're not so sure, Mr. West?" Zach queried. He must have noticed the differences in their reactions, as well.

"Peer pressure can be hard to battle at any age," Norman began, sliding a look across the table to his wife, "but our boy was never a fighter."

"He was calm and peaceful. But you have to admit, Norman, that he'd have followed that Jesse kid to the end of the world."

"No, I can't, and I won't."

"Colin wanted to please Jesse, but you don't think he did drugs?" Paige directed her question at Gloria.

"She doesn't want to get the boy in trouble," Norman interjected. His voice turned stern. "He's probably gone, Gloria. They don't care if he did drugs other than if it might help find him."

Gloria scowled at her husband. Maybe there *were* underlying currents of tension...

"Fine, he might have smelled like weed on occasion. He told me that it was Jesse smoking it, though." She fired a glare at Norman. It seemed to bounce right off him.

"The report says that you last saw Colin two days before he disappeared," Paige said, steering the conversation back to the facts.

"Yeah, we went over for a visit, and he seemed agitated. He and Jesse had just had a falling out. Jesse said he was moving out, and Colin didn't know how he was going to pay the rent," Norman explained.

"How did Colin support himself?" Zach asked.

"He was working as a clerk at Clancy's. It's a grocery store in town."

Paige made a note of this.

"I really think that Jesse did something to him, I always have." Gloria was shaking.

Paige would ask Pike if they'd looked into Jesse Holt after Colin's disappearance the next time she saw him.

Fifteen minutes and several questions later, Paige and Zach were loaded back in the SUV.

"I wish we had some answers for them," she said.

"That makes two of us."

"Speaking of answers…" She smiled over at him. "How long have you and Sheri…you know?" She wiggled her eyebrows.

"Ugh," he said. "I'd thought you'd have forgotten about that by now."

"You're not the only one with a good memory."

"Fine, fine. One year."

"One year!" she exclaimed. "Holy crap, Zach! You're practically married. Wait, you're not married, are you?"

He was laughing. "Ah, no. Well, not yet anyway. I was thinking of—"

"You were?" she interrupted.

His laughter died down.

"On Valentine's Day," she realized aloud.

He shrugged. "Yep, but duty called."

"Sorry, Zach. Did she understand you being pulled away?"

He nodded and smiled. "She's the most understanding person I've ever met."

"Ah, Zachy's been bitten by the love bug."

He rolled his eyes. "Oh, God help me."

CHAPTER

18

TELEVISION WAS FOR THE WEAK-MINDED, and he found the futility of sitcoms to be tedious and mind-numbing. His thoughts would always drift—as they often did anyway—to the freedom of the spirit, to being rid of the flesh that bound him to Earth. There was one program that held his attention, though, when he decided he felt like watching something, and that was the news. Events most people considered to be tragic, to be evidence of a world full of chaos, he rather enjoyed hearing about. The car bombs, the terrorist attacks, the murders—these things only proved how fleeting an earthly existence was and how the way one spent one's time mattered.

When he wasn't making sacrifices, he was usually thinking about them—either past offerings or those yet to come. There was a hunger that raged through him that made such sacrifices necessary, and the constant natter in his brain told him he was living his life with purpose and according to divine plan.

He went to the fridge, took out a bunch of grapes, and broke off a cluster. He put them into a bowl and then filled a glass with cold, filtered water. Sitting down in front of the television with the bowl of grapes on his lap and the glass of water on the side table, he was ready for the eleven o'clock news.

"Hey, honey." His mother padded toward the sofa, wearing a robe over her pajamas and slippers on her feet.

He smiled at her, yet felt nothing for the woman who had given birth to him. And she knew how he viewed her, how he didn't have the same feelings other sons had for their mothers, but she accepted him for who he was. She didn't try to fix him when the rest of the world saw him as a freak.

He'd had no friends in school and was teased excessively for being different, but that was a small price to pay for being chosen. It had taken him awhile to fully realize his purpose, but once he had, there was no stopping him. He lived on a higher plane of existence than his human peers, one they couldn't comprehend. He saw the entire spectrum from life to death and beyond.

"I see you got yourself a snack," his mother said. She put a hand on his head as she walked along the back of the sofa toward the kitchen.

The home was open concept on the main level. The kitchen was next to the living area, and the latter had no interior walls. Rather, the arrangement of furniture and a large oval rug defined the space. He'd often imagine his father sitting in the chair closest to the TV, but his imaginings would never become reality. His father must have been ashamed of him as he rarely came around.

The doctors had labeled him and wanted to medicate him. Some had wanted to institutionalize him. But his mother hadn't let those people near him. She was like a mother bear with a cub, and he really could get away with anything in her eyes.

He turned on the television, and its light was harsh against the otherwise shadowed living area. He and his mother preferred to watch in relative darkness with a couple of table lamps turned on.

The banner for the eleven o'clock news flashed on the screen, the station's logo prominently displayed in the center.

His mother returned and sat on the couch next to him with a bowl of premade popcorn and a caffeine-free soda.

Chemicals upon chemicals were always her choice of snacks. People considered a risky lifestyle one that consisted of sleeping around, smoking, drinking heavily, or a combination of the three, but what would end up killing them was the so-called food they put into their bodies.

"The FBI has been called in after more severed remains were pulled from the Little Ogeechee River," the news anchor stated calmly from the news desk.

His eyes snapped to the screen. More remains? What did they mean *more*? And what *remains*?

"Two weeks ago," the anchor continued, *"remains of two unidentified young males were found. On*

Monday, additional remains were discovered and tied to a third victim, also male, also unidentified. All of them were in their twenties. Savannah PD's homicide unit has called in the FBI as they believe this is the work of a serial killer."

His mother shifted on the sofa beside him but didn't say a word.

Why hadn't he heard about this before now?

He straightened up, and his mother was eying him in his peripheral vision, but he didn't turn to acknowledge her. He kept his eyes on the screen, listening to every word the reporter was saying.

"But that's not all. Investigators have found additional severed remains just earlier today and continue to search the Little Ogeechee River. We were able to catch this footage before local authorities forced us to leave the area."

A brief video showed an investigative team combing the river with local law enforcement. There were four individuals who stood out among them—three men and a woman. With their assured postures and pressed suits, they had to be the FBI.

The video went back to the news desk.

"The causes of death haven't yet been determined, and authorities are withholding comment in this regard. All they will confirm is that remains have been found and that they are investigating."

"No!" The scream burst out of him, startling his mother, but she only briefly glanced at him. He jumped up and raced outside to the edge of the property, where it neared the river. He let himself be guided by his intuition, his memory, and the moonlight as thoughts were rushing through his mind. *Severed remains?* That part didn't make sense to him.

His feet sank into the ground, the mire attempting to suck him in and stop him. But he trudged on, his heart racing. When he took his next step, something hard scratched his leg. Reaching down, he pulled out a bone. His eyes widened. It looked like an arm.

He let himself drop to sit in the mud, letting it encase his legs and lap, while he held the arm. They had been *his* offerings that had been found in the river. They must have washed out with the recent rainstorms.

This was what happened when he waited too long between offerings. If only he'd been back here in the last two weeks, maybe he could have prevented this.

What was he going to do now? The FBI were here.

Rage quivered through him, and he closed his eyes, calling upon a higher power for direction. At that time, he sensed the moonlight getting brighter, and when he opened his eyes, the moon was clear of all clouds.

Maybe this wasn't a horrible situation. It could just be his time to receive the ultimate glory he was due.

Yes, he'd make another offering, and this one he'd present in full to the FBI. They'd study and analyze it, and come to realize that the man they were after was much more than flesh and blood.

CHAPTER

19

MY WORKOUT HAD BEEN TOUGH, but it hadn't completely purged my thoughts of Becky. I'd slept better last night than the night before, but I had to accept that I was going to miss having her in my life—even if it was just to talk to. Right from the beginning, conversation had come easy for us.

I wiped my neck and face with a towel, knowing it was probably time to get ready. A glance at the gym's clock confirmed it was six thirty. Jack would be knocking on my door shortly.

I rushed upstairs to my room to find Jack already waiting in the hallway. His eyes traced over me, from my sweaty hair to soaked T-shirt, to my shorts and running shoes. "Why aren't you ready to go? It's seven."

I moved past him and slid my key card into the door. "I just left the gym, and it was six thirty down there."

"Well, then their clock is wrong." Jack pulled out his cell phone and shoved the screen in front of me.

7:03.

Shit!

"Give me five minutes." I went into my room without waiting for a response and closed Jack outside.

It took a little longer than five minutes. All right, closer to ten, and Jack was across from my room, leaning against the wall when I came out. He pushed off when my door opened, and he had his phone out again.

"You've never been good with time, Kid," he said and took off down the hall toward the elevators.

There it is again.

But I guess when I was thirty-one and the man was a dinosaur…

I pulled my door shut and jiggled the handle to make sure the lock caught.

We met up with Paige and Zach in the hotel parking lot and headed over to Savannah PD. Once there, we all filled up on coffee, and Jack started the conversation.

"Nadia sent me a list of people in the area who matched the criteria of being of Mexican heritage and a professional truck driver, but it's not really much of a list. We've got three names." Jack turned to me. "Stanley Gilbert isn't one of them."

"He fits other criteria, though," I defended.

"His phone could have ended up in the river for many reasons," Paige said.

I locked my gaze with hers. "And coincidently near an arm?"

"We have no way of knowing why the phone was in the river. You said his wife is controlling. Maybe he threw it in there so she couldn't reach him." Paige raised her eyebrows.

"He has an interest in the Mayan culture," I reminded her.

"He studied it in school," she fired back. "It doesn't mean he still has an interest in it."

"All right, that's enough," Jack said. "Before this discussion goes any further, Nadia also had some success with Stanley's financial records. On Monday, Stanley withdrew his full daily limit from a bank in Chattanooga, Tennessee."

Unbelievable.

"On Monday? Wait, why are we just hearing about this now?" I asked.

Jack stared at me. "Nadia just got access to the financials."

"The family's financials?" I tilted my head. "Darla told us she manages the money, yet she didn't mention this withdrawal to us either time we spoke to her."

"Maybe she didn't know," Paige suggested.

I thought back to the nervousness she'd shown when we went to leave the first time. But maybe it wasn't so much her nerves getting the best of her but rather a desire to protect her pride. To admit that Stanley had taken money out would be tantamount to acknowledging Stanley had left her. "Oh, she knew. And Chattanooga? He could be taking I-75 back to Michigan. Maybe going to his parents.'" I glanced at Jack. "We should have locals drop in and see if Stanley's been in contact with them, or at least have their place put under surveillance."

"Sounds smart."

I wanted to pat myself on the back but restrained myself. I could definitely get used to receiving praise from Jack.

"You do realize, though, that he could be anywhere by now," Paige said. "Then again, he could still be in Tennessee."

"And with no hits on the BOLO for his Prius, he's likely driving something else," Zach said.

"Well, if he ditched it, it tells me he has something to hide, if you ask me," I concluded.

"Nadia has narrowed down the list of truckers to one driver whose route transects where a few white twentysomething males went missing," Jack said. "Good news is the man is currently between runs. His name is Carlos Rodriquez."

I smiled. "A perfect Spanish name."

"He's also a feasible suspect," Jack said drily. "You and I will go to Stanley's work after we meet with Garrett Campbell about the torso." Jack then addressed Paige and Zach. "I want you to go see Carlos. I'll forward you everything that Nadia sent me on him."

Zach nodded. "Any update on the number of remains found so far?"

As if he'd read Zach's mind, Pike came into the room. "I've got the latest count. Three more legs, another torso, and another arm. All are in various states of decomp. Some of the remains are just bone. Everything's been sent to GBI."

Jack nodded. "We're headed there soon to see Garrett."

"Do the remains match up with previous finds?" I asked. "Arms and legs without skin, the torso with skin and covered in blue paint...a missing heart?" Nothing about any of this was easy to verbalize.

"The second torso didn't have skin." Pike swallowed, the idea seeming to sour his gut. "But the heart was missing again."

"We'll need to find out if they were removed before or after death. We could be looking at our cause of death," Zach said. "Hopefully, the medical examiner will be able to answer that. Any results on the blue paint?"

"Not yet. But I assure you it's a priority," Pike said. "Officers haven't had any luck on the streets so far when it comes to missing people, either."

"Where is he getting his victims?" The question came out louder than I'd intended and may as well have been rhetorical at this point. But it was a glaring piece of the puzzle we were missing and one we'd better find soon.

"Lieutenant, I have a question for you about Jesse Holt," Paige spoke up.

"The former plantation employee?" he clarified.

"Yes. We spoke to the Wests about their son Colin, who went missing five years ago. At the time, he was roommates with Jesse. They fingered him as being behind their son's disappearance. Was that angle explored?"

"I can certainly pull the file again and take a closer look."

She nodded. "Thanks. Let me know."

"Will do."

CHAPTER

20

I CALLED LANSING PD ON our way to see Garrett Campbell. There hadn't been any sign of Stanley going to his parents' place in Michigan yet, but they were monitoring the situation. There wasn't much more I could do from here, so Jack and I drove the rest of the way to GBI in silence.

We entered the morgue as the chief ME was gloving up. "My gross findings tell me that we're looking at multiple victims again."

"So how many is that now?" Jack asked.

"Seven. Should we get started?" Garrett bobbed his head toward the gurney and the dismembered torso. Not that I needed him to point it out. Still, my gaze followed his direction.

"It's not the prettiest thing to look at, is it?" He lowered his head to catch my eye.

"Not exactly," I said. "Nor to smell." The stench ran right up my nose, and I stamped out the nausea.

There was a glimmer in Garrett's eyes. "There are masks in the dispenser over there if you want one."

"I'll be fine." And really, I should have been. What he didn't know was that I had seen worse—*a lot* worse. I'd seen ground human intestines, decapitated heads, severed penises. Yeah, working for the Bureau was certainly wrought with less-than-pretty things to look at.

"Do you have any questions before I get started?" Garrett asked.

"When should we know what was in the paint?" Jack stepped closer to the gurney, while I remained a few feet back. I would have moved farther away if I wasn't certain both men would catch it.

"It's nothing you can pick up at a store, I can tell you that with certainty." Garrett brushed his gloved fingertips along the skin and rubbed at the paint before showing us his hand. Blue particulates stood out against the black latex. "It's quite durable as you can see. It's held up against the elements, and to the touch—" he put his hand over the torso again "—I say it has a texture much like clay. A sample was already sent to the lab."

"Finding out its composition is a priority," Jack said in a no-nonsense tone.

"As we are well aware." Garrett's eyes went from Jack, to me, and back to Jack. "Shall we start now?"

"By all means."

Garrett dove right in. Not the most delicate way of thinking about things, considering the hole in the victim's chest, but it was what it was. He cut the Y-incision and flapped back the skin. It was one thing I'd never quite adapted to seeing, but at least it didn't have the effect of making me want to vomit, so I considered that a good thing.

Garrett stepped back to take a photograph of the insides. "The killer wasn't delicate with what he was doing, but see these?" He pointed to a couple of ribs that showed deep nicks. "Given the fact that the victims were restrained, and the way the blade shifted—" he pointed to some marks that didn't fall in line with the other grooves "—I'd say we have our cause of death."

My stomach churned. "His heart was removed while he was alive?"

Garrett was looking inside the chest cavity. "There's no doubt in my mind that the heart was removed perimortem."

I was suddenly aware of each of my heartbeats and thankful for their existence and the air in my lungs. I couldn't imagine what this poor guy had gone through. His heart torn out while he was alive... It was barbaric and sadistic by modern-day standards. And more than that, this indicated that Zach was more than likely right about our unsub carrying out an ancient ritual.

"Do you believe the blade used here was the same as that used on the arm and leg found last week?" Jack asked.

"Too soon to tell, but I'll be doing what I can to determine that." Garrett leaned in closer to the torso, but he must have caught a glimpse of something as he pulled back. He took a pair of what looked like long tweezers from a side tray and plucked something from one of the grooves in the bone. He held it up to the light, and I angled to get a look.

It was dull and made me wonder if it was flint like Zach mentioned the ancient Mayans had used in their sacrifice ritual.

Garrett put the piece in a vial. "I'll have an analysis done on this."

He went back to the remains. "The other organs appear intact. I'll take samples and have a toxicology panel run to see if this victim was drugged." Garrett spoke with his eyes and hands on the torso. "Of course, any evidence of that could be long gone. The digestive system should tell us how long it was since he last ate. Calculating time of death, however, with nothing more than what's in front of me is going to be impossible…"

"You have my number. Call the minute you have any more findings," Jack said, stepping toward the door.

"Will do." Garrett was back in the torso.

Jack and I left the morgue, and while Jack was excellent at hiding his emotions, I was full of empathy for the victims. And curious what about them specifically had attracted our unsub.

CHAPTER

21

Carlos Rodriquez was a native Mexican who had immigrated to Savannah twenty years earlier. He'd buried two wives and was a registered gun owner. Currently, he was single and living in a mobile home community in a double-wide. There was a garden bed outside that was overgrown with wild flowers and whatever seeds had found their way to the soil.

"He makes regular runs back and forth to Alabama," Paige told Zach as she summarized what they had on Rodriguez. "Missing Persons indicates that there have been a couple white males abducted along his route during the time he's been with Buck's Cartage."

"And Jack's sending us in alone?" Zach smirked at her from the driver's seat, teasing her about her lament from a couple days ago when they were on the way to see Jesse Holt.

"We're just getting a feel for the man. Nice and friendly," she mimicked back.

They were already parked in Carlos's driveway

beside his Buick LeSabre and had been sitting there for about a minute. She reached for her door handle and got out of the SUV.

As they approached the mobile home, she noticed someone holding back the curtain in the front window, but with the sunshine glaring across the glass, it was hard to distinguish much beyond that.

Zach knocked, and they waited. No answer.

"Does he think we don't see him?" Paige knocked this time, harder than Zach had.

"Go away!"

"Mr. Rodriquez, it's the FBI." She had to talk loud enough for her voice to travel through the door but not so loud that everyone in the neighborhood heard her. "We need to talk to you."

Her request was met with silence.

"They don't have back doors in these things, do they?" Paige asked. "Because I'm getting a bad feeling…" She stepped off the stairs, and so did Zach.

He was already around the side when a gunshot cracked through the air, accompanied by smashing glass.

Shit! Paige ducked and moved against the trailer to seek cover.

The shot had come from inside the trailer home and the bullet exited out the front window. Who knew where it had ended up, though.

"I know my rights!" Rodriquez yelled. The distinct sound of a gun cocking hit the air.

"We just have some questions for you," Paige

shouted.

Zach had inched his way back around to the front corner of the home, opposite Paige. Rodriguez was still on the other side of the front window.

Somehow they had to get the situation under control. Get him to relinquish his weapon and see that they were on his side.

"Nice and friendly, right?" she whispered to Zach.

"Go away!" Rodriguez yelled again.

"We need your help," Zach called out.

He shrugged when Paige looked at him. He was apparently playing good cop.

Rodriguez barked a laugh. "Ain't no Fed needing my help."

"Please," Zach said.

"That's it, I'm calling this in," Paige stated harshly and loudly to play up the role of bad cop, even though she was dialing Savannah PD.

"If I talk to you, will you go away?" Rodriguez asked.

"You have my word," Zach assured him.

Paige got through to PD and backup would be here soon. She put her phone away.

"Come out with your hands up, just so we know you're no longer armed," Zach directed.

"How do I know you won't shoot me?"

Zach holstered his gun, and Paige shot him a glare. "What do you think you're—"

"I've put my gun away," he said to Rodriquez.

Paige angled her head to see in the front window, and Rodriquez was moving around inside. The front door opened, and he stepped out.

"Hands on your head," Zach said, inching closer to the man.

He complied, and Paige hurried up behind him and snapped a pair of cuffs on his wrists.

"Hey!" He jerked his torso, trying to buck her off, but she held on.

A crowd was starting to gather in front of the house, and the faint sound of sirens echoed in the distance.

"This is an FBI matter. Go back to your houses," Zach directed them.

The people didn't move, just started talking to one another.

Paige and Zach shuffled Rodriquez into the house.

"What do you think you're doing?" he complained.

"You shot at federal officers, Mr. Rodriquez. That is a crime." Zach continued to play nice with the man, and Paige admired his ability to act.

"I didn't mean to." Now he was pouting.

"We just wanted to ask you some questions, be civilized about it," Zach continued.

Paige was glaring at Zach. Rodriquez could have killed her or Zach, or any number of innocent people. God, she wished she knew where that bullet had ended up.

"You're here about my weed, aren't you?"

Paige glanced at Zach and then back to Rodriquez.

"My doctor's just being stubborn is all. I need it for medical purposes," he rambled on. "Some jerk neighbor probably smelled it and called me in."

"We're not here about that. We're here about something far more serious," Paige said.

He squinted at her. "What else could you want me for?"

Paige caught the flashing lights from the approaching police cruisers out of the corner of her eye. Two of them pulled up and parked out front.

Paige continued. "We'd like to know if you can tell us anything about the remains found in the Little Ogeechee River."

"Ah, I heard about that on the news. A serial killer in Savannah? That's all I know."

"You're sure that's all you know?" she fired back.

"What else do you think I know?" he asked.

"You drive a truck for Buck's Cartage, yes?"

He jutted out his chin. "That's right."

"And you immigrated here from Mexico twenty years ago?"

"So?"

"You take great pride in Mayan culture?" she prodded.

"I mean, I guess. But you're losing me. Why are you interested in me?" He no sooner asked the question than his eyes widened. "You think I'm a suspect or something? The Mayan thing ties into the killings somehow?"

"It's an open investigation." Paige stood her ground. "We need to know if you have any knowledge of this person." She let go of Rodriquez, leaving Zach to hold on to him. She pulled up a photo of one of the missing men on her phone and held it for Rodriquez to see. "Do you know him?"

Rodriquez leaned in as if he needed reading glasses. "No."

She brought up another. "Look at this one."

"No. Listen, there is no way that I did whatever it is that you think I did." One of Rodriquez's legs buckled, but Zach held him up. "Damn bum knee. That's why I need the marijuana. It's arthritis."

"Do you have any other properties besides here?" she asked.

"No."

"Access to any?"

"No."

"What do you make of this?" Paige showed him a photo of the blue-painted torso.

Rodriquez's face contorted, and his lips curled in disgust. "Please...*no más.*"

Paige put her phone away. Given what was before her, she didn't think Rodriquez was the unsub they were looking for, but then again, he might be a good actor. Still, the only box he really ticked off was that of opportunity. Means and motive weren't there. He didn't seem to have a place to carry out the torture and murder, and besides losing two wives, nothing in his file indicated a horrendous life event that would trigger him to start killing people.

An officer rapped on the screen door. When Paige looked in his direction, he asked, "Everything under control, ma'am?"

She glanced back at Rodriquez. "It is."

e the request.

h, sure. I'll have you move to the conference
." Elliott stood up. "There are seven people
worked closely with him. Do you want them to
in one at a time?"

at will be fine."

ott showed us to a room with an oval table
ght leather chairs. There was a credenza at the
f the room with a silk flower arrangement in
At the front, there was a whiteboard.

wherever you'd like. I'll send Benny Robbins
. He's an investment specialist like Stanley

t left the room, and within three minutes,
man entered. He had broad shoulders, an
jaw, dark hair, and intelligent eyes.

ld I close the door?" he asked.

e," I said.

vas watching the man, letting his gaze fall
, studying him, analyzing him.

seemed to notice and squirmed under
tchful eye. "You want to—" he cleared his
-ask me about Stanley?"

. Have a seat." Jack gestured to the chair
m me, to his left, and Benny sat down.

vell do you know Stanley?" Jack asked.

hough, I guess. We'd hang out sometimes."

across the table. "Is Stanley all right? Did
happen to him?"

how, we're just trying to locate him," I

The officer came in, and there was another
behind him. Paige and Zach handed Rodriquez
over to them and shook her head at everything that
had transpired. Two for two—first Holt was carted
off to jail, now it was Rodriquez's turn. And it hadn't
needed to go the way it had. It could have just been
nice and friendly.

CHAPTER

22

JACK AND I WERE ON the way to Empire State of the South Bank to speak with Stanley Gilbert's boss, and I couldn't stop thinking about Stanley.

"Stanley's been browbeaten for the entire seventeen years he's been married to Darla. A person can only take so much of that," I said.

Jack gave me a sideways glance, took a few more puffs on his cigarette, and tossed the butt out the window.

He apparently wasn't going to talk, so I continued. "I still find it interesting that he chose now to supposedly leave his wife."

"It might be nothing more than a coincidence. We need more answers."

Jack parked the SUV, and not long after, we were sitting across from the bank manager, Elliott Dunham.

Elliott was in his forties, and on the surface, he was average in every way possible—height, weight, looks. There was a framed photo of him and a

beautiful woman on a tropical be
filing cabinet behind his desk. Th
ring on his finger, and he had a
to him that told me the marriag

"I'm in shock Stanley too
Elliott shook his head. "He was
employee, going beyond what

"What were his work
remembering the unrealistic
us.

"Nine until five, Monday th
when I said he went beyond
I just meant—"

"Monday through *Thursd*
day out of the week when S
for.

"Yeah?" Elliott's brows
didn't know that already?"

I glanced at Jack, and I
clenched.

"Did he ever travel t
asked.

"He did use his vaca
he went away, I wouldn'
anything outside of wo
know him better than
that his wife is quite t
and pulled out on his

Everyone seemed

"We'd like to sp
coworkers, then." Ja

mad
"A
room
who
come
"T
Elli
and ei
back
a vase.
"Sit
in first
was."
Ellio
another
angular
"Shou
"Pleas
Jack
over him
Benny
Jack's wa
throat "
"We d
across fro
"How
"Well e
He leaned
something
"Right
replied.

Benny's face paled. "H-he's not— I've heard about those body parts being pulled from the river."

"Stanley had Fridays off," I said, getting right to the point. "Do you know how he spent them?"

"At his cabin, mostly. Sometimes he went on road trips."

I looked at Jack. *Where to start?*

"Where's his cabin?" Jack asked.

"Here in Savannah. Actually—" Benny pulled out his phone and pressed some buttons "—I put the— Here it is." He rattled off the street address.

"Have you ever been to his cabin?" I asked.

"Oh, yeah. I go every week or so."

It sounded to me like Benny and Stanley were closer friends than he'd originally let on.

"Although, it's been a few weeks at this point, and last week, his mother was in town."

So that's where she'd stayed... I'd have the registration on the property checked.

Benny went on. "Sometimes Duane would meet us there."

"Who's Duane?" I asked. "Does he work here, too?"

"No. I'm not exactly sure what Duane does, come to think of it. He lives at home with his folks."

I was getting the hint from Benny's tone that he found it odd that Duane lived with his parents. "How old is he?"

"Thirty-two." Benny said it as if he'd be completely embarrassed if he had the same circumstances.

"Do you know why he lives with his parents?"

"Why wouldn't he? His folks are loaded. They have as much money as God."

"What's Duane like?" I asked.

"I'd say quiet, kind of…off? He seems to be a deep thinker, very introspective, but not the most focused. You can be talking to him, but he might as well be a million miles away."

"And what's Duane's last name?"

"Oakley."

I raised an eyebrow. It was time to call Benny out. "You obviously know Stanley more than 'well enough.'"

Benny's eyes diverted from mine briefly, and he clasped his hands on the table. He was looking at me when he said, "I was just…nervous. And uncomfortable. I didn't know exactly why you were interested in him. If he did something wrong, you might think I was in on it with him."

"Yet the first thing you brought up was concern about his welfare," Jack said, his tone dry.

"Like I said, I was nervous."

It was a possibility he was telling the truth, so I let it go for the moment. "Does Darla know about the cabin?"

"God, no," Benny said. "Are you kidding me? She would have put an end to it right then and there."

"Where did Darla think Stanley was when he was at the cabin?" I asked, even though I was pretty sure I already knew the answer.

Benny shrugged. "At work or running errands, I guess."

"What did you do when you were there?" I kept the questions going.

"Just hang out. Nothing special. I'm happily married, and I need to get away and blow off some steam once in a while. Ya know, be with another guy, drink beer, watch sports, burp."

Maybe being single again wasn't a horrible thing. Heck, I could spend Saturdays in my boxers, scratching my ass if I felt like it. "I hear you."

Shit. I just said that out loud.

"You're married?" Benny asked, clearly trying to establish a rapport with me.

I smiled. "Happily divorced. Happily single." Both came out feeling like lies. At least the *happily* part.

Jack looked over at me and gave a subtle shake of his head.

Time to get back on track.

"Where did Stanley go on his road trips?" I asked.

"Not too far. He had to be back for Darla." He paused. "She thought he worked on Fridays," Benny added.

We thanked Benny and went through the motions with a few more of Stanley's coworkers, but none of them were as insightful as Benny had been.

Jack called Nadia as we walked toward the car. "Nadia, we need to know who owns this property." He gave her the address of Stanley's cabin while I looked up the location on my phone.

Jack unlocked the doors to the SUV, and we got in. He turned the ignition and started the air-conditioning.

Nadia was on speaker now, her fingers clicking on her keyboard. "Here we go. It's registered to Cecil and Arlene Gilbert."

"One more thing, and I need you on this right away. Revisit Missing Persons and focus the search on white males in their twenties who were reported missing on Fridays within a four-hour drive of Savannah."

"Jack?" she asked, sounding confused as to why we needed that info.

He relayed what we'd learned.

"As fast as I can," she said.

He hung up and tore out of the parking lot. "Call Paige and Zach, and tell them where to meet us."

"Before I do that, look at this." I held up my phone for him to see. "The cabin is right on the Little Ogeechee River."

CHAPTER

23

"WHAT WAS WITH THAT 'happily divorced, happily single' bit back there?" Jack lit a cigarette and then lowered the window—something I wished he'd done first.

"Nothing." My insides were twisting. I didn't need him to think I was losing my grip on reality or that I was having some sort of emotional breakdown.

"I thought you were seeing that detective from Dumfries. Becky Tulson." He didn't bother to look over at me.

"Not anymore." It hurt a bit to admit out loud.

"You have bags under your eyes. You're up and in the gym before the sun's up. You spaced out at the precinct yesterday morning." Jack was talking to me—I mean, I was the only person in the car—but his gaze was frozen on the road.

"I often work out in the morning. I'm fine, Jack."

"Are you trying to reassure me or yourself?"

Mind games. At least I wasn't nibbling on the bait. "Have I done something that makes you think that I can't handle this case?" I asked.

Jack looked over at me now, taking a long inhale from his cigarette. "I never said you couldn't handle it. I just want to make sure that your head's here in Savannah."

"It is." I looked out the windshield and had to fight every urge to cross my arms and sink into the chair like a sulking teenager.

Jack nodded. "That's all I need to know."

"What about you?"

Oh, sometimes I spoke without thinking… And I really wished I hadn't asked *that* given the way the skin around his eyes wrinkled. He wasn't squinting because of the sun. Rather, this was a tell that I was encroaching on territory that was none of my business. But seeing as I'd already put the question out there, I might as well continue to hang myself. "You're smoking more than ever. You've have a rough few months." Really, it was more than a few, and there were a lot of hard weeks in a row. It started with his mother's death and ended with him almost being killed.

"Do I need to explain myself to you, Kid?"

I wasn't sure how I had expected Jack to respond, but I figured whatever he'd say would carry disdain and anger at intruding on his personal space. But his tone of voice, while firm, wasn't rough or heated.

"We have each other's back out here, Jack." I matched his friendly tone. "We all have the right to know that our team members are—" I didn't want to say *emotionally stable*. What was a good alternative?

"—doing all right. You went through a—"

"Don't start." Now his voice carried a harsh edge.

"You almost died." Saying that out loud, I wondered if I had been more affected by his experience than I'd realized. I sincerely cared for Jack despite his gruff exterior. You could say that I respected his tenacity and his demand for perfection, despite it being a high standard to measure up to sometimes. But it served to make me a better agent, to give me something to strive for.

Jack remained silent, finished off his cigarette, and tossed the butt out the window. "You don't have to tell me."

I'd almost forgotten what I'd last said by that point.

And those words were all he said the rest of the way to Stanley's cabin. I guess there wasn't much else for him to say. Really, he'd told me more than I'd expected he would. With those six words, he'd revealed that his experience was on his mind, that he was reliving that day over and over again. For some reason, I often regarded Jack as being larger than life, something other than human, but at times like these, I saw a glimmer that told me he wasn't much different from the rest of us.

Jack pulled into the driveway of the cabin, and not long after, Paige and Zach parked behind us. There was no sign of Stanley's Prius and no garage.

The cabin itself wasn't much to look at from the outside. It was vinyl-sided and compact—probably no more than five hundred square feet.

Paige and Zach went around to the left of the building. The right side was tight against a hedge. I went with Jack to the front door. He banged, but there were no sound coming from inside.

I looked in the window next to the door. Its curtain was pulled back. "It's just a living room."

Jack and I crept to the back of the house where Paige and Zach were peering through the windows.

Zach pulled back from the last one. "Haven't seen anything that stands out, Jack."

We all looked at Jack for our next step.

"Spread out and look along the river," he said.

I looked at the soft ground. Was he serious? We were all in dress shoes and nice clothes. Not to mention the closer we got to the water, the greater the chance of encountering an alligator. Back in Virginia, the biggest threat in my backyard was a rabid squirrel.

I pulled up my pant legs and treaded carefully, but my shoes still sank into the mud.

From what I could see, no areas screamed of recently dug graves or disturbed ones. The edge of the river was lined with bulrushes, but between the waving stalks, I saw the remains of what had been a boat dock. Time had settled it at a sharp angle, and the bare wood had been bleached by the sun. It didn't stop an alligator from lounging on it, though.

That was it. I was out of there. I turned around to head back toward the cabin.

Paige laughed. "It's just an alligator, Brandon."

Nope, we'd come, we'd looked around, and there

was no sign of human remains poking out of the mud. There was no Stanley, and from what we could see, there was no indication that any murders had taken place inside.

"I'm glad I'm here to provide some comic relief," I said to her.

Jack's phone rang then, and when he hung up, he said, "We're going in."

"Jack?" Paige asked.

"That was Nadia. She got a hit in Missing Persons that could be one of our victims."

Jack didn't normally act on could-be's. He acted on warrants and legal cause.

I locked eyes with Paige, then Zach, but they both followed him so I did the same. Jack stepped aside for me to pick the lock.

"You sure you don't want to wait on a warrant?" I asked.

"Brandon, get us in there or get out of the way."

I held up a hand briefly, then got to work. Less than a minute later, we were inside.

Instead of getting the chills that usually shot up my spine when narrowing in on a killer, I felt like I was trespassing and invading someone's personal living space.

Just as I had concluded from the outside looking in, the place was dark and the furnishings sparse. In the kitchen, there were dishes on a drying rack. There was a TV in the living room, and it had cable. It seemed like an ordinary cabin, but the air was fresh, indicating that the place had been aired out recently. Maybe first impressions here hadn't painted an entirely accurate picture. He could have just cleaned things up for his mother.

I headed for the bathroom, not certain I really wanted to see it. There'd been a past case where we'd found a severed head in a toilet bowl, and I'd barely made it through seeing that. If someone was going to rip out a beating heart, there would be a lot of blood, and that would make a bathtub the easiest place to clean up. I stepped inside the room and resumed breathing.

"No tub, just a shower stall," I called out to the team. I didn't want to look in the toilet, but I inched my way toward it and lifted the lid with my shoe. Nothing but water.

Jack came to the doorway first.

"I just don't see how Stanley would have the room to work here," I said. "Where would he have stretched out his victims? Cut off their hands and feet? Buried them? There don't seem to be any bodies in the muck we waded through. No blue paint, either."

Jack remained silent for a few seconds. "I agree," he said, already heading to the door.

So now we'd entered the man's cabin, left our muddy shoeprints everywhere, and were walking away with nothing.

"It's time to fill us in, Jack," I said. "What makes you so sure that Stanley was involved with the missing person case Nadia told you about?"

"We'll discuss it back at the precinct."

"And we're just leaving his place like this? Unlocked?"

"I'll get someone to take care of it." Jack and I locked eyes. Peering into his, I couldn't help but question if he'd been telling me the truth when he'd said he was fine.

BACK AT THE PRECINCT, Jack tossed a printed copy of the missing person report on the table. "His name is Eric Morgan. He was reported missing by his wife, Kelly, in Atlanta last Friday."

"Atlanta's less than four hours from here. Close enough for a Friday road trip," I said.

Jack gave me an I-told-you-so look—raised brows, tight lips—telling me that's why he'd justified entering the cabin.

"The man is married?" Paige stated rhetorically as she passed the report to Zach to read.

"I'll want you and Zach to go speak to the wife," Jack told Paige, "show her Stanley's picture, see if he looks familiar."

Zach looked up from the report. "Locals investigated but didn't turn up anything."

"Let's hope we can do better," Jack replied.

"Eric is also a father to a seven-year-old girl," Zach continued. "The family was at Perimeter Mall and it was around noon when he went missing. His wife said he disappeared when the family split up to go to the restroom. Under distinguishing markers, it shows a tattoo on his chest—a heart with the initials *E* and *K* inside."

"At this point, if we've found pieces of him, we wouldn't know," Jack stated somberly. "I've already requested that Stanley's picture be distributed among the media immediately. While I was doing that I got a message from GBI. The results on the blue paint…" Jack handed Zach a printout.

Zach exchanged one report for the other. His eyes barely hit the page. "Oh…"

I didn't like the sound of that. "It's a match to what they believe is in Mayan Blue?"

"Yep. Copal resin, leaves from an indigo plant, and a type of white clay called palygorskite."

Pike had mentioned that the Mayans may have made their blue paint from ingredients found in Georgia. "Let me guess, all of that is found here?"

"Copal resin can be found in sweet gum trees, and both it and indigo plants are indigenous to Georgia. And attapulgite, a composite of smectite and palygorskite is mined in Attapulgus, Georgia, a five-hour drive from Savannah." Zach continued as if this were all routine to him. "And the blue paint is quite resilient."

"As we saw with the torso," Jack said.

"I hadn't mentioned this before now but some sacrifices were painted blue and tossed into wells to appeal to rain gods," Zach went on. "A sacred cenote in Mexico had a blue residue on the bottom that was fourteen-feet thick."

"From the sacrifices?" I asked. Wait, why was I encouraging this history trivia session?

Zach nodded.

Paige turned to Zach. "If our unsub is applying the blue with his hands—"

"He'd have blue hands," Zach finished for her. "Unless he used gloves."

"Where would he get the clay?" Jack asked. "And can we tie these components to Stanley Gilbert?"

Zach let out a deep breath. "Attapulgite is used in several over-the-counter medications to treat diarrhea, and it's added to lime mortar."

"Which is?" I asked.

"It's used for period-home restorations." Zach really was a walking encyclopedia.

We were in Savannah, Georgia, established in the early seventeen hundreds, with its share of old homes and buildings. If Stanley wasn't our unsub, we'd really have fun narrowing things down.

Zach touched Paige's arm. "Palygorskite is also a component of cement."

"Jesse Holt works at Savannah Cement," she said.

Jack shook his head. "For now, we're going to focus on Eric Morgan's wife. I want you and Zach to go speak with her in Atlanta, show her Stanley's picture—Jesse's, too, if you want—see what you can find out. Brandon and I are going to talk to Duane Oakley, one of Stanley's friends, and see if we can connect Stanley to another person or location where he might be carrying out the ritual."

CHAPTER

25

THE OAKLEYS' PROPERTY DEFINITELY SHOWED that they had money, just as Benny had told us. There was a gated entrance, and the house was set back from the road with a long, gray-brick driveway leading up to it. The house matched the stone of the driveway and was a single story, although I'd guess the ceilings weren't a standard height of eight feet but rather ten to fifteen. The landscaping was done by a professional, possibly a crew, even, and there was a paved path into the gardens with a bench that overlooked them.

I pressed the doorbell, and a piece of classical music played inside the home. Before the song finished, the door opened and a fiftysomething woman was standing there in an apron.

Jack held up his credentials, as did I. He made the introduction. "We're special agents with the FBI. I'm Jack Harper, and this—" he gestured to me "—is Brandon Fisher. We'd like to speak with Duane Oakley."

Her face fell and her mouth made an *O*. She held up a finger and excused herself. She left the door wide open. The interior of the home was certainly posh. High ceilings, as I'd imagined, crown moldings, chandeliers—

Another woman came to the door. She had a thin frame and an oval face. Her hair was pulled back into a loose bun, and I wouldn't be surprised if it reached past her shoulder blades when it was down. "Why do you want to speak with my son?"

"We have some questions for him about Stanley Gilbert," Jack replied.

"I just saw Stanley's picture on the news," Mrs. Oakley said. "What's this about?"

Jack held his ground. "We'd like to speak with Duane directly, ma'am."

"Fine." She teetered off in a huff, and a man in his thirties came to the door.

"Hello?" The word was arched, as if he wasn't sure who we were or why we were there.

Jack made the introductions again. "We need to talk to you about Stanley Gilbert."

"Yeah, sure. Come in." Duane led us to a sitting room with twelve-foot coffered ceilings and wainscoting. The trim was white, and the walls the color of butter. The afternoon sun was streaming in three large windows and somehow brightened the yellow.

Jack and I took a seat on a couch, and Duane sat in a chair.

"Mom said he was on the news," Duane said.

"How well do you know Stanley?" Jack asked right away. He wasn't getting sucked into a meaningless sidebar.

"Pretty good. We'd get together and have beers usually at least once, if not twice, a month."

It was time to get more into Stanley's character. "Did you ever see him lose his temper?" I asked.

Duane laughed. "Not in the two years I've known him. He probably catches flies and releases them somewhere they can't bother him."

"How did you meet?"

"I had some investment needs, and it so happened Stanley worked where I banked. He helped me."

"What do you have in common?"

"Not much." A small chuckle. "But he's a calm and relaxed person, and I have a hard time around high-strung people."

"Did you ever go to his cabin?" I asked, wondering if he'd lie to me.

"Sometimes."

"And you'd just hang out there, have a couple beers?" I relaxed into the conversation to set Duane at ease.

He smiled. "Yeah, exactly."

"You said you sometimes went to his cabin, but did you go anywhere else together?"

Duane shrugged. "We have drinks downtown at Patty's Pub on occasion."

Why would Stanley risk going out in public and getting busted by Darla? Was there something special about Patty's Pub?

"What about anywhere else?" I asked.

"Nope."

It was time to press a little harder. "We understand that Stanley sometimes takes day trips on Fridays. Do you know where he goes? Any place he enjoys going regularly?"

"Besides his cabin, he likes to go to Blue Heron Plantation. Beyond that, I don't know."

"Does he have access to any properties besides his house and cabin that you're aware of?" Jack asked.

Duane shook his head.

"Not to any that you or your parents might own?" Jack was the one pressing now.

"No. My parents own this house and a place in Florida, but Stanley's never been."

We might have left Duane more confused than we found him, but it went both ways. We still couldn't connect Stanley to a property where he could make the sacrifices and dispose of the bodies.

CHAPTER

26

THE MORGANS LIVED IN THE middle of a high-class suburban paradise. All the houses were nestled close together with similar architecture on dime-sized lots. Every detail of the homes was thought-out. Even the garages didn't have the typical roll-down steel doors. Instead, they were gable-style with some square windows at the top.

The Morgans' house was a powder blue with crisp white trim. Zach pulled the rental SUV up to the curb in front. In the driveway, a woman was helping a young girl out of a minivan. She stopped when she turned and saw Paige and Zach.

The woman was wearing dark sunglasses, despite it being early evening, and Paige could see her trying to make sense of who they were. She carried on, though, unloading some grocery bags from the backseat and helping her daughter to the house.

Paige's heart was breaking for Kelly Morgan. "I can't imagine what she is going through."

"Me either. And it's only been a week." Zach cut

the engine and got out of the vehicle.

Paige followed his lead. It was best to get this over with as fast as possible. But she had to focus on the reason they were there: they had a potential lead in her husband's disappearance.

Zach lifted his hand to knock, but Kelly had the door opened before he could.

Her shoulders sagged, and up close, with her glasses off, grief was etched into her facial expression. Bags lined her eyes and told of little sleep. "You cops?"

Paige held up her credentials. "FBI."

"Are you here to tell me my husband left me, too? Because if you are, you can leave." Kelly crossed her arms.

"No, we're not." Paige held eye contact with her, hoping that Kelly would get the message that they were there to listen and to help.

Kelly stepped back inside her house and gestured for them to enter. Zach closed the door behind them.

"I'm Paige, and this is Zach." She wanted to do whatever she could to set the woman at ease; she'd been through so much already.

"Kelly... But I guess you know that." She shook her head. "Let's go into the living room."

She led the way and took a seat on one end of a sectional couch. Paige sat beside Kelly, Zach next to Paige. Framed pictures on the wall showed a happy family of three in different poses and settings.

"Where's your daughter?" Paige asked, not seeing

the little girl.

"She's in her room. I could tell you were cops... or something. I gave her a cookie and told her to go play." Kelly's face paled as she met Paige's eyes. "Have you..." Her chin quivered, and tears seeped from the corners of her eyes.

"No," Paige said softly.

Kelly wiped her cheeks and then twisted the wedding band on her finger. "I know he's dead. I can just feel it." She put a hand to her chest, and the sadness emanating from the woman was enough to labor Paige's breathing, but she had to detach from the emotions. That was probably the most difficult aspect of the job for her.

Paige summoned some strength and asked, "Can you walk us through the day your husband went missing?"

"You mean the day he was *taken*?" Her tone was sharp, bitter. Not at Paige or Zach, but at the situation she found herself in. She was living a nightmare that no one wanted to have.

Paige nodded. "Yes."

"We were just at the mall, walking around. It was actually Eric's idea to go that day." Kelly paused and made eye contact with Paige. "How is that even right?" She let the rhetorical question sit out there for a few seconds. "Brianna—that's our daughter— wanted ice cream for lunch." She stopped talking, and an odd smile touched her lips.

"Mrs. Morgan?" Paige prompted.

Kelly looked at her. "Eric spoiled her rotten. She

loved her father."

Past tense. It was probably a way of preparing herself for the news of his death that she figured was coming.

"Brianna wanted ice cream... Then what happened?" Zach asked.

Kelly glanced at him. "We all went to wash our hands." Her eyes glazed over.

"In the public restrooms?" Paige clarified.

"Yes. If only I hadn't insisted that we all—" Kelly choked up.

Paige continued. "Local police investigated your husband's disappearance—"

Kelly scoffed. "If you say so. Seems to me they gave up awful quickly. Said there was no ransom demand, and without any real cause to suspect foul play, they had nothing to go on. They told me that missing persons aren't actively investigated. As if they had done me a favor by looking into it the bit they had. And then they turn around and tell me that Eric probably left me. *Probably?* And that's insane because Eric would never do that to me or to Brianna." Kelly was trembling now.

"Did you see anyone suspicious hanging around your family that day? Someone you kept seeing maybe?" Paige asked.

"Not that I can remember." Kelly ran a hand across her forehead. "God, I wish I could."

Paige pulled out her phone, brought up a photo of Stanley Gilbert, and held the screen out for Kelly to see. "Do you recognize this man?"

Kelly took the phone in her hands. "He doesn't look fam—" She enlarged the image and dropped the phone to the floor. "Oh my God, yes! Yes, that's him. The janitor. He was the one. It's his eyes. I recognize his eyes."

Paige picked up her phone. "He looked different otherwise?"

"Um, yeah, he had a—" Kelly closed her eyes for a second. "He had a mustache. Who is he? Why did he take my Eric?" She started shaking, and Paige moved closer to her and put a hand on the woman's forearm.

"His name is Stanley Gilbert," Paige explained.

"I don't know him. And why my Eric? Why?" Desperation and hysteria mingled in her tone.

"We'll do all we can to find out," Paige reassured her. "Where was he when you saw him?"

"He was standing near the Dairy Queen eating. I figured he was on his lunch break."

"And he was alone?" Paige was thinking about Jesse Holt, even though they hadn't been able to connect him to Stanley.

"Yes."

Showing her Jesse's photo right now would just set things off course. "And the last time you saw your husband he was going into the restroom?"

Kelly ran a hand over her forehead. "I…I never saw him go in. Brianna and I were ahead of him. Maybe he never did… God, I don't know."

"Where are the restrooms in relation to DQ?"

"Right there, pretty much."

The picture was starting to come together. Stanley, impersonating a janitor, had been standing there poaching, waiting for the ideal and unsuspecting white male in his twenties to come along. He'd probably snatched Eric in the restroom.

Kelly looked at Paige, her eyes bloodshot, her cheeks tearstained. "Do you think Eric's dead?"

Paige hated the direct question, but she had to retain as much professionalism as she could. "Until we know what happened, it's best to stay positive."

"Is it?" Kelly spat. "That's what you'd do? Who is that man, anyhow? I'd never seen him before that day. He'd have no reason to take Eric. Unless..." She looked at them as if seeing them for the first time. "You're with the FBI... Doesn't the FBI only investigate serial killers?"

"Please, Mrs. Morgan. Let us do our jobs. We will get you answers." Paige hoped she could live up to the promise.

Kelly shifted on the couch to face Paige. "You have a body, don't you? And you think it might be Eric's."

Unfortunately, Paige couldn't avoid this disclosure. As gently as she could, she said, "We have found unidentified remains."

"Oh God!" Kelly started sobbing.

Paige rubbed Kelly's back. "Shh," she said, trying to be soothing. "We don't know anything yet."

"And we could really use your help," Zach tiptoed. "You mentioned that you thought Stanley was a janitor. Why?"

Paige glanced at Zach and subtly bobbed her head. If he hadn't asked, it would have been one of her next questions.

Kelly took a few heaving breaths. "He had one of those large garbage bins on wheels."

"What did it look like?" Zach asked.

"It was black."

He nodded, jotting down what she recalled. "Was there garbage already inside it?"

"Uh, I don't know. It had a lid."

"What was he wearing?" Zach asked.

"Gray coveralls, I think?" She sniffled. "That's all I remember."

"You've done great, Mrs. Morgan," he assured her.

"I never told any of this to the local police." She hiccupped a sob. "I didn't think about him. And now...he could have been the one to take my Eric." She cupped her face with her hands.

Traumatic situations played wild tricks with the mind, and she likely hadn't considered the janitor a threat. "None of this is your fault," Paige told her.

Kelly let her hands drop away. "How do you know?"

Paige made sure to look in Kelly's eyes as she spoke. "Given the setup and where he was standing, it would have happened to someone regardless."

"Is it sad to say I wish it was someone else?" Pain was tattooed into her expression, her limp body language, her lack of energy.

"It's natural to feel that way." Paige gave it a few seconds before continuing. "Do you need us to call anyone to come be with you?"

Kelly shook her head and wiped her cheeks. "No, I'll be fine."

"We will keep you posted."

"Uh-huh." It wasn't so much laced with disbelief but heartbreak.

"Here's my card." Paige extended one to her. "Call me if you need to."

Kelly nodded, and Paige and Zach excused themselves.

Out in the SUV, Zach got behind the wheel. "A garbage bin with a lid doesn't sound right to me. Normally, they're open."

Paige thought back to the last one she'd seen. "You're right. He probably put Eric in there and wheeled him right out of the building." She turned to Zach. "Was there any note in the file about the locals requesting surveillance video from the mall—inside or outside?"

"Not that I remember."

He had an eidetic memory. She flashed him a brief smile. "Then they didn't."

"We'll ask Perimeter Mall about that and the bins, but I made another observation in all this."

"Shoot."

"There's no way Stanley could have loaded the bin into his Prius. So either he left it behind or he was driving something else."

"I'd say the latter is more likely. But there are no other vehicles registered to him. And he couldn't have rented one or it would have shown up in his financial records. Most rental companies require a credit card. Nadia would have caught that."

Zach winced. "Not necessarily. She was focused on what happened since Monday."

"Nah, we've been told Darla's in charge of the money, and she would have noticed the transaction."

"So where does that leave us?"

"Someone else is involved. Has to be."

"I think so, too."

The case had just gotten a little darker. It had merely been an idea before, but now they were pretty sure they were searching for more than one unsub.

"Well, the rituals were not a solitary affair, either," Zach said. "When the Mayans performed the sacrificial ritual, it involved the man who ripped out the heart, a priest, and four blue-painted attendants. On top of that, you had the crowds who observed."

She nodded. "I'll have Nadia take a look into vehicles owned by Stanley's friends, Duane Oakley and Benny Robbins."

"Absolutely," Zach said. "And the BOLO on Stanley's Prius hasn't had any hits yet, so maybe Stanley is driving the vehicle he used for the abductions."

"Which is what, though? We have no idea," Paige lamented.

"We're not completely without leads. It would have to be something large, like a cargo van, for instance."

"True," she agreed. "Okay, I'll call the mall, but

I'm going to make another call first."

"To Jack?"

"Nope, to Lieutenant Pike. He hasn't updated us on Jesse Holt and Colin West." She dialed his cell number, and he answered on the third ring. "It's Paige. How did you make out researching Jesse Holt?"

"I was going to update you when you came back in, but I spoke to the detective who looked into the Wests' case originally. Jesse Holt was cleared as a suspect. He had an ironclad alibi. He was in Cancun that week. Tickets, passport, all of it was verified."

"And the Wests would have been told this?"

"They absolutely were." Pike paused a few beats. "Some parents have such a hard time in this situation—their child goes missing and they want quick answers, so they're blind to the truth. They want someone to point a finger at."

She wasn't sure she appreciated Pike's lesson as she was already aware that was a possibility. "Thanks." She hung up, looked over at Zach, and shared everything Pike had told her. "Holt's not behind Colin's disappearance."

Zach flicked a glance at her. "Then who is?"

CHAPTER

27

HE WAS DRESSED IN BLACK, a god in human form. The offering was naked before him and bound by chains. He chanted as he dipped his hand into the mixture, his fingers coming out coated in blue. He started with the offering's face, pressing the paint to his forehead and working his way around his temples, down his cheeks, along the length of his neck, the back of his neck, behind his ears, *on* his ears…

The offering let out a moan, and his eyelids slowly fluttered. When they fully opened, he screamed incoherently, and it was then that he must have realized his tongue was gone. His eyes widened, and tears fell, streaking the blue paint.

He began again, first touching up the offering's cheeks and then smearing the blue over his shoulders, his arms, his hands, his back, his buttocks, his privates, his thighs, his calves, his feet. All this time, the offering remained quiet and still. Broken. Succumbing to the reality of his fate.

When all the paint was applied, he stepped back

to admire his work, the time for sacrifice upon them. The act itself fed his soul like a walk in nature did for some people. But he wasn't "some people." He was above the masses, and he'd evolved through his awakening. He no longer had to close his eyes to elevate above this flesh-and-blood existence. But as it was, he was stuck inside this form—five foot eleven, black shoulder-length hair, brown eyes, alabaster skin. Yet, he also appreciated having touch and taste, which came with being entombed in flesh, and breathing, the sound of doing so and the feeling of oxygen filling up his lungs.

He inhaled deeply, feeling it enter his lungs, expand his diaphragm. As he emptied his mind, he let his eyes roll back in his head, savoring the moment for a few seconds. He then looked on his offering. The man was weak and feeble, submissive, conquered, without voice.

He removed the restraints, and the offering, who hadn't eaten much of anything for days, had no strength to hold himself up. The offering's legs were like a rag doll's beneath him as he guided the man to the outer room. Without the strength to resist him, the offering stumbled onto the sacrificial stone. At this point, he restrained the offering to another contraption that would stretch out his body and elevate his chest. The offering was bound once more at the wrists and ankles.

A smile teased his lips as he observed the offering watching him, his gaze indicating that he was already drifting partway into the next realm. Yet, the offering managed to yell and buck with remarkable strength now. The chain was being wrenched, but there was no way he could break free of his bonds. And there would be no one to hear his screams.

The protest was short-lived, and the offering retreated again into silence, a calm serenity, a state of detachment and observation.

This offering was perfect. A young man of strong will, a former protector, and a provider. He had been a worthy opponent.

"You will ascend soon. The time is near." He left his offering for a few seconds and procured the sacrificial knife.

The offering thrashed feebly, tears running down his cheeks in sheets, as he cranked the ratcheting system to tighten the constraints. As the chains pulled on the offering's arms and legs, bones popped, separating limbs from the joints, the cries became bloodcurdling howls. They reached his ears like music, praise to the gods. This was the sound of the defeated. But the offering wouldn't suffer for long, and until then, he would bask in the ritual process.

He stopped the ratcheting system and peered at the offering. The man mumbled, not a word of it coherent. The offering was likely pleading for his life and his freedom, though. Probably adamant about how he'd be found, how his murder would be atoned for, full of threats—none of which would see fulfillment. Not when it was divine purpose that he died.

Beautiful.

"You have fought courageously, yet you are not strong enough." Closing his eyes, he inhaled his own majestic nature, his godliness. The sound of beating drums and cheering rang in his ears.

He smiled as he was about to embark on his finest hour. After all these years and countless offerings, he was finally going to get praise and admiration for his hard work. Not that he'd ever required it before—at least not from the earthly realm. His accomplishments were appreciated by those in the heavenly realm, the place where he belonged.

His heart pumped fast with anticipation as he spoke in Spanish to call upon the heavens for their blessings for his safe return and to express his faith in divine timing. While he was stuck in this human body, it would not be for much longer.

The offering's cries were dying down, and he feared the man might have passed out. He slapped his face to rouse him. He needed the offering to be awake for the next step.

"Prepare yourself for the afterlife." He took the knife and thrust it into the offering's chest, his other hand closely following it, and he came out with the man's still-beating heart, blood dripping from his hands.

Tremors ran through him, and he felt the divine present with him. He closed his eyes briefly and then opened them, his head tilted heavenward. He held the still-beating heart over his head for a moment and then placed it on a silver plate.

He let out a yell at the victory, at the release, at

the sacrifice. He smeared blood from his hands on the faces of four idols he had placed near the stone. Four represented stability and the God of the Sun and Warriors.

He started chanting again and returned to the offering, who had now crossed over. Taking the knife, he cut off the hands and feet, plucking the bones from the flesh, and set them on a silver plate.

He then moved the body to the floor and worked at peeling off the offering's skin, starting with the scalp so he could take the man's face. He proceeded to the arms, and chest, and legs, chanting the entire time, praising the gods.

Once he'd finished, he laid the skin of his sacrifice over his own, in effect dressing himself with the offering. Carefully, he performed the dance that represented the rebirth of life, but then his movement stopped.

Standing there, a calm swept over him, as it always did at this point, and he let his mind gravitate up and away from the earthly realm. This was his reward for carrying out the sacrifice. But the feeling of absolute bliss didn't last long.

The clock was ticking, and he didn't have the time to savor this offering.

He ripped the offering's skin from him and tossed it to the ground.

He roared in sheer frustration, but now it was time to implement the second part of his plan. He had to place the remains somewhere they'd be found quickly, preferably at first light.

CHAPTER

28

THE SUN CAME UP THE next day, and we had one priority: finding Stanley Gilbert. Something that was easier said than done when we had no idea where he was. Yet. Last night, Paige had updated Jack and me about their visit to Atlanta. The Perimeter Mall was sending Nadia surveillance videos pulled from their parking lot and food court cameras from last Friday for the window of eleven in the morning until one in the afternoon.

Hopefully, we'd come away with another vehicle that we could track down, but at least we were now armed with the knowledge that Stanley had used the ruse of being a mall janitor to abduct Eric Morgan. It was quite likely that he'd used this tactic more than once in different places. The video from inside would make for terrific evidence when the case went to court.

Despite the hope that we'd get some solid leads, Jack was in a sour mood. "We need to find out where he is carrying out the ritual and burying the bodies. Heck, there's a lot we need to find out."

"It's going to have to wait," Pike said as he entered the room. "A body was found about half an hour ago." He took a few heaving breaths.

Not another one...

"It was found on Grove Point Road near Shore Road," Pike added. "In a ditch, next to a culvert."

"Not too far from where Stanley lives," I said.

"Where was it? Just out in the open?" Paige asked.

"Yep."

I looked at the team, and they were all likely thinking the same thing I was: dumping a body like this didn't seem like our unsub's work. "Who found the body?" I asked.

"A bicyclist." Pike was already on the move. "Follow me."

TWENTY MINUTES LATER, we were on scene, and I was dying for the comfort of the room back at the precinct. Looking at crime scene photos and dissecting the psychology of our unsub seemed like a cakewalk next to what was before me.

The body of a male was laid out on a plastic sheet. His skin had been removed from his entire body, including his face. There was a hole in his chest, his ribs were sticking through the muscle tissue, and his heart had been removed. His hands and feet were also missing.

Strips of skin were next to him and were blue, likely coated with the same paint that had been on the torso found two days ago.

The smell was rancid, and flies were buzzing around.

I dry heaved and then burped. It was time to call upon my training, upon the need to detach. I was hoping my adrenaline wouldn't fail me now. But taking a deep breath wasn't an option. If I inhaled that... Oh, my mouth was salivating... I turned away from the remains, certain I was going to vomit in front of everyone. Sadly, I'd been sick at a crime scene before—more than once, truth be told, and it had to stop happening.

"We're obviously looking at a secondary crime scene," Pike said, setting his hands on his hips.

"And there's no way that the body could have been here for too long without being spotted," Paige added.

"He likely would have acted under the cover of night to at least eliminate some of the risk involved with dumping the body," Zach said.

"I'd say that we can rule out the skin removal as part of something he's keeping as a trophy," Paige reasoned. "Though he's deviated from his regular MO on this one. He doesn't normally put his victims on display."

"He wants our attention now," Zach said.

"Well, he's got it," Jack fired back.

"You said a bicyclist found him?" I asked, trying to focus on the case itself and not the remains.

"Yeah. About seven this morning. Name's Heath Pierce. Said he was biking for exercise." Pike pointed toward a cruiser with two men inside. For privacy purposes, on-scene statements were often taken in police vehicles. "Officer Phelps is with him now."

My eyes drifted to the remains, but I didn't let my gaze linger there.

What nightmares are made of... The words that would forever be associated with my first case as an FBI agent. It applied today as much as it had then. That investigation had required us to hunt a killer who had ritualistically killed and buried his victims, even went so far as to grind up his victim's intestines, but today... Looking at what was before us, this was pretty much just as bad.

I swallowed an involuntary lump of bile, and bitterness coated my mouth and throat.

Zach must have caught the sour expression on my face, and he was smirking at me. I swear he'd be laughing if he felt it appropriate. How he kept himself composed given the situation, I had no idea.

Then I heard the retching, the heaving...

An officer was bent over some long grass, and a few seconds later, he came up wiping his mouth.

"Based on the dump location, our unsub wanted this body found, but it was placed in such a spot that it would be hard to see from a car just driving past," I concluded.

"The unsub was going at it from a shock-factor standpoint. He carries out his ritual in an intimate manner, and while he seems to be looking for acknowledgment for what he's done, he also wanted the person who found his victim to have an intimate experience." All this came from Zach, and it made sense to me.

"If that's the case, he'd want to see the reaction of the person who found the body, of our reaction," Paige added.

Zach glanced over the area. "He'd want a front-row seat. He could have dumped the body and hung out, waiting."

"That's brazen." The words just came out.

"It is, but we're not exactly looking for a man who is shy about what he does—at least not anymore. Make sure to have your officers on the lookout for Stanley Gilbert," Jack barked to Pike.

"On it." Pike walked off in the direction of several officers.

"If Stanley's behind this, either he's back in Savannah or his partner is acting solo," I surmised. My gaze went back to the victim. This time I managed to keep my stomach calm. "What is the killer doing with their hearts?"

"He could be eating them," Zach said with a shrug.

I supposed nothing at this point should surprise me.

Moving on…

We weren't any closer to identifying the other remains, and the reconstruction of the face from the skull found on Wednesday still hadn't come through. We just knew it was another male in his twenties. Had that been Eric Morgan or were we looking at him now? We'd have to wait to find out.

"It would probably be a good idea to make sure

the back of the victim's skin is swabbed for foreign DNA," Zach said, and we looked at him. "If he's doing the Mayan ritual, he'd be laying the skin over himself."

No one said anything to that. I was just trying to hold myself together. Jack was standing back, appearing like a stone wall, like nothing could penetrate him no matter how horrible or heinous. And Paige was staring at the body.

"I'd say we should get authorization to forward this to a private lab," Zach added.

"I'll make the call," Jack said.

When Pike returned to us, Jack asked, "When is the medical examiner expected to be here?"

"Should be soon."

"We've got to rush the autopsy on this," Jack said.

Pike nodded. "Yes, I know, and I'll make sure that Garrett realizes that."

Crime scene investigators swarmed in like locusts over the area, combing each blade of grass for evidence that could provide a lead. Two came over to the body—one taking photos and sharing her observations, the other looking on and making notes. They carried out their jobs as if they saw this sort of thing every day.

The one taking pictures hunched next to the body. "The victim's heart was removed." She took some images and then touched the victim's facial tissue with a gloved hand and opened his mouth. "His tongue has been removed."

Another picture.

Paige turned to Zach. "Was tongue removal part of Mayan culture?"

Zach shook his head. "No, but it seems our killer allows for some diversion from the ritual, remember?"

"Like what else?" I asked.

Pike's head was going back and forth following our conversation.

"The skin for one. Sometimes he removes it, sometimes he doesn't," Zach replied. "Then the tongue. Without having other remains, we can't say if he always does this. If we are looking at someone else working with Stanley, that could account for the differences. Each killer would vary the ritual slightly."

Pike was staring at Zach. "Why do you think he cut the tongue out of this victim?"

"As I mentioned, it's hard to know if it's this one specifically or if it's always the case," Zach replied.

Pike nodded, but I wasn't satisfied.

"Is he trying to keep them silent? Is it literal or more symbolic? Did he remove the tongue when the man was alive?" The questions were pouring out of me, and I found it hard to stop. Our job was to assign logic where there didn't appear to be any, and so far, we were failing.

CHAPTER

29

JACK ASKED PAIGE TO SPEAK to Heath Pierce, the man who had found the body. Zach followed her to the patrol car where Heath was inside giving his statement to an officer.

Another officer, seasoned and probably nearing retirement, stepped toward them. "He's a real wreck. Can't stop shaking. We've offered to call an ambulance for him, but he's adamant that he's fine. But that boy is far from fine." The officer hitched up his pants. "I can't imagine being in his shoes, coming across that. Lord Jesus." He was shaking his head and seemed lost in a world all his own.

"No one should have to witness something like that." And when Paige said *no one*, she literally meant just that.

"Did you run a background on him?" Zach asked the officer.

"Yeah, a quick one. No marks against him." The officer paused there, but Paige saw in his eyes that he seemed to debate whether or not to say something else. A few seconds later, he came out with it. "Are you thinking he's behind the murder? I mean, first person to find the body is usually a suspect, but I thought you had a person of interest. Stanley... Gilbert? Something like that? I saw the BOLO and the picture issued to the media."

A reporter was creeping his way closer to the cruiser. Paige glanced at Zach to keep the man back.

Zach went over and held up his hand. "You're going to have to leave this area."

"The public deserves to know the truth. Is Stanley Gilbert a killer? Did he strike again?"

"Go. Now. If you don't leave on your own, we'll—"

"What? You'll make me?" the reporter scoffed.

"If you want to go to jail, fine by me." Zach made a move toward him.

The reporter held up his hands and retreated. "Fine."

Zach returned to where Paige and the officer were standing, and the driver's-side door to the cruiser opened. The officer who had been speaking with Heath regarded his colleague briefly, then spoke to Zach. "I have his general statement. He's having a hard time dealing with all of this, though."

"I'll just be a minute or two," Paige said.

The officer looked at her. "Be sure to keep to that. We're going to be taking him to the hospital to have him checked out."

She nodded. The officer stepped to the side, allowing her to slip into the driver's seat.

Heath Pearce was in his twenties with dark hair

and green eyes. He was biting his lip until she looked directly in his eyes, at which time his mouth froze, his teeth stuck to his bottom lip, and they slowly slid off and released.

"My name is Paige." She offered a pleasant smile. "I'm with the FBI."

"Heath."

She nodded. "I understand that you've already given a brief statement to the local police, but I was hoping you could talk to me for a few minutes."

"Uh, sure." His voice was shaky, uncertain despite his words, and he was fidgeting.

"Given what you've witnessed, it's perfectly normal for you to be having a hard time processing it," she said.

He bobbed his head. "Yeah."

"Can you tell me why you were going by this stretch of road this morning?" She treaded delicately so he wouldn't get stressed out and raise his defenses.

"I always ride along here in the morning for exercise. I don't work until three in the afternoon." His eyes met hers as he spoke. "I'm an early riser."

"Is there anyone who can verify this?"

"My roommate."

"And who's your roommate?"

"Jeff Martin."

Paige made a note of his name. "Where do you work, Heath?"

"I'm just a stocking clerk at Clancy's."

Paige's breath hitched. Colin West had worked at

a grocery store by that name. Could this Clancy's be the same place? She'd bench that line of inquiry for a minute. "So you were just riding along and spotted the deceased?"

"Yeah." His eyes glazed over then. "I didn't know what it was at first. I just knew it wasn't…" He didn't finish his sentence.

"Did you touch the—"

"Yuck." Heath started rocking back and forth. "Absolutely not."

Paige pulled up a photo of Stanley on her phone and held it across the console for Heath to see. "Do you know this man?" As he looked at the picture, she studied his reaction for any small tells of recognition but didn't see any.

Heath shook his head. "I've never seen him."

"Does the name Stanley Gilbert sound familiar to you?"

A few seconds passed, and Heath shook his head.

They'd verify his exercise schedule with his roommate, but she didn't think Heath was hiding anything from her. All that would change, though, if they found his prints on the remains, seeing as he'd said he never touched them.

"I have another question for you, Heath. Do you know Colin West?"

His voice contorted as he seemed to give it some thought. "The name sounds familiar."

"It might be a reach, but he used to work at the same grocery store as you five years ago."

"Ah, that's why I recognize it. Yes, I knew him. He

just up and disappeared or something. Rumor was he took off to Hollywood, wanted to be a star."

Paige's heart sank. "His parents think he might have met with some trouble."

"All that was rumor as I said. I don't know for sure."

"What was he like?" She was curious if there'd be any discrepancies between what the parents thought and a peer's impressions.

"He was the life of the party. All the girls wanted him, and all the guys wanted to be him."

"He was sure of himself? Confident?"

"Absolutely." Heath looked away briefly. "I'm not sure how to say this, and it doesn't really matter, but he wasn't in the best physical shape."

Paige recalled the picture of the overweight young man. "From the sounds of it Colin didn't let that bother him."

"Not at all."

"You would never describe him as a wallflower, someone who was passive?" Paige pushed once more.

A small chuckle and it was like Heath had forgotten why he was in a squad car to start with.

Paige smiled at him. "I guess not."

Heath nodded. "You guessed right."

"What about drugs? Did Colin use?"

Heath's eyes went beyond her to all the cops in the area.

"No one is going to get in trouble. Just tell me."

"Yeah, he used. Weed, cocaine, whatever came to

him."

"Thanks." She got out of the car and gestured for Zach to come over. "Heath has an alibi we'll check out, but it turns out he works at the same grocery store Colin West did, and they knew each other."

"Really? Small world."

"That's what I thought, and Heath had a completely different opinion of Colin than his parents did," she said.

"Not a complete surprise."

Paige nodded. "We know that Jesse Holt was in Cancun when Colin went missing." She attributed finger quotes to *missing*. "Holt used drugs, and Heath said Colin did as well. What if it was just something as simple as a drug dealer taking Colin out and disposing of the body?"

"Could be, Paige, but that's not our case."

"I know, but you saw how broken up the Wests were. I just wish we could get them some answers."

"Have Pike get someone on it," Zach suggested.

And she had every intention of doing just that.

CHAPTER

30

HE WATCHED THE POLICE AND investigators as he drove slowly past the crime scene. Officers were directing traffic and merging flow from both directions into one lane. But he felt safe as one of many vehicles driving along this stretch of road. Word of the murder must have already circulated among the gossipers and was bringing people out. Normally this area wasn't heavy with traffic. He was happy it was today, however. It gave him more time to observe what he had created.

Nearing the location where he'd dumped the body, he spotted the same four Feds he'd seen on the news. They were all standing there looking pensive as they tried to analyze both the murder and the man behind it. He'd love to know what they were thinking.

His heart was pounding in his chest from the pure exhilaration of watching it all. Who would have thought he'd enjoy having his work out there? But he did. Again, the divine knew better than he did who was grounded in the physical. The flooding had actually been a blessing.

While he had been robbed of the sacredness of this ritual, there were some benefits. He would finally receive the honor, praise, and acknowledgment.

And he should have been fine to leave things like that, to walk away, to go back to the way things used to be. But he was starting to like the thought of becoming infamous, of being feared, of being hunted.

Ah, yes.

His smile took over his face. He would show them all that he was more than a conquering warrior. They would bend at the knees before him and beg him for mercy, but he would turn them away.

He was looking out the window, and he met the gaze of the youngest agent. A redheaded guy. He seemed to stare right through him.

Did he somehow know? A sliver of human fear creeped through him. What if he was found and stopped before he was done?

Center yourself, dear one…

He approached the end of the detour, and a hoard of press was gathered behind the police barricade. All except one, who had finagled his way past. His microphone had the logo of a local radio station.

He tuned in as he merged back on to the open road.

"…body found along Grove Point Road near Shore Road. Avoid this area as traffic is being constricted to one lane. It's unknown who the victim is or the state

of the remains. We have to wonder if this is related to the remains pulled from the Little Ogeechee River…

"The FBI have a prime suspect and a nationwide manhunt is underway for a man named Stanley Gilbert. His picture can be found on our website. If you see this person, call the FBI or police immediately as he's believed to be dangerous…"

"No!" He yelled and smacked his palm against the steering wheel. How could they believe that? This work was his and his alone!

His breathing became labored, his nostrils flaring with rage.

He sped home, parked in the garage, and closed the door. Rushing to his private room, he logged onto his computer and brought up an Internet browser and searched *Stanley Gilbert FBI.*

Results filled the screen and confirmed his fears. Everything the reporter on the radio had said was verified before him in black-and-white.

How dare Stanley receive the credit! The glory!

While he struggled to assume control over his thoughts, the darkness took over—or was it the light? There was no time for lying low now, nor did he want to, and he knew exactly who he was going to sacrifice next.

CHAPTER

31

"WE *NEED* TO FIND STANLEY GILBERT," Jack roared that afternoon back at the precinct.

I hated to point out the obvious to Jack, but we'd been trying to do exactly that for days now with no luck. At least his request to have the DNA from the roadside victim tested and processed by a private lab had been approved. I didn't want to imagine what his mood would have been otherwise.

"We also need to tie him to the three ingredients in the paint," I said.

Jack cast me a sideways glance as he paced the room.

I was either brave or stupid to bring up something else we needed to do in connection with Stanley.

"Just a quick interjection here, Jack," Paige said.

"What is it?"

"I was able to verify Heath's alibi with his roommate."

Jack nodded.

Paige looked at me. "Going back to Stanley,

though, I think we should take a look at his home, not just the cabin."

"I'm pretty certain he's not burying bodies there," I said. "Darla would know it and have no problem turning him in." An image of her strangling Stanley flashed in my mind.

Jack's phone rang, and he answered on speaker. "Go ahead, Nadia."

"I dug further into Missing Persons looking for twentysomething men reported missing on Fridays within a four-hour drive of Savannah. The search results came back with eighteen, in addition to Eric Morgan."

Holy crap!

Nadia continued. "Unlike Mr. Morgan, though, not all of them were married with families, but they were all in good physical shape."

"Worthwhile adversaries," Zach chimed in.

"If that's the case, Colin West likely didn't fall prey to our unsub. He was overweight. We might never know what happened to him," Paige added sorrowfully.

"Uh, guys," Nadia weaseled back in, claiming the lead in the conversation. "Eleven of the men went missing from malls in South Carolina."

Some areas of South Carolina were close enough to be a day trip from Savannah.

"Send everything on this to all of us, Nadia," Jack directed.

"Will do." All our phones chimed with notifications of new messages.

"So what triggered Stanley four years ago to start doing this?" Paige asked.

"He and Darla moved to Savannah five years ago," I was quick to say, not yet sure how it factored in to figuring out Stanley's motive.

"There's got to be more to it than a move. Something happened four years ago that had a huge impact on his life," she retorted.

"Unless he had abducted and killed prior to then and we just haven't tracked down the missing person," I said, hating that without more our hands were tied in this regard.

Jack stopped pacing. "We just have that cold case from Lansing, and we know Stanley was living there at the time."

"If that was Stanley, though, his victim criteria has changed drastically. Why go from killing people who live a high-risk lifestyle to family men and those who would be reported missing?" Paige asked.

"More questions…" Jack grumbled. He pulled out a cigarette and perched it between his lips. "Any update on the video from the mall, Nadia?"

"I don't have it yet, but I followed up. It should be here this afternoon."

"It is afternoon. Press them to send it right now," Jack bit out.

"I'll call them again." Nadia hung up, leaving the three of us staring at one another.

Jack was on the warpath, and I couldn't blame him. Eric Morgan may have been taken by our unsub a week ago today, but if his body was found while we were in Savannah that would eat away at Jack as if he—*we*—should have been able to save him.

"Let's start looking at what we *do* know," I said, my mind going back to the roadside crime scene and the way the body was left for us to find. "At the most recent crime scene, the body and skin were placed on clear plastic." I held up my hand to Zach, who looked like he was going to interject. "I'm sure he could have picked it up anywhere, if that's what you were going to say."

"Yep," Zach conceded.

"That's not why I brought it up, though. I was thinking about how the body was disposed of. It shows our unsub took care with it. He could have just dumped the remains haphazardly, but it was placed there, *presented* to us." I stamped out that last part, and chills ran through me.

"That would also mean he took time at the dump site. He wasn't afraid of being caught. He took a risk," Paige offered.

"He's escalated," Jack said. "He's gone from burying his victims to displaying them on the side of the road." He took a few steps. "He's not afraid anymore."

"He wants to be stopped, then?" I asked.

"Not necessarily." Jack aligned his gaze with mine. "But if that's the case, he might be hoping for suicide by cop."

Jack's statement fell heavy over the room. There was no way any of us wanted to assume that responsibility. No matter the evil we witnessed, when we faced the unsub, the last thing we wanted was to decide if he lived or died. Still, there were times we were forced into that position.

The silence stretched on for a bit, and then I picked up on my earlier train of thought. "Going back to laying the victim out with care… I'd almost say whoever dumped the body did so lovingly, with respect for the deceased."

Zach nodded. "In Mayan culture, being a willing sacrifice was considered an honor and those who offered themselves were respected."

"I doubt he was willing," I shot back.

Zach rolled his eyes. "Even conquered warriors who didn't hold their beliefs or values garnered a level of respect from the Mayans."

"And that was demonstrated by throwing their bodies down the temple stairs and skinning them?" I asked.

God, how do I ever sleep at night?

Jack pulled the unlit cigarette from his mouth. "Our unsub's revealed a lot of himself to us this time. Why? Is it because he wants to get caught? Killed by us? Or is there something larger going on here?"

Jack had us going quiet again.

"We brought up the possibility of there being more than one unsub," I said. "And we've never been able to determine where Stanley carries out the ritual or buries the victims, so what if it's occurring on Stanley's partner's property? We did speak to two of his friends, but we haven't really dug into them beyond simple background checks and vehicle registrations."

"But we do know that neither of them live next to the river or own additional properties," Zach said.

"Hmm."

We all turned to Jack.

"Maybe we're not as dry for leads as we thought." He made eye contact with me briefly. "When Brandon and I spoke with Duane Oakley, he mentioned he'd sometimes meet up with Stanley at a place in town called Patty's Pub."

With all the twists in the case—and the new victim—I'd somehow shoved my curiosity on that matter aside. "What made him take the risk of going out in public and getting caught by Darla?"

"Let's go find out. And while we're doing that, I want you two—" Jack eyed Paige and Zach "—to see about the man who was reported missing before Eric Morgan."

Zach consulted his phone. "His name was Elijah Lewis, reported by his wife, Tanya, three months ago. She's in Hampton, South Carolina."

Jack snapped his fingers. "Let's get moving."

CHAPTER

32

PATTY'S PUB WAS LOCATED IN the Historic District and had the feel of a classy establishment from the sidewalk. The building was pale redbrick, but the face of the pub was hunter green with gold accents. It was two in the afternoon, and some patrons were seated outside on the patio.

"For two?" A brunette stood behind the hostess stand and reached for a couple of menus.

My stomach growled, and I was hoping that Jack would let us mix business with nutrition.

Jack glanced at me. "Sure."

The hostess smiled, and so did I. "Follow me." She led us through the space to a table for two tucked away in a corner. "Your waitress will be over soon."

We both sat down, and she handed out the menus. I opened mine right away as Jack watched me intently.

"Thanks, Jack. I am starving."

"So I heard." His eyes lowered as if to indicate my stomach. Had the growling been that loud?

"I just know we're on a case and—"

"We'll always have work to do, but if we don't eat, we're going to run out of energy. And I need us to have energy right now."

I nodded, feeling for Paige and Zach who would be on their way to speak with Tanya Lewis in South Carolina while Jack and I would be stuffing our faces. Or at least I would be. Real meals were hard to come by when working a case, and I was going to take advantage of this.

"Just order something quick, though," Jack said.

Did he know me? That's how I preferred to dine on any given day. Going out for a long, drawn-out meal was never my idea of a fun time. Another advantage of being single again.

Ironically, a pang of sadness hit me as the thought sank into my gut. I was single…again. I wondered how Becky was doing. She never called after Valentine's Day, not that I'd expected her to. If anything, it was probably in my hands to mend the relationship, but why should I change who I was for anyone? I'd lost my wife because I chose my happiness. Maybe it wasn't so much the job that resulted in my becoming a bachelor. Maybe it was an inadvertent choice that I had made. I wasn't sure if that made me feel better or worse, though. And what exactly had I chosen?

Jack set his menu down, ready to order, and he flagged down a nearby waitress. Who knew if she was ours—we hadn't seen one yet.

This one came to the edge of the table and was

grinning.

"We'd like to order." He looked at me. "You ready?"

I wasn't really. It was a matter of being too hungry to decide. But if I had to choose… "I'll have the open-faced roast beef sandwich." What was I thinking—carbs and gravy? I must be stress eating. I handed her the menu.

"Good choice." She turned to Jack. "You?"

"I'll have the same." She took Jack's menu from the table and left.

I was surprised Jack didn't give her a spiel about the hurry we were in, but maybe he had an ulterior motive. And really, if we were extra nice to her, she might have something to share with us about Stanley Gilbert. We'd love to know how often he came here and with whom. Was it only with Duane Oakley or other people, too?

Jack and I met eyes, and I drummed my fingers on the table.

He looked down at my hand. "Something wrong, Kid?"

I stopped thrumming.

"No. I thought we had this conversation."

"Hmm."

"What is it, Jack?" My voice rose without intending for it to do so.

"It just seems that something is preoccupying you."

"I assure you, I'm not preoccupied." He didn't need to know about the thoughts that creeped in about Becky, how I was always alone, and how the feeling that I was doomed to spend my life solo went back to childhood when my mother couldn't have any other kids after me. Sure, I grew up spoiled and the center of attention—both aspects that I enjoyed—but sometimes there was nothing I wouldn't have given for a sibling to argue with, to compete with, to protect.

To protect...

Was that the issue here? Was I single because I smothered those around me? No, that was ridiculous. If anything, my actions would lean more toward aloofness. But what if all that was to protect *me*? The need to protect would account for my career choice to serve, if nothing else.

"You seem pretty deep in thought for it to be 'nothing.'" Jack was looking me in the eye, and there was no hiding it.

"You've told me many times that our relationship is a professional one, Jack." I don't know why I kept saying his name. Maybe to tone down the message, insert more respect. But really, we weren't that different from each other. "Well, I have a hard time with that sometimes. We're screwed up, the both of us. But it is what it is."

He smirked. "I think everyone's screwed up just a little."

"Suppose so."

As I looked at him, the realization that he was a single man, too, drilled into me. His story, from what I knew of it, painted him as a military hero who was too busy serving his country to commit to anyone.

He'd even missed out on his son's childhood. So the question was, what was Jack protecting himself from? Or was it a different issue for him?

"You know I'm single again, and I know I told you I was fine with it, but I'm not sure I am." Man, the feelings were just pouring out of me. "But I can assure you that it will have no effect on how I do my job."

"Oh, it will," he said. Not a judgment, just matter-of-fact.

I tilted my head. "How's that?"

The waitress returned then to fill up our water glasses, and I couldn't wait for her to leave again. I didn't need Jack backing out of this conversation.

As soon as she had left, he said, "Everything we go through in life changes us, makes us who we are."

Was I really having this deep of a conversation with Jack of all people? A man who preferred emotions didn't exist?

"I have my own demons," Jack continued, nodding. "Yes, yes, I admit it. But I wouldn't be the person I am without them."

"You almost died just six months ago." I took a deep breath, realizing again just how fond I was of Jack.

He shrugged. "I didn't, though."

"You're telling me you don't think about it? That it doesn't affect you daily?"

He met my eyes when he said, "It does. But it's how I choose to handle it that matters, and I'm certainly not going to let it define me."

I didn't know what to say in response as I was too busy trying to figure out how his point applied to me. I had chosen to be single to protect myself from getting hurt and had gone so far as to bury myself in my career. These things were defining me... I had a career, I was an only child, I was divorced. Was this what I wanted to be remembered for?

I cleared my throat.

"Here you go." The waitress set our orders in front of us, and I had never been happier to see carbs and gravy.

Jack and I ate quickly without any more conversation, and if it wasn't for the fact that I felt more comfortable with the man than ever, I wouldn't have believed it had happened.

The waitress slipped a billfold onto the table. "Whenever you're ready."

"Ready now." Jack pulled out a credit card.

"I'll be right back." The waitress returned a bit later, a smile on her face. "So are you visitin' from outta town?"

Jack opened the billfold and signed his receipt. "You could say that. We're with the FBI."

"Oh," she said as he handed it back to her. "You here about the bodies that were found? Heard there was another one this morning... You working that case?" With each question, her voice got louder.

Jack just had to look at her in his certain way, the one that exuded authority, and she put a hand over her mouth for a moment. "Sorry. I'll keep it down."

I pulled out my phone.

"We have some questions for you," Jack said.

"Uh, sure." She glanced over her shoulder. She was probably concerned because she had other customers in her section.

I smiled at her. "It won't take long."

"All right. What can I help you with?" She shifted her weight to her right.

"Do you know this man?" I showed her a picture of Stanley on my phone.

"Stanley? Sure. But I don't know where he is."

Jack's eye twitched. "Why would you say that? You normally would?"

Her face paled. "No, not that. I just know that you're looking for him. I saw it on the news."

"You know him well enough to be on a first-name basis," I began, her attention turning from Jack to me.

"Means nothing," she said. "He comes in most Friday afternoons."

"Most?" I asked.

"I'd say so."

"And does he come with anyone?"

"Uh-huh. A couple different friends, but he never brings them together."

I fished through my phone for a photo of Duane Oakley. "He one of them?"

She glanced at the picture. "Yeah."

"What does the other man look like?" The hair on the back of my neck was already standing up. We came in hoping for a lead, and we were getting exactly that.

"He's got dark hair. Don't think he's quite six foot. And he's got very pale skin. He's quite a bit younger than Stanley, probably in his twenties?" The waitress looked to the corner of the room, and I followed her gaze to a woman who was watching her. I'd guess it was her manager. I held up my badge for her, and she slunk into the back.

I looked back at the waitress. The description she gave us sounded familiar to me. "One more picture."

She looked at the photo I brought up of Jesse Holt.

"Is that him?"

"No."

I raised an eyebrow. "That was fast."

"I'm just absolutely certain that's not him."

"A couple more questions," Jack began. "You said he'd come in on Friday afternoons. About what time?"

She bit her bottom lip, thinking. "Probably around four or so? He'd have a couple beers and then leave."

"Was he here last Friday?" I asked.

She nodded.

So he'd abducted Eric Morgan in Atlanta, had driven back to Savannah, had done who knows what with him, and then had gone out for a couple beers?

I sat up straighter. "How did he seem to you?"

"What do you mean?"

"His normal self? Stressed out?" I fed her a couple of options.

"His normal self *is* stressed out." She gave a small smile. "He's wound tight all the time. Especially when he's with that younger friend of his. Nothing can make him smile when they're together."

Jack pointed to the ceiling. "Do you have surveillance video set up in here?"

The waitress rubbed a cheek on her shoulder. "Yeah, we do."

"We'll need to see it," Jack stated.

"I can't help you there. You'd have to speak to the owner."

"Would you get him for us, please?" I asked.

She shook her head. "It's a *her*, and she's not in."

"We'll need her number, then." Jack wasn't taking no for an answer.

"One minute," she said and walked away.

She came back with a piece of paper, which she handed to me.

Her name was Patty Haven, and I was already dialing her as we left the restaurant.

CHAPTER

33

IT'S A GOOD THING TRAVELING didn't bother Paige. Jack was sending her and Zach all over the countryside with this case. The GPS indicated that they were five minutes from the Lewis household where they'd be talking to Tanya. They'd called ahead so she was expecting them.

Paige frowned as they pulled up to the house. It was big—two stories and probably three thousand square feet—and the couple hadn't had kids so that meant Tanya lived in this huge house all alone now. Somehow that made Tanya's situation feel so much worse.

Luckily, the front door opened for them by the time they got up the walk, and she couldn't dwell on it any longer.

"Agent Dawson?" asked the woman just inside the door, presumably Tanya.

"Yes, but please, call me Paige." She smiled. "And this is Zach."

The woman nodded. "I'm Tanya. Thank you for

coming."

Paige glanced at Zach before walking in. Tanya was calm and collected considering everything she'd been going through.

They took seats in a living room stuffed with photos. There were framed ones on the walls, on the fireplace mantle, on the end tables. And on the coffee table in front of the couch where Paige was sitting, there was a homemade wedding album. It had been covered with satin, lace had been hot-glued around the edges, and another piece of lace was being used to tie it shut. The pictures around the room were mostly of both Tanya and Elijah, except for the ones on the mantle, which also showed a younger man on his own. Paige guessed they must have been childhood photos of Elijah, as the resemblance was unmistakable.

"You said on the phone that you wanted to talk about Elijah." Tanya crossed her legs, remaining extremely calm.

"You reported him missing three months ago from Columbiana Centre, is that correct?" Paige asked.

"That's right. If I hadn't been so stubborn about dragging him along that day, maybe he'd still be here." Tanya looked Paige in the eye. "The police told me he'd left me, wanted to start a new life, but none of that made sense."

"Why's that?" Paige asked.

"Everything was going great for us. And I mean *everything*. We won this house in a lottery a few months before. He'd recently been promoted at work. We were talking about having a baby." Only with that last statement did her strength seem to crack slightly.

Zach leaned forward, putting his elbows on his knees. "Can you run us through that day?"

"There was a major shoe sale going on... I love my shoes." She forced a small smile. "I told Elijah that we could make a real outing of it—go shopping, have a nice lunch out, and spend the night at a hotel. Columbia is about two hours from here so it also makes for a nice getaway. I told him the day would be my treat. We keep our accounts separate," she apparently felt she needed to add.

Paige picked up on the present tense and a stab of sympathy struck her. "Where did you last see him?"

"I sent him to get us cinnamon buns." She bit down on her bottom lip. "If I had known he'd never come back, I would have happily forgone the bun and kept him with me..."

"And where were you?" Zach asked.

"Trying on shoes." She attempted a smile again, but it faltered partway through.

"What time of day was this?" he continued with his line of questioning.

"About noon." Tanya apparently didn't need to think her response through. "By the time twelve thirty came around, I was really starting to panic, wondering where in the hell—oh, sorry for that. I mean, where he'd gone. I tried calling his cell, but it kept ringing and ringing."

"Did he ever keep it on silent?" Paige inquired.

"I don't think so. His parents are older, and he always wanted to be accessible." Tanya's energy dipped now, and she continued in a more somber tone. "Going through all this is killing them."

"Understandably," Paige sympathized. "You seem to be holding yourself together rather well, though."

"Only because of Him." Tanya pulled a crucifix out of her pants pocket. "God, Christ—they give me strength."

"It's nice that you've been able to find some peace through all this," Paige said.

"I just have to keep the faith that he'll come back to me." Her eyes lowered to the cross she pinched in her fingers. "If he doesn't, well, then that's something I'll have to deal with, I guess. But it never hurts to hope."

"No, it doesn't." Paige's eyes drifted to the mantle. "Are those photos of Elijah?"

Tanya brightened at that. "Yes, they are."

Paige got up and walked over to take a closer look. The pictures captured Elijah in different poses, but there was a theme. "He must have loved his sports," she said.

"That he did," Tanya replied. "Especially baseball. He was a really good pitcher, too, or at least that's what he told me. His parents said so, too, but parents always think their kids are amazing. Look at those talent shows, like *American Idol*. Whoa. Kids come on there to audition after being told by everyone around them that they are the best, and then they croak like something's dying."

Paige chuckled.

"Did he ever go on to play baseball as an adult?" Zach asked.

Tanya turned to look at Zach, who was walking toward her and Paige. "No. After he broke his arm, he wasn't much good at pitching anymore."

Paige's gut twisted. The anthropologist had said that the arm found on Monday had been broken when the victim was a teenager. She took a steady breath. "When did he break his arm?"

"He was in his teens. I'm not sure exactly when. I could ask his mom, though."

Paige put a hand on Tanya's. "No need."

Tanya's eyes widened. "You know something, don't you?" She started rubbing her crucifix.

The truth must have touched Paige's eyes. She was quite certain that they'd found Elijah, or at least a part of him, but it was too early to say for sure. The doctor who had treated Elijah would hopefully be able to provide an X-ray of the break so the anthropologist could confirm the ID. If not, they'd be waiting on DNA. Either way, the verification process wouldn't be a fast one.

"Honestly, Mrs. Lewis, I don't," Paige said. "But I will be in touch if we learn anything."

Tanya studied Paige's eyes and eventually nodded.

"There is one more thing we need to ask you." Paige proceeded to take out her phone. She brought up a picture of Stanley Gilbert and extended it for her to see. "Do you recognize this man?"

"No." Tanya dragged out the word. "Why are you asking me this?"

"Another woman's husband has gone missing from a mall, as well, and—"

"The poor thing." Tanya was rubbing her cross. Paige wasn't sure if she was referring to the husband or the wife.

"She'd seen this man in a janitor getup," Paige continued. "He had a mustache." She'd kept the photo held out for Tanya to look at, and her gaze drifted there.

Tanya shook her head. "I'm sorry, but I've never seen this man."

"Did you spot any janitors when you were there that day?" Zach asked.

Tanya took a deep breath, her chest heaving with the effort. "Not that I remember."

"Sometimes we can be so focused on what we're doing, we don't think we notice what's going on around us. Usually we remember more than we think." Zach paused. "What about any man that you saw more than once?"

Tanya took her time mulling over her answer to that one, her eyes cast down at the floor. Suddenly they shot up. "Actually, there was one. I saw him at the front doors to the mall, and then I saw him again at... Oh, where was it? I don't remember which one, but he was standing outside one of the stores."

"Did he seem to notice you both times?" Zach asked.

"He was holding a book, flipping through it."

Tanya looked at Zach. "But yes, yes, he did." She pointed to Paige's phone. "But it wasn't that man."

Paige pulled up a picture of Jesse Holt and showed it to Tanya. "What about him?"

Tanya looked at the photo and shook her head. "I wish I could say yes."

Paige put her phone away.

"Can you remember what he looked like?" Zach asked.

Tanya curled her lips. "Nothing really stood out about him."

"What about hair color? Skin color? Height?"

"He was a white man. I think he had brown hair, and I'd say he was at least six feet tall."

All right, so that would describe a lot of men in America. But still, it gave them more confirmation that Stanley Gilbert wasn't working this alone.

Paige and Zach managed to excuse themselves a few minutes later.

When they were back in the SUV, Paige said, "We found her husband's arm—I just have a feeling." She adjusted the air-conditioning vent so it wasn't blowing directly on her.

"You can't be positive until the testing is done," Zach reminded her as he drove them back to Savannah.

She was well aware of that, but there was such a lightness that came with the thought of providing closure to someone. The people who missed these men deserved to have that, to know what had truly befallen their loved ones, no matter how ugly it was.

But in the meantime, Paige would take what she could, and for now that was a description of their second unsub, no matter how generic it might be.

CHAPTER

34

STANLEY HATED IT WHEN THINGS didn't go according to plan. It made him nervous and uneasy, his stomach full of butterflies. *Such an odd expression...*

Why was he back in Savannah? He must be insane. He'd left everything behind, and he'd made a run for it to be free and clear. But he'd only made it as far as Nashville before he'd heard the news. Body parts were being pulled from the Little Ogeechee River.

He remembered how his breath had frozen when he'd heard that. Talk about fortunate timing that he was out of reach, but it was his knack for attracting bad luck that had made him toss his phone in the river that day. That's probably why they wanted to talk to him. Yes, they'd found it, that was all. Or that's what he was telling himself...

When he'd ditched the phone, he thought he was making a bold statement that he didn't want anything to do with his life anymore—at least not the one he'd been living. Darla was enough to tip him past the breaking point, and abducting men, although not something he did for himself, did bring him some stress relief. In the kidnapping scenario, he held the power. He wasn't browbeaten. A man could only withstand being chastised, manipulated, and disciplined for so long before he had to get the anger out of his system somehow.

He had planned to go to his parents in Michigan until he'd heard the news about the remains. If the investigation came to his door, his parents' house would be one of the first places the cops would go. No, there was no sense involving them, and when he'd seen his face on the news, he was assured he'd made the right decision to stay away from them.

Being wanted by the FBI left him with two choices: go back and defend himself, or keep running. Both had benefits; both had weaknesses.

He didn't trust himself in the face of experienced Feds, but he also wasn't equipped to keep running. He'd always had a stable home life, even if it had become skewed over the last few years.

He tried to downplay the Feds' interest in him, but the words *nationwide manhunt* were being used and he didn't like the sound of that. The Feds must have had proof of his involvement.

How though? How had they figured it out?

A taunting rhyme rattled through his head: *What a tangled web we weave when first we practice to deceive.*

That could sum up the last four years of his life. The FBI must have just started pushing until they found the holes and then picked at them until they revealed the evidence they needed. By now they likely knew everything, and it was in his best interest to stay far away from Savannah. So again, what the hell was he doing back here? Curse his sense of responsibility.

Stanley pulled into the driveway, and his anxiety ratcheted up further. Tremors laced through him, trying to warn him that he was making the wrong decision. His mind was screaming, *Run*! But he ignored it and continued up the lane, parked his vehicle, and let himself in.

The house was quiet and felt empty.

"Hello? Anyone home?" he called out.

The pinch came to the back of his neck, and his legs instantly weakened. He fumbled around for something to hold himself up and ended up leaning against a column. He had to get out of there before it was too late. He hadn't come back to die.

Shit!

"Why?" he cried.

His words met with no response. He sensed a shadow looming above him, and as if it suffocated him, it took all his strength and he fell to the marble floor. If he could look at his attacker, hopefully he could get them to feel something, to stop.

But his eyelids fell closed, and he knew then that he'd made a deadly choice.

CHAPTER

35

GARRETT'S FACE FELL WHEN HE saw us and Pike. He was probably getting about as sick of seeing us as we were of seeing him. There was far too much death so close together, and it threatened the sanest and most seasoned people in law enforcement.

The roadside remains were laid out on two gurneys—the skin on one, and body on the other. It was a lot easier handling the sight of it here than it had been in the ditch with insects buzzing around. But it was nine o'clock at night, most of the building was empty, and it was dark outside, making it a little more unsettling than usual. I didn't think there was ever a good time to be next to a cadaver, though, particularly when it had been mutilated.

Garrett turned his back on us and scrubbed his hands before putting on a pair of rubber gloves. His eyes were dark and sullen, no doubt a reflection of the rest of us. "Here's what I have to tell you so far." He paused. "I've been able to confirm the deceased as an Eric Morgan out of Atlanta."

"By his tattoo?" Paige's voice was small as she guessed.

Garrett nodded.

Paige lowered her gaze to the floor, and she touched her cheek. I could sense sadness coming off her in waves. Feeling so much empathy for others was both her strength and her weakness.

Garrett looked at us each in turn. "I'm guessing this isn't a complete surprise."

Jack locked his jaw and shook his head.

Garrett took a deep breath and continued. "The body was scoured for insects, and fly eggs were found but no maggots."

"They start to emerge after twenty-four hours," Zach said.

Garrett nodded. "That's correct."

"So Eric was killed within the last twenty-four hours," Paige deduced. "But he was taken just over a week ago. What was the killer doing with him all that time?"

"Pure and simple? He was tortured." Garrett walked toward the body and pointed at the head. "His tongue was removed."

"Yes, we found that out at the crime scene." Jack's gaze took on a steely intent. "Was it cut out while he was alive?"

"It was. I can tell this by the amount of healing that has taken place."

There were a few seconds of silence.

"You said he was tortured…" Paige swallowed audibly. "What else was done to him besides cutting out his tongue?"

"As with the previous remains, restraints had been placed around the wrists and ankles. An earlier microscopic examination showed evidence of healing in some areas. It seems plausible that whatever the killer used to subdue the victim was loosened at times and then retightened." Garrett turned the body over and directed our attention to the back of the neck where there was still skin. He pressed a finger to point out a small pinprick. "Now, it's quite tiny as you can see, but I believe this is a puncture wound from a needle."

"He was drugged," I spat.

"Appears so, but toxicology will confirm. Since the body is less decomposed and—I hate to say it this way—*fresher*, we'll have a better chance of knowing for sure. And that's assuming it was in his system at time of death."

"The other remains didn't indicate the victims were drugged, but it does make sense as a means of controlling them if our unsubs held and tortured them for a period of time." I was holding on to the opinion I'd come up with days ago.

"What else?" Jack sounded as if he were ready for more bad news to drop.

"We were able to conclude from the other torsos and their digestive systems that they hadn't been fed for days before their deaths."

"What about Er— him?" Paige put her hands in her pockets.

"I will let you know, but I wouldn't be surprised if

it is the same for him."

My gaze drifted to the body or what was left of it. It was hard to believe that this had once been a vibrant man in his twenties. "We have an entire body this time, limbs attached…" I made eye contact with Garrett. "Were his limbs removed from their sockets?"

Garrett nodded. "They were, and given time to decompose, his arms and legs would have become detached just like the other remains we've examined."

Paige stepped closer to Garrett. "Do you think this was part of the torture?"

"I can't honestly answer that without taking a closer look at the body to see if it happened before or after death," Garrett said softly. "As I've been made aware of, the testing for DNA in this case is going to be handled by a private lab. Included in what I'll be submitting is a swabbing of the back of the deceased skin." Garrett looked at Zach. His recommendation to do precisely that must have made it back to the chief ME from the roadside crime scene.

"What about any other trace evidence from the scene?" Jack asked.

"I've got a list of everything collected," Lieutenant Pike said, speaking for the first time since we'd arrived. "Just came in before we got here. A printed list is back at the precinct."

Jack seemed to look through Pike. "We need everything the second you get it."

Pike squared his shoulders. "You'll be getting it

now."

Jack straightened to his full height, and his eyes locked on Pike, who looked away. Jack addressed Garrett. "We'll need the results as soon as humanly possible."

"And you will get them." He let his gaze drift over us. "Are you all staying for the autopsy?"

Jack clasped his hands behind his back. No one else moved.

"All right, then." Garrett stepped closer to the body.

"Actually, Jack..." Paige's voice cut through the room.

Jack faced her, and she continued. "I'd like to give notice to Eric Morgan's widow."

He shook his head. "Local law enforcement can take care of that."

Her cheeks took on a pink hue, and while the other men turned away, I watched her talk to Jack.

"It would mean a lot if I could do it," she said. "We're waiting on results anyway."

"No, Paige. I can't let you go right now."

Her face fell, and she blew out a breath that had her hair fanning outward. She chewed on her bottom lip and nodded. To those who didn't know her well, she might have appeared slightly broken, but I detected a lick of anger in her eyes. No doubt Jack, who had known her longer than me, saw it, too. But apparently it wasn't going to sway his decision.

Garrett proceeded with the autopsy, and a couple of hours later, we were leaving GBI.

In the parking lot, Pike yawned. "You coming back to the precinct?"

I'd glanced at the clock before we'd left the morgue, and it was after eleven. My body was certainly ready for bed, and as frustrating as it was, there wasn't much that could be done tonight. As Jack had mentioned earlier in the day, he needed his team to have energy, and if looking at Paige, Zach, and even Jack was any indication, we all needed rest.

Jack shook his head. "Have that list ready tomorrow morning. We'll see you at seven." He headed toward one of the SUVs.

Pike saluted Jack and went for his vehicle, as well.

Paige stood in front of Jack. "What about Kelly Morgan?"

"I'll make the call to have someone go by."

"Tonight, Jack. She deserves to know."

Jack put a hand on her shoulder. "Tonight."

Paige held his gaze for a few seconds and left for the other SUV.

I watched Paige as she walked ahead of me. Her shoulders sagged and her feet seemed to drag. She was more than physically exhausted. She was taking this part of the case personally.

CHAPTER

36

THE NEXT MORNING, I was happy to see that Paige seemed her normal self again. The weariness that had been etched into her eyes and weighting her stride was gone.

Caffeine was buzzing through my system, but that's what happened when I drank two coffees in fast succession. But there was no getting around the fact that I needed something to perk me up. Sleep hadn't come easy again last night. Paige's face when the roadside victim had been identified as Eric Morgan kept replaying in my mind. Interspersed with that was the horrific display of the body and scattered thoughts of Becky. I finally managed to nod off at about three but had a restless sleep full of idiotic dreams that made absolutely no sense.

The team was in the meeting room and so was Pike. As he'd promised Jack, a printout of the list of items Forensics had collected at the crime scene yesterday was available to us upon arrival. In fact, he had four copies on the table.

The list of possible evidence was long, and while most probably wouldn't factor into the case, more was always better. Fingerprints were missing, but that just told us our unsub—or unsubs—were careful and likely wore gloves. The list did include, however, carpet fiber and hairs.

"The lab is determining the makeup of the carpet and hopefully can connect it to a manufacturer and whether it came from a vehicle or a home," Pike said. "There were a few hairs found. Some were on the back of the skin, so it seems likely they won't belong to the victim."

"And there are usable skin tags?" Zach asked.

What most people failed to realize was that hair could tell investigators a lot about the person it came from—region and diet, for example. But without a skin tag, there was no way to pull DNA.

Pike nodded. "At least one does."

"Tell us more about the fiber," Jack requested.

"It's coarse and a dark-charcoal color. That's about all I know." Pike was standing and put his hands on his hips as he looked around at us.

There was a knock on the door then, and Detective Rowlands came in with a report and handed it off to Pike. "The results from the phone company on Stanley Gilbert's account," he said and swiftly left.

Pike skimmed it and said, "Calls came in regularly from a local number—before and after his disappearing act—from a number registered to Patty Haven."

"Seems that Stanley might have been having an

affair," I theorized.

Pike pressed his lips together. "If so, what do ya know? He had some backbone to him."

Jack looked at me and I read the unspoken question in his eyes. Yesterday when I'd tried to reach Patty Haven, my efforts had resulted in leaving a voice mail. I shook my head. "She hasn't returned my call."

Jack nodded. "I must admit it seems odd that he'd frequent Patty's Pub. We need to establish a personal connection between the two of them and, if there is one, find out how far back it goes." Jack glanced at Pike. "Let's start with her background." Jack left with Pike and minutes later, they both returned.

Jack gave us a recap. "She was born Patricia Long and was originally from Lansing, Michigan. Her father was a senator for the state. She moved to Savannah ten years ago. She got married to a Wayne Reed not long after coming here, but the divorce went through five years ago. She then immediately changed her last name, and that of her now twenty-three-year-old son Joshua, to Haven. Joshua's father was marked as unknown. Here's Joshua's file." Jack handed it to me, and I opened it.

The eyes staring back at me were ones I remembered seeing before. "I've seen this guy!"

"Calm down, Brandon, just tell us where and when," Paige said.

"At the roadside crime scene. He was driving by watching everything. We made eye contact." My heart was racing.

"What was he driving?"

"A white van." I thumbed through the report. "Nothing's registered to him. What about Patty?"

Jack opened the folder and shook his head. "Just a Lexus sedan."

"He was there because he wanted to see the investigation, I can feel it. And Patty was from Lansing like Stanley, and the kid's father is unknown? It might be a stretch, but come on!" I was getting a bit worked up.

"Call Stanley's parents," Jack instructed me in a calm but stern voice.

I got up and left the room. The phone rang three times before a woman answered. "Is this Arlene Gilbert?"

"Yeah, who are you?"

"I'm Brandon Fisher, an agent with the FBI, and I have a question about your son, Stan—"

"I've seen his face and name all over the news. You ought to be ashamed of yourself. He wouldn't harm nobody."

"Ma'am, I—"

"Don't you *ma'am* me. Tell me what you want."

There was no way I could give her any indication, no matter how subtle, that we had proof of Stanley's involvement or she wouldn't say a word to me. "We'd like to talk to you about girlfriends Stanley might have had before he went off to college." About one possibility in particular, really, but I had to pace myself.

"Stanley never had girlfriends. He was quiet, kept

to himself. Was a good student. He got straight As."

"Often good students are bullied. Was that the case with Stanley?"

"Well, yes, but he could handle himself. He had some friends who stuck by him. There was one who was a girl, but not a girlfriend, no. I think he had a crush on her in high school, though. What was her name again? Cecil!" she yelled out, failing to turn away from the phone. Her screechy voice sent a sharp pain through my head and had my eardrum aching. "Who was that girl Stanley liked when he was growing up? Patricia? Something like that?"

A man was mumbling incoherently in the background.

Arlene came back to the phone. "Patricia… something. I'm sorry but I don't know her last name."

"Long?" I asked, going with her birth name.

"Yes, yes, that's it." There was a lightness to her voice at the beginning, but it darkened when she said, *that's it*. "My boy would never do what you think him capable of."

Parents never thought the worst of their kids.

"Thank you for your help, Mrs. Gilbert." My gratitude was met with a dial tone.

I returned to the conference room and shared everything that I had learned from Arlene. "Patty and Stanley were close as teens, and from the sound of it, he had pretty strong feelings for her. So it's quite possible he's the father of her son."

Pike dropped into a chair.

"I take it you had no idea Stanley had a son," Jack stated.

Pike shook his head. "No clue whatsoever."

"It's quite possible that Stanley and his son are working together," I said.

"The phone number that called Stanley was registered to Patty, though," Pike lamented.

"It is possible that all this involves the mother somehow, too. We know Stanley had an interest in Mayan culture." Zach crept into the conversation. "What if Joshua was trying to impress his father?"

Jack didn't say anything.

"He could have figured it was a way to get his father's attention," Paige ventured.

"I'd say it's likely Stanley wasn't aware he had a son until four years ago when all the killing seemed to start," I suggested.

"Hmm." A sideways glance from Jack. "What made an ordinary—and seemingly upstanding—citizen aid and abate a serial killer?"

Zach shrugged. "We know the parental bond can be very strong."

"Stanley could have gotten involved to protect his son," Paige said.

"If Stanley wasn't united with his son until four years ago, he could have been riddled with guilt—whether he knew about his existence before then or not," I suggested. "He'd want to bond with his son."

Paige glanced at me. "They abducted and murdered together in order to *bond*? What's wrong with that picture?"

"It's sad, I get it," I said. "But it's also possible."

"Brandon and I will visit Darla and see if she has anything to say on the subject of Stanley having a son." Jack turned to me. "We also have more than enough now to justify a warrant to look around the place."

"And we'll be looking for what exactly?" I asked.

"Any more links that tie him to the murders, further evidence of a secret life, or anything that might tell us more about Joshua or Patty." Jack looked at me. "You said she didn't return your call?"

"That's right."

"Not a surprise, considering." Jack mumbled.

CHAPTER
37

"YOU'RE BACK AGAIN?" Darla bemoaned our presence while stepping out of the way to let us into her house.

"We need to know what you know about Stanley's son," Jack ground out as he brushed past her. I stuck close behind him.

She gaped at us. "A son? I don't know anything about him having a son. We've been married for seventeen years. You remember my telling you that, right?"

"How long were you together before you got married?" I asked.

"A few years."

"But your relationship started in college?"

"Yes."

"And you and Stanley never took a break, saw other people?"

She glared at me. "No."

"Well, the facts remain. Stanley does have a son," I said, stretching the truth, but we might learn something.

Darla lifted her chin. "Doesn't matter. I've filed for divorce. He didn't deserve me in the first place, and now you're telling me he has a son?" Darla scoffed, letting out a puff of air. "Jackass."

I wasn't giving her any satisfaction by acknowledging her tantrum. "Do you know who Stanley dated before you?"

"A better question would be, do I know of anyone?" She snickered. "He got a lucky break with me."

Again, Darla could make me feel empathy for a man involved with serial murder.

"It's important that you think long and hard here, Mrs. Gilbert," Jack began, "and tell us of anyone Stanley might have dated."

Darla's body stiffened. "He told me that I was his one and only."

"He made you think he didn't have other girlfriends before you," I stated.

"Yeah, I guess so." She raised her hands in the air. "Obviously the man is a sack of lies. I hope you nail his ass to the wall."

"You and Stanley moved here five years ago, correct?" I asked to reestablish the facts.

"Uh-huh."

"And it was your idea to move here?"

That met with an eye roll. "Yes."

It didn't seem like a coincidence that the murders had started a year after Stanley had moved to Savannah. He could have met his son not long after coming here or known about him before and just hadn't bothered with him. It wouldn't have been easy to hide a long-distance relationship from Darla. "What did Stanley think of the move?"

She shrugged. "He was fine with it."

"Just fine?" I pressed. "What does that mean? He was excited? Indifferent?"

"He didn't fight me on it. He knew it was important for me to live in my folks' house."

"And once you moved to Savannah, was he the same man you'd known back in Michigan?"

"I'm not sure what you mean."

"Did he become moody?" Jack elaborated. "Quiet?"

Darla closed her eyes for a few seconds and let out a deep breath. "Come to think of it, he did become quieter. I just thought he was unhappy being here. And he seemed to lose his appetite, hardly eating anything for dinner."

Maybe he'd been snacking before coming home or had more than a couple beers at the pub on Fridays…

"Did you ever ask him if he wasn't happy here?" I asked.

"Nope."

And the wife of the year award goes to…

"Do you think that his son lives here? In Savannah?"

"It seems likely. Yes," Jack stated without emotion.

"He didn't work the long hours he told me, did he?" A statement that would come out sounding heartbroken from most wives had left Darla's mouth with indifference. She was looking at Jack to answer her.

"No, he didn't."

"Oh, that lying sack of—" Darla balled her fists. "He better not come back here."

It was a good thing Jack didn't mention Stanley's Fridays off or the existence of the cabin. If he had, there might have been another murder, but then again, she'd have to find Stanley first.

Hey, maybe she could lead us to him…

Jack stood. "We'd like to have a look around."

Darla crossed her arms. "As I told you before, not without a warrant."

"It's a good thing we have one, then." Jack pushed it toward her as he started to move through the place.

Darla kept up with him. "What are you looking for?"

"It's all in the warrant."

The truth was, there was nothing specific noted in the warrant, but it permitted us to have a look around the property for evidence of his involvement in the murders. Jack and I didn't know exactly what we were looking for, just that we'd know it when we saw it.

Jack turned to Darla. "Is there a space in the house that was mostly Stanley's?"

"You mean like a man cave?"

"Precisely," he replied.

She shook her head. "Stanley was with me whenever he was home."

CHAPTER

38

HAD PAIGE AND ZACH stop what they were doing return to the precinct. He'd caught them on the to Patty Haven's house. They'd already been to pub but hadn't met with any luck.

ack handed Stanley's laptop over to Zach. He had ired up and was in, the password requirement no eterrent for a wizard like him.

"We need to have everything in order and be absolutely certain we're looking at the right guy before we head over to the Havens," Jack said. "What have you got, Nadia?"

She was on speaker again. "I made it through the video from Perimeter Mall. The good news is it shows Stanley at the back side of the parking lot pushing a lidded garbage bin toward a light-colored GMC Savana."

"And the bad news?" Jack asked gruffly.

"The bad news is twofold. First of all, DMV records don't show a Savana registered to him. It's not a rental because nothing is showing on his credit

Of course, he was…

Meeting his son and becoming involved with serial murder was sadly an outlet Stanley had probably come to see as a release. In the very least it was an escape from this woman.

"Where's your bedroom?" Jack continued moving through the house.

"Upstairs."

"Where—"

Darla pushed past us and led the way.

Their room was the second on the right and of a generous size with a large window overlooking the river. It was decorated with furniture that I could see having belonged to Darla's parents, given the bulky frames and oak wood that spoke of thirty years ago. If it wasn't Darla's parents', she and Stanley must have picked it up from a yard sale or auction.

"If you would stay in the hall, please." Jack backed Darla out the door.

She narrowed her eyes at him and scowled, but complied. Her hands shot to her hips.

I walked through the room. There was an en suite with a Jacuzzi big enough for two, and the spacious walk-in closet had two clearly defined areas for his and hers. The latter took up far more square footage.

I put on gloves and opened some doors on Stanley's side but spotted nothing of interest. Jack was rifling through some drawers.

"Everything looks normal. No signs of—" I had spoken too soon. I had just opened another closet door and inside on hangers were a few pairs of coveralls, a couple in navy blue and one in gray. I moved them along the rack, looking at the fronts. None had names embroidered on them.

"Jack?"

"Yeah?"

I shared my findings with him. "I doubt he had any need for these as an investment banker." We both knew he'd worn coveralls to pose as a janitor to take Eric Morgan, but I was curious why he'd kept them here when he could have stored them at the cabin.

Jack left me to speak to Darla in the hallway. "Do you know of any reason Stanley would have coveralls?" I heard him ask.

"He'd wear them when he worked in the yard," she answered.

Jack returned to me, and I had moved on to some drawers. The thing was, if Stanley was keeping evidence of his son in his home, it wouldn't be anywhere easily found. The same went for a tie to his involvement with the murders. The coveralls were probably the closest we'd get here.

And about two hours later, after working through the entire house, Jack and I made that same conclusion. We collected Stanley's laptop and were about to head out.

"Wait a minute." Darla was pointing at the computer under my arm. "You can't take that."

"We can, and we are." Jack gestured for me to continue out the door.

I sensed the heat coming from her, even with my

back to her.

Jack and I g
feeling in my b
appetite since liv
the car into gear, c
already had a cigare
to light it.

"The window first," l
He conceded with a su
"Now, I don't know if it'
or help us figure this whole
that Stanley seemed to lose his
here, and we know he visited th

Jack was looking at me with a s
in his eyes.

"It doesn't explain a smaller app
of the week, but if Stanley got some
the pub, he wouldn't be hungry for din

Jack took a long draw on his cigarette.
you headed with this, Kid?"

"Darla said she managed the money
household. But if Stanley paid at the pub by d
credit card, she'd know. That means that Stanley
to pay cash. The question is, where was he gett
the cash from if Darla kept track of every penn
coming into and going out of the household? The
son wasn't always at the pub with him to cover the
tab, so who paid for his food and drink?"

card history. And second, the plate isn't clearly readable and will need to be enhanced by someone more technical than I am."

It wasn't very often that Nadia had to delegate a task.

"When should we have it?" Jack asked.

"Probably a couple hours, if that."

"We know who the likely unsub is," he disclosed. "It seems possible that Stanley is working with his son, Joshua Haven."

"His son?" Nadia sounded as surprised as the rest of us had been when we'd come to that conclusion.

Jack gave her a quick rundown.

"Wow, that's quite the development," she said when he was done.

"That it is. Call once you have the plate." Jack ended the call and looked around at all of us.

This was one of those extremely frustrating situations that required a great deal of patience. I made eye contact with Paige, and she seemed as weary as she had the night before. She wanted this case closed and put to an end. And she wasn't alone in that desire, that was for sure. I wished we were already on the move to the Havens', but I understood Jack's desire to be armed with all the facts before we rushed in. Still…

"What if there are more victims fighting for their lives?" I asked.

Jack's hardened gaze settled on me. "We do this by the book. We get our facts, and then we move in."

There was zero room for negotiation based on the

set of Jack's jaw.

"Lieutenant, can you send officers over to watch the Havens' house?" Jack asked. "Tell them to be discreet."

"I'll do that now." Pike pulled out his phone and made the request. He hung up. "They're heading over there right away."

Jack nodded. "We need to find out more about this man she was married to, this Wayne Reed."

Pike had a precinct laptop in the room and started tapping on the keys. "Wayne Reed is forty-eight. Lives in Savannah and he owns Reed's Restorations."

"Wow, people are creative with business names around here." The words came without thought and warranted me a glare from Pike and Jack.

Zach continued, not looking up from Stanley's laptop. "Do they specialize in period restorations?"

Pike glanced at the computer. "Ah, yeah."

"Meaning they'd have access to lime mortar and, by extension, palygorskite clay," I said.

"Good. We have Wayne connected to the clay. Does he have a Savana registered to him?" Jack asked.

"He does," Pike stated somberly. "And a Toyota Corolla."

Paige cradled her coffee cup. "So how does he fit in? He provides the wheels and the clay to Stanley?"

"We can't rule out any level of involvement from any of them," Jack reasoned.

Pike looked up from his laptop. "Wayne's van was reported stolen."

Zach, who had been clicking away on Stanley's laptop, looked up now.

"When?" Jack asked.

"Just this morning," Pike said.

"Get a BOLO out on it," Jack directed. "And what properties does he own? Anything next to the river?"

"Only the building where he has his business, and from the records, he lives above the shop. And to answer your other question, it's nowhere near the river," Pike responded.

And with that, Jack was up and on the move. He addressed our team. "The four of us are going to talk to Wayne Reed. And Pike?"

"Yeah?"

"Get a couple officers to join us as backup."

"Uh, guys?" Zach was still seated at the table. "There's a file here on Stanley's computer that I can't get into." He addressed Pike. "Do you have someone here who can work their magic on this thing?"

Pike nodded. "I have just the man for the job."

CHAPTER

39

REED'S RESTORATIONS WAS SET UP in a large heritage house. The main level had been turned into the company's office while the upstairs was Reed's residence, as Pike had told us.

The four of us gathered outside the building, Pike hanging back from the group. Two uniformed officers were at their cruisers.

"We're going in casual and cautious," Jack told us.

Meaning we'd leave the guns in our holsters and the four of us would be entering the front door together. *Check.*

"Now, we have no idea how involved Reed might be or even if he is," Jack continued.

I learned a long time ago not to prejudge any situation on a snippet of fact, despite the human tendency to do just that, as if life was all about reaction time, not the consequences. In the FBI— just like life in general, I supposed—we were accountable for all the results whether they were favorable or not. And Jack, well, he preferred his team didn't fall under scrutiny from the higher-ups.

Before we entered, Jack said, "I'll take the lead in there."

A chime sounded when Zach opened the door for us, and inside stood a man who matched the DMV photo for Wayne Reed.

"Good day, can I—"

We all held up our credentials, but Jack took the lead toward Reed. "We're special agents with the FBI, and we have some questions that need answers."

Reed was calm, especially in the face of four Feds. He leaned against the counter. "Shoot."

"You reported your Savana stolen this morning," Jack began.

"Yeah."

"Not really a question. This is, however… How long has it been missing?"

Now Reed seemed to clam up, his eyes drifting over us, showing the first sign of nervousness at our presence.

"You need to start talking." Jack obviously smelled blood in the water. "Do you know Stanley Gilbert?"

"I am sort of friends with him."

"Explain sort of."

Reed's Adam's apple bobbed with a rough swallow. "He's a friend of my ex. You probably know about Pat—"

Jack nodded.

He took a deep breath. "Well, she asked me if I'd help him out."

"Help him out, how?" Based on the heat in Jack's

voice, I was happy that I wasn't on the receiving end.

"She said that he did some restoration jobs around town."

I knew looks could be deceiving, but pictures of Stanley didn't indicate a man I would peg as built for manual labor.

"You still haven't answered my question. How would you help him out?" Jack asked.

"I'd lend him my van sometimes," Reed said.

That came too easy to be the full story. Besides, it raised other questions, such as when did Stanley last borrow it and was Reed covering up more than he was letting on?

"How often?" Jack asked.

"Fridays." Reed must have sensed that mattered to us because he was quick to continue. "That's the day he did renos…usually."

"Usually?" Jack wasn't letting him off that easy.

Reed worried his lip.

"When did you last let him borrow your van?" Jack pressed.

"This past Monday."

"And when before that?"

"The Friday before." Reed held up his hands; Jack must have been glaring at him. "Fine, I confess. I heard on the news that you're looking for Stanley."

Jack tilted his head. "Then why didn't you call in?"

"I didn't want to get him in trouble. Guess you could say I was protecting a friend."

"Well, that *friend* is involved with serial abduction

and possible murder."

"Oh…" Reed grabbed his stomach, and he was rapidly shaking his head. "No, that can't be."

"Maybe you reported your van missing because you wanted to separate yourself from Stanley," Jack said.

"Not at all. I had no idea he was…"

"You sure?" Jack punched out and let the question sit there for a few beats before continuing. "We're quite certain that he used your van two Fridays ago to abduct a man from Perimeter Mall in Atlanta."

"I just can't… Wow. Really?"

I was a few feet away from Jack, and I sensed his energy shift. He was annoyed by Reed.

"I didn't call in because I… Well, I didn't know where he was. I know that his Prius is out back in my garage."

Jack clenched his jaw and glanced over his shoulder. He slowly turned back around to face Reed. "How long has it been here?"

"Since Monday when he picked up my van."

Jack tapped the side of his right thigh, a trait of his that didn't present often but it worked for him almost the same way an elastic around a wrist could be snapped to calm the temper of a person with anger-management issues.

"And you have no idea what he did with the van?" Jack was seething now.

"No, I swear. Stanley's so calm. Are you sure he—" His words stopped there, and I imagined Jack's famous stare homed right in on Reed.

"Besides lending him your van, were there other ways you helped him?" Jack asked.

"I'd sell him lime mortar sometimes. I get a good discount on the stuff."

Reed had no idea just how helpful he was in aiding murderers. Or did he?

"Now tell us about Patty's kid."

Reed's chin tucked in at the abrupt change of subject.

"What's he like?" Jack asked.

"He's not really a kid. He's got to be in his twenties."

Jack was silent, visibly not impressed.

"He's a little..." Reed's eyes shifted over us. "A little out there."

"Meaning?"

"Meaning that he should be locked up, on meds, something. There are definitely screws loose."

"Why do you say that?" Jack asked.

"He'd talk to himself, walk around the house mumbling. It was like he was two different people— or more. Honestly, he was the reason I had to get out of there."

"How did Patty react to your feelings about her son?"

Reed scoffed. "Oh, he could do no wrong."

Jack looked at me. "Have Pike get his men in here to stay with him."

I just nodded and did as I was told.

CHAPTER

40

Stanley had been trying to move for a while now, but his arms and legs didn't seem to be getting the message. His head felt like it had been struck by a Mack Truck, and his eyelids, like his body, refused to move.

How did he get here? Where was here? What had happened to him? All he had were hazy, jagged images that were dispersed in his mind as if they had been blown to bits in an explosion. But they began to form a picture...

Savannah, Georgia.

He was driving...

Wanted by the FBI.

Oh, it hurt to think. A tapping migraine afforded him no release to clear, coherent thought.

He tried to link together what he did recall, and slowly, it started to take shape.

He'd come to see Joshua and Patty...

He winced as his neck throbbed, firing heat through his body.

Was he standing up?

If he could open his eyes, maybe he could see where he was. But doing so wasn't going to come easy. It was as if his eyes were sealed shut.

"Help!" he cried out, but it came back to his ears garbled.

He struggled some more and managed to get his eyes open—or were they closed? He couldn't see a thing. His heart started beating fast. He was going to have a heart attack!

"Hello?" The voice didn't sound like his own. Did what he said even make sense? Did it come out as *hello* or something else?

Then the jagged edges of the images started to smooth out. He was here to put an end to the mess he'd gotten involved with, and it was time to turn himself—and all of them—in. Had he been given a chance to explain himself?

Why had he been so stupid? He was naive to think they'd be for that.

But part of him felt he didn't have the chance to let them know why he was back.

A bright light came on overhead, blinding him.

"Rise and shine." This voice was different from his own and didn't circle inside his head, but it sounded very distant, almost like an echo. It was a man talking to him.

"Wake up," the man said, and now something was also touching his cheek. It felt gauzy, as if he were having a dream or interacting with an apparition.

"I said *wake up*." The man was more insistent now,

demanding a response. But Stanley couldn't get his eyes to stay open. His mind was drifting, despite the touch to his cheek becoming more persistent, harsher, more painful.

Stanley's eyes shot open, but the brightness of the light had him closing them again.

"Look at me!" The man was unrelenting, and the touch he was feeling, he now realized, was the man slapping him. Pain seeped into Stanley's awareness.

He opened his eyes and looked at the man. *Joshua.* He was wearing all black and around his neck were…bones?

His own son…the monster. But was this a bad dream? Had he fallen asleep at the wheel and was actually lying in a hospital in a coma somewhere, none of this real? No, the throbbing in his cheek was real. He could wriggle his fingers, but his arms weighed a hundred pounds, and he couldn't move them.

Looking over, he saw his wrists bound in iron clasps connected to a chain. Looking down, his legs were ground to the floor, clasps around his ankles.

Joshua must have drugged him.

And then the memories came crashing over Stanley. He'd shown up, and before he'd had a chance to speak, he'd lost consciousness. And now he was here… Was this what his son did to the men he brought to him? He'd never come in here or watched.

"What are you going to do to me?" Stanley asked.

"You don't get to ask the questions, Stanley."

Hearing his name come from Joshua's lips sent shooting pain down his spine. His body remembered clearly now the fall to the marble floor.

"Dearest Daddy, you are getting the credit for my work. And I don't like that one bit." Joshua left him to move around the room, which now that it was illuminated, Stanley could see was rather compact. Maybe eight feet by eight feet. There was a table in the one corner. There was something on it, too, but Stanley couldn't make out what as his eyes weren't fully adjusted yet.

"Let me go. You don't want to…" Any strength he had mustered was quickly failing him.

"I can't let you go, Daddy. The FBI thinks you're behind the offerings." Joshua broke out into a bout of laughter. "They must have a sense of humor. Me, on the other hand, I don't. I take this very seriously."

The words weren't all making it through—at least not on a level he could comprehend. He didn't understand why any of this needed to happen to him. Why had his son strapped him in here? Was he planning to—

"You can't be running around pretending you are me." Joshua stared at him intently. "How dare you?"

He didn't want to be Joshua. He wished he'd never met the boy. "I'm not claiming anything, Son," Stanley said.

The smack across his face was swift and hard. It shoved Stanley's teeth into his cheek, and the taste of metal filled his mouth.

"Don't call me *Son*." Joshua squared his shoulders,

clasping his hands in front of himself.

Shit, this wasn't looking good. Any familiarity in Joshua's eyes was gone. Instead, within lurked a stranger, a demon. Stanley was going to die. Here, like this, bound in chains.

"What are you going to do to me?" he asked, trembling through his core.

A smile crept onto Joshua's face. "You are going to be the ultimate sacrifice."

"Sacrifice?" The one-word question slipped out, but the past rushed over him. Not long after first meeting Joshua, who was nineteen at the time, he had presented him with a gift. If one wanted to call it that. The memory of the dead animal still made his stomach curdle.

"I am a Mayan priest, Father."

Joshua had said it over and over with the beaming smile of a young child who'd drawn a picture or crafted a gift with his own hands.

All this was Patty's fault! If she hadn't kept the boy a secret from him, if she hadn't told him that his father had left them to study ancient cultures—specifically mentioning the Mayans—none of this would have happened. He wouldn't have allowed himself to get all caught up in this nightmare—a father protecting his child when he should have been protecting the world from that child instead. But he had found himself eventually taking some pride in the boy. He had created another living being, and really, who was he to judge? He'd been judged all his life. So he'd agreed to keep the family secret, that his son was a serial killer in the making, and instead, Stanley bonded with the boy. But it quickly took a turn he hadn't anticipated, and the truth was more complicated than he'd originally thought. And when he'd become involved, there had been a part of him that had enjoyed the power over others. He might not be able to take their lives, but he could control them. Plus, when Joshua had something to occupy his time, he was calmer.

"Let me go, Son. We can talk." He couldn't just give up on his life.

Joshua gave a sinister grin and shook his head. "It's far too late for conversation, Offering."

His mental illness had advanced, and what Stanley saw before him was "the Other." At least that's what he called it. And it was coming out more often. That was partially why Stanley had decided to run on Monday.

"The FBI think you're behind everything. It's time to prove who I am." The Other's eyelids fluttered, and he took deep breaths, drawing Stanley's attention to the tiny bones around his son's neck.

"You will no longer take credit for my work. You will no longer pretend you are me."

"Please, I never—"

The punch to the gut came so quickly that Stanley didn't have time to prepare for the impact. But his body barely moved, given the tight restraint system he was in.

Stanley vomited, barely missing the Other, who had jumped back. But instead of disgust showing on the Other's face, there was amusement.

"You think you're strong, Stanley Gilbert?"

"I'm your father."

The Other spat on the ground. "You are not my father, human."

The Other went to the table and picked something up. When he turned around, Stanley could see that it was a rudimentary knife. It made him think of the blade the Mayans had used for the heart-extraction ritual.

Oh God. No! No! No!

He swallowed bile and his mind slowed.

The Other was about six inches from him now, motionless, except for his eyes that traced his face.

If only he could think clearly, he'd bring back his studies of the Mayan culture beyond the human sacrifices that involved such brutality and bloodshed. How could he appeal to the Other? One word kept coming to him: submission.

"I am yours." The words came out jumbled, and the Other's brows contorted in confusion.

How could he word this in such a way as to keep his life? Stanley's stomach tightened and so did his chest. He had to think!

The sacrifices were usually high-ranking prisoners of war—warriors. Those who didn't qualify or who were of lower status were used for labor. Yes, that was it. His weak nature finally had something positive to offer.

"You don't want to sacrifice me. I am not worthy." Yes, that was it. That should work, or at least make the Other think about what he was planning to do, how Stanley was far from an ideal sacrifice.

The Other didn't say anything or move. Was he even breathing? Did he need to breathe? Nonsense. His son was in there…somewhere.

"Please, I am weak. I always have been." Stanley's head was clearing, thank God. "I've been living a double life. You know this. Saddled with a vindictive woman for seventeen years. I should have been with your mother." Maybe he could make the Other disappear and bring his son back. "The FBI wouldn't have known a thing about me if I hadn't decided to toss my phone in the river."

"I couldn't reach you." There was the glimpse of his son in the eyes now, and a single tear fell down his cheek.

"Please, Son. I love you. I've done so much for you."

"No!" He roared, his eyes clouding over and the darkness moving in. "You have not."

This was it. Stanley was going to die. He never thought he'd wish for the FBI to come for him— turning oneself in always had a better consequence— but he prayed to God they would find him before it was too late!

His breathing was becoming erratic and signaled the onset of a panic attack. He didn't need this now. He had to quiet his mind, his nerves.

He was heaving, pulling on the restraints with his body's efforts to derive oxygen.

The Other was observing him, angling his head.

Was he trying to read Stanley's mind? Maybe a panic attack wouldn't be a bad thing. It would support his claim of inferiority. Hopefully, buy him his freedom long enough for the FBI to rescue him.

CHAPTER

41

PIKE, MY TEAM, AND I, along with a couple officers, were on a side road near the Havens' property waiting on some last-minute items to fall into place before we moved in. Jack had Nadia pulling medical records for Patty and Joshua Haven and seeing if she could dig up anything else that might prove useful.

SWAT was called in to assist, local traffic would be detoured from the neighborhood, and an ambulance would be standing by. We had the blueprint of the house spread on the hood of Jack's rental and warrants were in process—two arrest warrants and a search warrant. Officers had already confirmed that Patty Haven was home.

Jack was sucking on his cigarette like it might be the last one he'd ever have. "We'll need to approach this slightly differently than we normally do," he said. "They have a large property, and the backyard is gated." He was primarily talking to his team, but he glanced at Pike, regarding the fence.

"At least seven feet high," Pike pitched in.

"The property backs against the river..." Jack paused, giving his strategy some thought.

"I'm not sure if the fence goes all the way to the river or not," Paige said.

"We need to bring backup in and position them on a boat."

"Good idea." Pike signaled to one of the officers to arrange it. "Put them undercover and give them fishing rods."

Jack addressed his team. "We're all going to the front door. We'll knock, announce ourselves, and head in, then spread out. Brandon and I will cover the main level. Paige and Zach, you two take upstairs."

"Sounds like a plan," Zach said.

"Keep alert. Joshua and his mother will likely do whatever's necessary to protect their secret."

"With a house this big, they might have staff," Paige offered.

"We'll need to approach with caution, then," Jack replied.

His phone rang, which he answered on speaker.

"The license plate from the mall's parking lot came back. The van is registered to Wayne Reed," Nadia said on the other end of the line.

No one on the team said a word. It was an answer we'd expected.

Nadia went on. "And Joshua was diagnosed with DID, but he's never been treated with medication."

"And what does that mean for his condition?" I asked.

"Dissociative identity disorder," Nadia explained. "Joshua has at least two personalities, maybe more. It's usually caused from sustained abuse over a period of time. It's how the victim seeks comfort outside of himself or herself."

"So what happened to Joshua?" Paige asked.

"Patty Long would have paid to have her and Joshua's legal names changed to Haven," I began. "And a haven is—"

"A safe place," Paige finished.

"Yes. So maybe Patty moved here to get her son away from someone," I concluded.

"Nadia, check if there's any evidence that Patty or Joshua were abused," Jack directed.

"Will do."

"I'd also like to know where she got all her money," Jack continued.

"I'll do my best to find out."

"Remember how I said that cutting out the tongue wasn't a part of the ancient ritual?" Zach asked suddenly. "We figured it just might have to do with more than one person being involved in the actual ritual process, but that's not necessarily the case. It could carry a deeper meaning. One of Joshua's personalities could feel suppressed and want to be more dominant than it is, but one of his other personalities is, in effect, silencing it."

"Do you think his secondary personality is the one behind the murders?" I asked.

"His second, third, who knows? We should prepare for the distinct possibility that he won't be

Joshua Haven when we go in, though."

"Zach," Paige began, "you also mentioned at the crime scene the other day that it could be a way of silencing his victims, taking their voices. In cases of child abuse, the kids are often told to keep quiet."

"Nadia, you still there?" Jack asked.

"I am."

"Dig into close family relatives of Patty and Joshua, too."

"Okay."

"Is there anything else you can tell us about Joshua at this point?" he asked.

"From the file, all I can see is that he and his mother moved to Savannah when he was thirteen."

"He would have been pulled out of school." That could be hard on some kids.

"Not the case for Joshua. He lasted for half a year of kindergarten in a public school, but then he was homeschooled."

"Mom was sheltering him from the world," Paige said.

"Or trying to shelter the world from him," I countered.

"How far back does the abuse go?" The thought made me sick.

Pike's phone rang. A few seconds in with his caller, he said to us, "The undercover officers are in position."

An officer came hurrying toward us. "We've got the warrants."

"Stay safe," Nadia said before disconnecting.

Jack dropped his cigarette butt and extinguished it with a twist of his shoe. "Let's go."

Jack, Paige, Zach, and I headed up the Havens' driveway by foot. Savannah SWAT were in position to enter the garage, and they'd go into the house from there.

Jack banged on the door. "FBI! Open up!"

He paused and was met with silence on the other side of the door.

"Open up or we're coming in," Jack bellowed into the evening air.

We heard the rushing of feet inside. It was hard to distinguish how many people. They weren't headed toward the door, though.

Glass shattered inside, and a woman cursed.

Where did she think she was going that we couldn't catch up with her?

An officer spoke over the comms. "There's a white van in the garage."

Probably Wayne Reed's. That meant Stanley Gilbert was likely inside.

Jack turned to me. "Now."

I knew that he was inferring that I should bust the door. It was wood so I did it the old-fashioned way with a strong leg and a well-aimed foot. It took one kick, and I thanked my exercise regimen for that.

We stepped inside and set out as per the plan. Jack and I stuck to the main level while Paige and Zach headed upstairs.

My heart was beating fast, but my mind was clear and processing my surroundings.

The house was beyond fancy, every accent the touch of a professional decorator. The door opened to a large room with fifteen-foot beamed ceilings and windows that went the full height of the wall. The furniture layout and area rugs designated different parts of the space, including one that served as a living room and had a TV. It was on at a low volume, suggesting that at least one person had been watching. On the floor, next to a side table, was a broken vase. It was probably what I had heard smash when we had been outside.

Jack and I made our way to the back of the home, where the kitchen was located.

Muffled screaming found my ears.

I hurried toward a door that was to the left of the kitchen. Opening it, I saw nothing but darkness.

CHAPTER

42

MEMORIES OF THIS MAN, his father, kept washing in and blending with rage. It was difficult to distinguish his feelings, his perceptions, from each other. There was a tug of mercy and then, in a flash, all-consuming hatred.

He had come back to turn them in. That could be the only explanation for his return. He was going to desert them. Yet Stanley kept looking at him as if he had something more substantial to say. All that was coming through, however, was him pleading for his life. And did he really think it necessary to proclaim himself as being inferior? He didn't possess the strength to carry out the ritual himself. He simply abducted the offerings and handed them over.

Yes, Stanley was weak. It was a choice he had made.

While Joshua might have been viewed by outsiders as a misfit, it wasn't like he had made the decision to be this way. He had been chosen. He didn't belong here. And not just in Georgia, but on

Earth. He was above human form while Stanley was simply pathetic.

"Do you honestly think you can talk me out of sacrificing you?" Joshua said. "I would take honor in your death."

"You..." Stanley seemed to have lost his strength to speak after the full-blown panic attack he'd experienced earlier.

Joshua got up in his face. "You what? What about me?"

Stanley's eyes closed briefly. "You are not a strong warrior..."

Rage slithered up Joshua's spine, and he felt his body becoming cold. "I am—"

"You are a...god."

Any anger that had swelled melted away. He stepped back, never having expected those words to come out of Stanley's mouth. "Why do you say that?"

"I can tell."

He couldn't gauge if Stanley was bullshitting him and just saying whatever it took to be freed, but it felt amazing to hear. He was being recognized. None of his other offerings had a clue. They had been conquered mentally and physically, and had given up not long after they'd had their tongues cut out, as if they had resigned themselves to death, knowing there would be no escaping it.

Joshua's gaze hardened on Stanley. There would be no release for him. He needed to account for his failures, and Joshua was not a merciful god. He was one who demanded blood sacrifice.

He went to the table to retrieve the knife, and the door to the outer room opened.

What was all that racket? Who dared come down here when he was in the middle of preparing an offering?

The door to the inner room opened and his mother was standing before him.

"What are you doing here?" he asked.

"The FBI are here," she said. "They've figured it out."

He didn't know what he should feel in that moment, but a radiant calm spread over him. Maybe the next phase of his life was close at hand. Maybe it was time for him to transcend.

"We've got to go…" His mother was spinning in a circle.

Joshua steepled his hands. "We stay."

Then, as if his mother saw Stanley for the first time, she hurried over to him and touched his arm. She turned on Joshua. "He's awake?"

He stared at her blankly.

"Let him go."

What gave her the right to boss him around? He didn't answer to her.

He went over to her and gripped her around the neck. Her eyes bulged and she slapped at him, but his hold grew stronger.

"Stop!" Stanley yelled, and Joshua looked him square in the eye as he continued to squeeze. He felt the bones crushing in his mother's throat.

He closed his eyes, breathing in his power.

"Help us!"

Stanley's screams yanked Joshua out of his reflection, and then he heard hurried footsteps coming toward the door to the outer room.

Joshua let go of his mother, and she collapsed to the floor, touching her neck and coughing, heaving for oxygen.

"You led them here!" Joshua snarled, holding the blade to Stanley's throat.

JACK TOOK OUT HIS FLASHLIGHT, his weapon at the ready, and used it until he found a light switch. Through the door next to the kitchen there was an area that had black-out shades covering the windows. And within the space, another room was sealed off.

"Stay here," Jack whispered to Paige and Zach, who had cleared the second floor and were with us now. He nodded for me to enter first.

The door to the inner room opened, and Joshua Haven emerged. He was dressed in black with a necklace of bones around his neck.

"You have arrived," he stated calmly.

I didn't care for his words or the way he was presenting himself to us. He was far too docile for it to be a good thing.

"FBI! Put your hands in the air!" I shouted.

Jack and I continued to approach, and Joshua didn't move. As we got closer to him, I noticed that there was a makeshift sacrificial altar opposite the side room. A round stone and idol statues were positioned near it.

"Joshua—"

"I am Huitzilopochtli," he boomed.

The Mayan deity...

That could be another reason why he made exceptions to the ritual. He was, in effect, offering the sacrifices to himself. Or so he believed.

"We are here for you," I said.

Joshua smiled. "Yes."

"Get down on the ground with your hands in the air." My heart was racing, pumped full of adrenaline.

Joshua continued smiling and got down on his knees, doing exactly as I had asked. "You are here to free me from my earthly bonds. And Stanley is going to cross over, be reborn."

Hairs rose on the back of my neck, and tingles crept down my spine.

Jack moved to go past me, but I had a horrible feeling and put my arm out to stop him. Joshua had mentioned us being here to free him; he mentioned crossing over and rebirth. Something told me it wasn't just about Stanley. He did want suicide by cop, and I wasn't in any mood to facilitate his desire. I holstered my weapon.

"What are you doing? Free me." Joshua looked upward and closed his eyes.

I swept in quickly and snapped a cuff on his wrist.

"No!" Patty Haven was running toward me, holding a blade and screaming. "Leave him alone!"

My hands were busy with the cuffs, and I tried to

hurry. Where was Jack? What was he doing?

I glimpsed over my shoulder to find Jack standing back about five feet from me and Joshua. He was just staring as Patty was closing the distance.

Shit! My hands weren't cooperating, and my thumb was hooked on a cuff.

"Jack!" I yelled.

He was frozen in place.

Patty was about five feet away when a shot sounded and she crashed to the floor. The knife slipped out of her hand and skittered across the floor. It stopped to Joshua's right. I was on his left. I had to move for it, and fast.

But I didn't make it in time, and Joshua got hold of the knife.

I backed up and drew my gun. "Put the knife down!"

Joshua smiled as he slashed his own throat from ear to ear. Blood was spurting everywhere, and there was so much of it. He dropped to the floor, motionless.

Joshua Haven was dead.

I turned to look at Jack, and he was standing there, dazed. It hadn't been Jack who'd saved my life. It had been Paige.

He was all right, my ass.

CHAPTER

43

THE PARAMEDICS CONFIRMED MY SUSPICION, announcing Joshua dead almost as soon as they'd arrived. His mother, though, would survive. Paige's bullet had struck her in the arm so that she'd released the knife but wasn't in any life-threatening danger. Stanley Gilbert had been freed and was being checked over by paramedics before officers were to escort him to the hospital for further testing where he'd be cuffed to the bed and under twenty-four-hour surveillance.

The white van in the garage had been confirmed as Wayne Reed's and the lidded garbage bin Stanley had used to abduct Eric Morgan was in the back.

Crime Scene Investigators were swarming the Haven residence inside and out. The undercover officers in the boat were never called into play, but when they docked, they did find some human remains mired in mud.

"And why didn't anyone see this days ago when boats and officers were sent out?" Jack hadn't gotten his edge back. He sounded almost as if he didn't care.

"It was just far enough back and hidden in cattails that the officers couldn't see it," Pike said, defending his brothers from Savannah PD.

We were inside the room where the rituals had taken place. I was still trying to shake the fact that Jack had left me back there—at least mentality. I had to put some space between us for a bit or I'd say something I couldn't take back, and that would probably wind up biting me in the ass.

Death was palpable in the space as I walked around, and it wasn't because Joshua had just died here. It was as if the screams of his victims resonated off the walls.

A CSI was processing the contents of a locked cabinet where bones from hands and feet were kept inside glass vases. Add to this find, the many bones around Joshua's neck, and I didn't envy the people directly responsible for ascertaining how many victims we were looking at. The number of missing persons Nadia had found wouldn't be near enough to account for all these bones.

Inside the room where we had found Stanley, there was a table with a container of the blue paint, the ingredients for which CSIs were still looking.

I walked over to where Joshua had made the sacrifices. The idols next to the round stone had smears of dark crimson on their faces, and I assumed it would test positive for human blood. There was a sort of ratcheting system set up around the stone, too, and I angled my head to figure out how it worked.

"That's how he stretched the victims out and dislocated their joints," Zach said, coming up behind me.

I straightened out. "Thanks for making that graphic for me."

"I'm sure it's not the worst image you've had in your head since you came in here."

"True," I mumbled.

"He wouldn't have let anything happen to you, you know."

I turned to face Zach. "He froze. If it wasn't for—"

"We're all human, Brandon. Even Jack."

I studied his eyes. How could he not see it? Jack wasn't the same man he had been before he almost died. "He's changed. I'm not sure he can handle the job anymore."

"You know that's not the truth." Zach squeezed one of my shoulders. "He'll be fine. Give him time."

I nodded, but my teeth were clenched. After all, this was my life we were talking about here. My thoughts shifted from dwelling on my mortality to the boulder I was staring at. It was enormous. It certainly would have been heavier than two men could carry. Even adding Patty Haven into the mix, there wouldn't have been enough brawn.

Then there was the matter of Tanya Lewis in South Carolina. She hadn't recognized Stanley, but she'd described a dark-haired man of at least six feet. Sure, that could include a lot of men, but I had a particular one in mind. I walked back to where Jack,

Paige, and Pike were.

"Wayne Reed has to be in on this," I said. "For one, there are a lot more remains here than the eighteen missing men from the last four years. There could be more prior to then, too. Ones that Reed could have helped with. Think about it—we haven't found the components for the paint. At the very least, Reed could be mixing that. But I'd wager he's more involved. There's no way a couple people could get that boulder in here." I was pretty much winded by the time I'd gotten all that out. My heart was racing so fast. "And if that's not enough, he's had Stanley's Prius all this time. He also admitted to knowing we were looking for Stanley and decided—" I attributed finger quotes "—to keep quiet."

"Have the officers watching Wayne Reed bring him in for questioning," Jack directed Pike.

Pike stepped away, his phone to an ear, but he didn't say anything into the receiver. He spoke to us. "I'm not getting any answer."

CHAPTER

44

THE TEAM TOOK BOTH SUVs, and Jack had Pike on speaker. The two officers who were left to watch over Reed were Officers Poole and Weaver.

"Dispatch can't reach either officer," Pike said. "Neither of them pushed the panic button on his radio. More backup is on the way, as well."

Jack turned into Reed's driveway so fast that the vehicle's frame rolled and had me reaching for the oh-shit bar. He parked it on an angle parallel to the building, and we both got out. Pike was right behind us, as were Paige and Zach.

All of us gathered by the passenger side of the SUV, using the vehicle as cover between us and the house.

"He doesn't have any guns registered to him," Pike said.

"But if he's overpowered two officers, you can be certain he's armed now," Jack stated. It was a sad likelihood, but I just hoped that both officers were alive.

Backup arrived in the form of four cruisers with two officers per vehicle.

Jack looked at each of us. "Ready?"

Pike nodded immediately. I took a deep breath and nodded. Then Paige and Zach did, too.

Jack directed Paige and Zach to go around back with Pike, and he and I took the front.

The door was unlocked, and the chime that had sounded friendly before now came across as menacing. Jack and I entered the house stealthily, our guns at the ready.

Inside, it was quiet…too quiet. Tile samples were strewn all over the floor, indicating there had been a struggle.

Behind the service counter, an officer was lying on the floor, leads from a Taser still in his chest.

I hurried toward him, holstered my gun, and felt for a pulse. I nodded at Jack and spoke through the comms so Pike would hear. "Officer Poole is alive." I let out the breath I had been holding.

"Thank God," Pike said. "Any sign of Officer Weaver?"

My eyes followed drops of blood toward a closed door. I pointed it out to Jack and drew my gun again. Holding it in one hand, I turned the door knob. Jack was standing there, braced to fire.

"We've found Officer Weaver," Jack said over the comms.

"Is he…?" Pike didn't finish his question.

The officer was slumped over, chin to chest, but his head was rising and falling.

"He's alive, too," Jack replied.

I holstered my weapon again and got down next to the officer. I lifted his head back. He was out cold. Then I looked at the side of his neck and around the back, where there was a small prick in the skin.

"He was drugged," I said. "Probably the same thing used on Morgan, and likely the other victims."

Pike, Paige, and Zach joined us in the front.

"No sign of Reed?" I asked.

Paige shook her head. "Or his Corolla. Stanley's Prius is in a garage out back, though."

Pike passed his gaze between his two officers, looking from one to the other. "Thank God, they're alive."

The wailing sirens of ambulances were drawing closer.

Jack pointed to the floor. "Let's rip this guy's life apart and find out where he might have run off to. Lieutenant, make sure that all of Savannah PD knows about the manhunt and to issue a BOLO for Reed's Corolla."

The paramedics entered the house in a rush and attended to the officers. They weren't with them long before the one paramedic said, "We're going to load them up and take them to Memorial Hospital."

By that time, Jack had Nadia on the phone. "We need anything and everything on Wayne Reed right now."

"What did he do for work in the past? Any evidence of travel?" I asked.

Jack nodded. I'd impressed him again.

"Give me a few seconds…" Nadia told us.

That, of course, turned into more than a few.

"Nadia, give us something," Jack pressed.

"Okay, okay, no criminal background," she said.

"How long has he owned the restoration company?" Jack asked her.

"Fifteen years, and before that he worked at Cox Incorporated for five years—the entire time he was married to Patty. Cox is a—"

"A prestigious law firm downtown," Pike interjected.

"How does he go from a career in law to owning a restoration company?" I asked. "What did he do for the law firm?"

"Oh, it says that he was a pilot." Nadia's voice lowered.

More tingles down the back of my neck. How many more victims might we be looking at? "We need to know where he went during that time."

"Who's the owner of the law firm?" Jack asked, superseding my question.

"Benjamin Cox," Pike answered. "The company is huge. They have clients all around the world. As a pilot, Reed could have gone anywhere and abducted people. But wouldn't flight manifests and customs be an issue?"

"There are ways around everything, and a motivated and organized killer could figure them out," Zach spoke up.

Jack looked at me. "We need to find out where Reed's travels took him. But let's also talk about where Reed could have gone now."

"He's got to know that we'll issue a BOLO on his Corolla, so he'll ditch it the first chance he gets," I said.

"I agree," Paige said. "He'd likely exchange it for another mode of transportation entirely—bus, train, plane."

"All we need is him hopping on a jet for a non-extradition country," Jack snarled. "I'll have him grounded." He turned to Pike. "Get some men checking bus and train stations for him. Tell them not to go by the parking lot, as he might not have driven the Corolla that far."

"Makes sense," Pike said.

"Brandon and I are going to go speak to Benjamin," Jack added.

"Try his office first," Pike suggested. "It might be Saturday evening, but that doesn't matter to a man like Cox. He works twenty-four seven."

Jack turned to Paige and Zach. "You might have to wait around a bit, but you two go to the hospital and see what you can get out of Patty or Stanley as soon as you can."

"You got it, Jack." Paige turned toward the door, Zach on her heels.

CHAPTER

45

PIKE HAD BEEN RIGHT ABOUT Cox Incorporated. All the lights were on and some people were working. At least there was a woman at the front desk. She didn't strike me as too happy to be there on a Saturday evening. Or maybe it was Jack and me standing in front of her holding up our badges that she didn't like.

"Supervisory Special Agent Jack Harper to see Benjamin Cox," Jack said.

The woman scowled. "He's in a meeting, and he's not to be disturbed."

She was definitely a gatekeeper, and she was probably paid handsomely for her ability to keep most people away from her employer. But Jack wasn't most people, and we were with the federal government following a lead in a serial murder investigation.

"A former employee is suspected of murder, and he's missing," Jack said. "We need to talk to Mr. Cox. Now."

The woman tilted up her chin and ran a hand down her neck. She pressed a button on the phone. "I know you said not to… Yes… This is an exception." Her gaze was going over Jack and me. "It's the FBI. They need to talk to you about…murder." She pulled off her headset. "He'll see you now." She got up and led us down a narrow hallway to an office the size of my first apartment.

The flooring was a blond hardwood that reminded me of a basketball court, though that also might have had something to do with the hoop that was mounted to one wall. The walls were exposed cinder blocks, and the office had a modern, minimalistic feel to it. Cox's desk was all sleek lines—black and glass. A sofa and matching chair were set up on an area rug that probably cost more than I'd made last year.

Three men were in the room when we stepped inside, but two excused themselves, leaving us alone with Benjamin Cox.

His pale skin would easily burn when exposed to sunlight or freckle immediately. I was someone who could recognize that curse. He was at least six four and lean. It wasn't a surprise that he had an interest in basketball.

Cox's tongue flicked out between his lips, and he steepled his fingers in front of his chest. His mouth relaxed into a scowl. "What can I do for you?" He was clearly unimpressed and irritated by our interruption.

"Wayne Reed," Jack spat.

"What about him?"

"He used to be your pilot," Jack said.

"That's right. Why are you here about him?"

"He's a suspect in an open investigation, and we're looking for your cooperation."

Cox straightened his tie. "Fine. What do you need to know?"

"You own a jet, yes?" Jack asked.

"A Bombardier Global 7000, to be precise." Spoken like a true elitist. "Why?"

Jack shuffled right past Cox's prideful statement. "We need a list of all the destinations he flew to."

"I'm not sure that I—"

"Do you have something to hide?" Jack stared the man down, and after a few seconds, Cox lowered his shoulders.

"I don't." He tugged down on his jacket. "But he did. I fired him because it came to my attention that he was making flights without my authorization."

"How did you find out about these other flights?" I asked.

"We were burning through fuel much faster than we should have been. I hired a PI to follow Wayne Reed's movements. They found out that he was hijacking my plane."

"How many times?" I asked.

"At least a dozen before I caught on."

Enough dancing around the matter. "We need to know exactly where he went and when," I said.

Cox's gaze went back and forth between the two of us. "Let me make something perfectly clear.

Whatever you suspect Wayne Reed of has nothing to do with me. Do you understand?"

Jack stepped toward Cox. "Do you understand that Wayne Reed is dangerous and on the run?"

Jack and Cox stared each other down. Jack won.

Cox sighed. "After he was caught red-handed, I had my PI investigate further. He came back with a number of airports where my plane had touched down. The one I remember off the top of my head is in Albuquerque, New Mexico."

I realized that New Mexico wasn't *Mexico*, but it seemed to strike close to this case. It was hard to accept that Joshua's stepfather flying there was a coincidence.

"I can tell by the way your eyes are lighting up that this means something. I assure you I'm not hiding a thing," Cox said calmly.

"As you've made clear," Jack stated. "We'll need a list of all the places he took your plane unauthorized."

Cox walked to his desk and pressed a button on the phone.

"Mr. Cox?" It was the woman from the front desk.

"Please print off the list of unauthorized flight plans that Wayne Reed piloted."

"Right away. Is that all?" she asked.

Cox turned to us.

"Have her send a copy to Nadia Webber." Jack rhymed off Nadia's e-mail address.

"Mr. Cox?" The woman spoke to her boss for confirmation.

"Do as he says."

Cox disconnected the call. "She'll have that ready for you in mere seconds. Glad I could help."

I wasn't sure whether he was being sincere or not.

Jack led the way out of Cox's office, and we collected the printout from the receptionist before leaving the building. There were three pages of flights over the course of Wayne Reed's five-year employment.

Once we were outside, Jack called Nadia. He explained everything we'd learned and that she'd be getting a full list.

"For now," Jack instructed, "start with New Mexico."

CHAPTER

46

AFTER JACK AND I HAD called Nadia, Paige had reached us with the news that Stanley Gilbert had been treated and that he'd walk away physically fine. His psychological health would be another issue. He was being carted to the precinct now, and that's where we were heading, too.

We'd have a bit longer of a wait for Patty Haven, who was having surgery to remove the bullet. But it had been a good shoot on Paige's part.

Jack and I met up with Paige and Zach in the observation room.

Through the one-way glass, we saw Stanley secured by cuffs to a table in an interrogation room. That must have felt great on his already-tender wrists, but the combination of knowing what he had done and now being face-to-face with the man was enough to make me lose any earlier inclinations toward empathy. He'd led numerous men to their deaths.

Jack had asked me to handle this interrogation,

and Stanley barely lifted his head when I entered the room. His eyes held a blend of sadness and confusion.

I pulled out the chair opposite him and sat down. "Why did you do it, Stanley?"

"Why did I do what?"

I settled back into the seat. "All right, you want to play stupid?" I pulled out a still from the security footage at Perimeter Mall showing him pushing the lidded garbage container toward the van and slid it across the table to him. "And don't think of telling me that isn't you. We know it is."

There was heat in Stanley's gaze. "How would you know?"

"The wife of a victim ID'd you."

Stanley paled but remained quiet.

"Also, that van you were driving belongs to Wayne Reed. And you know who he is."

Stanley scratched at the table with his left index finger. "Yes."

I pointed to the bin he was pushing. "You know who is inside that?"

His eyes drifted to the photo and back up to meet my eyes. "I do."

"Good, so you're not denying your involvement in the murder of Eric Morgan."

Silence.

"Now, let me ask you again… Why did you do it, Stanley?" There were so many questions we had for him, and this was merely a place to start. We needed to understand why and how his phone had ended up in the river and where he had been for the past six days since he'd seemingly disappeared from Savannah.

"I had to." His chin quivered now, and a single tear fell down his cheek.

"That's not who you are, is it? The type to abduct people and take them to be murdered?" While it was true that we didn't know if Stanley was directly involved in the ritual, it was advantageous to proceed as if we thought him innocent in that regard.

"No." He glimpsed at the one-way glass.

"So why did you do it?" Was my asking the third time the charm?

He met my eyes. "I didn't kill anybody."

"You helped to—"

"That is a lie!" He raised his voice.

I raised a hand. "I'll rephrase. You *abducted* men for *your son* to kill."

Silence.

"Come on, Stanley, you're already caught."

He sliced me a glare. "I did it to protect my son."

"I can understand protection. What were you protecting him from?"

"He is a killer, Agent. I knew it from the first time I met him. Well, pretty much right away."

"Tell me about that," I said. "When did you meet him?"

"Patty came into the bank one day. We hadn't seen each other since high school."

"You were sweethearts?" I was doing my best to be his buddy now and pulling on all my acting skills to do so.

Stanley nodded and gave a partial smile. "We were."

"But then you went away to college."

"I did."

"And her life went another direction. That must have been heartbreaking."

Empathize.

"It was," he said. "I loved her."

I picked up on the past tense. "Do you still?"

Stanley started scratching at the table's surface again. "No."

"Why not?"

He stopped all movement and looked me straight in the eye. "Because she is evil. Just like Joshua."

"Your son."

"I suppose he was."

Stanley would have known that Joshua was dead, but he didn't show any indication that it bothered him at all. Ironic, as he had been willing to abduct people for him. "You said that you did it to protect Joshua, but please help me understand how abducting people for him to murder accomplished that."

A blank stare. "If I hadn't done it, he would have, and he'd have been caught. He's not…well. Sometimes he seems normal, but he's far from it. He has a demon that lives inside him."

"Your son had been diagnosed with DID but was never medicated," I pointed out.

"I know."

"Why not help him and protect others by getting him medicine instead?"

"Patty."

My brow furrowed. "I don't understand."

"She doesn't believe in medicine," he said. "She believes in *herbs*."

"Homeopathic remedies?"

"Yes."

Not that I was in any position to judge the medical treatment a person chose, but I couldn't imagine homeopathic treatments having any real benefits for a person with mental illness. "You could have fought her on that. Told her that Joshua needed help."

Stanley was shaking his head. "No, she wouldn't listen. Joshua was perfect the way God made him."

I had to take pause and collect myself as I recovered from that statement. Perfection was a serial murderer? Now I'd heard it all.

"I was going to turn myself in…to you, the FBI," Stanley continued, looking past me to the one-way glass again. "But I went to see Patty and Joshua first. I wanted to convince them it was the best thing to do."

"Why now, after all this time?"

"I don't know, but it probably had to do with the fact that you'd find us. You were already on to me. It wouldn't take you long to figure out I wasn't working alone. It would look better to turn ourselves in."

"So if the remains never washed up in the river…?"

"You'd have never known. Life would have carried on."

Or death...depending on how one looks at it.

There was no remorse in Stanley's gaze, and for all his claims that abducting men for murder wasn't *him*, it had at least become part of who he was.

"What was your first clue something was wrong with Joshua?" I asked.

"He...uh...presented me with a gift."

"Presented? That sounds like an offering."

Stanley nodded. "He'd taken his cat, skinned it, and ripped out its heart."

I vomited a little in my mouth.

"He said, 'I am a Mayan priest, Father.'" Stanley licked his lips, then bit on his bottom one briefly. "He told me it was the Mayan heart-extraction ritual and asked me if I was pleased."

"Were you?"

"No, of course not," Stanley shot back.

"What did you say, then?"

"I was in shock and scared to death. Patty was there when he presented it, and she was smiling. I feared for my life."

"But you talked to Patty about it afterward?"

"I did, but she laughed off my concerns." Stanley fell somber. "She told me I'd been a horrible father and it was about time I made this up to Joshua. But I didn't know about him, I swear. Not until after she came into the bank."

"Do you know why he thought that killing a cat would please you?" I asked.

"I figured it out." Stanley waited a few beats. "Patty had told him that I wasn't in his life because I had to go away and study the Mayans."

The hairs rose on my neck. "He developed an interest in Mayan culture because his father had one?"

"Yes."

"And then when he met you…"

"It was the natural thing for him to do, I guess."

Natural to kill a furry family member?

"You said you came back to turn yourself and them in, but had you never thought of doing that before?" I asked.

"I was afraid before."

I thought back to finding Stanley naked and chained in that room. "For good reason."

"You—the FBI—were going to catch us. I knew it. I could just feel it. I took a stupid gamble and almost paid for it with my life. Thank God, you guys got there in time."

"Why keep bringing Joshua men to kill?"

"It would calm him down. He was in control of himself more than his other personality."

"And that personality was Huitzilopochtli?"

Stanley made eye contact with me. "I called it the Other."

Shivers laced down my spine. Sometimes I wondered how I ever cleaned the bad energy off me.

"Tell us about Wayne Reed," I said.

"What about him? He was married to Patty."

"Did he know about Joshua's illness?"

Stanley wasn't looking at me now.

"Stanley," I said more forcibly.

Nothing.

I snapped my fingers, and Stanley jumped. "Did he know about Joshua's illness?" I repeated.

"Oh, he more than knew. Before me, he used to get the men."

I rose to my feet.

"Where are you going?"

Ignoring Stanley's question, I left him and went into the observation room where I found Jack by himself. I wondered where Paige and Zach had gone, but before I had a chance to ask, Jack spoke.

"Nadia called while you were in there, and she had some luck with Missing Persons. Three twentysomething white men went missing from areas within reasonable driving distance of Albuquerque, New Mexico coinciding with flights Wayne Reed made there. And news has come back from the hospital that Patty Haven has been cleared, so Paige and Zach are going to talk to her now."

"Good," was the only word I could get out.

CHAPTER

47

PAIGE AND ZACH ENTERED PATTY Haven's hospital room.

She was lying on the bed at an angle, an IV line running into her hand. Her gaze was directed straight ahead of her, but she wasn't looking at the TV, which was off. Rather, she was just staring into space, smiling.

She didn't look at them when they entered, but she said, "He's free now."

"We're agents with the FBI," Paige said, ignoring her. "I'm Agent Dawson, and this is Agent Miles."

"He didn't mean to hurt anyone." She drew her gaze to look at them. "He honored their souls, sent them home. He was gifted."

Paige slid a sideways glance to Zach. It wasn't completely unheard of for parents to support and cover up the horrid actions of their children, even when it involved murder, but this woman had taken things one step further. She not only hid her child's actions from the world but she facilitated them.

"How long has he been *gifted*?" Paige thought it best to proceed with the woman's terminology and caught a glimpse of a silver cross on a chain on the bedside table.

Patty smiled at her. "All his life." Her gaze drifted to a spot in the back of the room. "I'm so proud of you."

Paige looked over her shoulder, then back to Patty.

"That's right," the woman said. "He's here now. He's crossed over directly to heaven."

Paige didn't know much about Mayan culture beyond what she'd learned during this investigation, but she found it hard to believe that a people who had such a respect for death would go straight to heaven if they'd committed suicide. And if that was the case, it led to another question...

"If he knew he would go straight to heaven," Paige began, "why didn't he kill himself before now?"

"Divine timing, dear."

Chills swept through Paige, leaving goose bumps in their wake.

"And he had a gift to share," Patty went on. "To help others cross over."

"He killed out of love," Zach interjected.

"Yes, that's right." She gave another smile that had Paige squirming from head to toe.

"Why did you involve Stanley in this?" Paige asked.

"What do you mean *in this*? Stanley was Joshua's father."

"I mean, covering up the murders and abducting innocent men."

Patty laughed. "Innocent? We are all imperfect. We all sin. In the heavens, there is nothing but perfection and bliss."

"Why didn't you abduct men for Joshua to sacrifice?" Paige inquired.

"Oh, no, that was not my role." Patty shook her head. "I didn't get directly involved."

"You are directly involved," Paige ground out. "You are an accomplice for murder many times over."

Patty was smiling at that space behind them again. And to think that her mental health was apparently sound. At least from a medical diagnosis standpoint, that was.

"We know that Wayne Reed helped you, too," Paige added.

"Yes. He is a good but weak man."

She didn't even deny it…

"He kept your family secret after the divorce," Zach said.

Patty looked at him. "Of course he did."

"Is he still involved?" Paige blurted out.

Patty wouldn't look at her but kept smiling at the empty corner of the room.

Maybe if Paige approached it from another standpoint, picked on the one thing Patty loved more than anything. "Wayne said that Joshua should be locked up, that he has screws loose."

For the first time since they'd entered the room,

Patty's face fell into a scowl. "You're lying."

"No, I'm not." Paige gestured to Zach.

"I heard it, too. He also said Joshua should have been on meds," Zach added with a head bob.

"That piece of shit. Fine, yes, he's in on all this. He lets Stanley use his van, he gets the sedatives we need, and he makes up the blue paint." The smile returned.

Wayne Reed had said that Stanley got lime mortar from him. Probably to throw the investigation off himself.

"We need to find him," Paige said.

"How nice for you."

"Can you help us?"

"Why would I?" Patty asked. "He is still family to me."

"You just threw Wayne under the bus."

"Nah, you have to prove all that I said." This woman was batty.

"He's the one who led us to you and your son."

"No!" Patty screamed and ripped out her IV.

Machines started beeping.

Patty was crying hysterically and slamming her fists into the mattress at her sides, the metal of the cuffs clanging against the bedframe. The chain with the cross fell to the floor.

Paige picked up the necklace and was going to put it back on the table when her fingers dipped into an engraving on the back. She turned it over.

Two nurses ran into the room and worked to sedate Patty.

"You're going to have to leave," one of the nurses told Paige and Zach.

Paige backed out of their way, not looking up, but kept her eyes on the inscription on the cross: *To my sweet Esther.*

In the hall, she shared the find with Zach. "We've got to get a hold of Jack."

CHAPTER

48

I'D GONE A FEW ROUNDS with Stanley Gilbert and wasn't getting a confession beyond the abductions. Jack and I were in the observation room when Paige came rushing in, Zach behind her.

"We think Joshua murdered Esther Pearson." She dangled a necklace from her hands. "There's an engraving on the back that says, *To my sweet Esther.*"

"But Esther Pearson was murdered ten years ago," I said.

Zach was nodding. "That's right. Joshua would have been thirteen."

"Mommy Dearest moved him to Savannah around that time." Paige was practically breathless now.

"Maybe Joshua had killed Esther and she was running to protect her son." There was such a thing as an unhealthy bond between parents and children, but this case was a good example of just how wrong things could go in that regard.

"Investigators might find the bones from Esther's

hands and feet on the Haven property. But that isn't all we have… You want to share, Zach?"

"Sure," he said. "Patty told us everything that Wayne Reed did to help Joshua. She went so far as to say he was in on all of it. She specifically mentioned letting Stanley use his van, sourcing the sedatives, and he makes the blue paint. How did you make out with—" Zach gestured to Stanley through the one-way glass.

"Not that well," I said.

Pike stormed into the observation room. "Two things." He glanced at Zach. "One, techs got into that laptop and found something you'll want to see, but there is something more important to attend to right now. Plainclothes officers have found Reed. He's at the Savannah train station."

We were all on the move behind him.

"Have them stand back. We don't need to spook him," Jack directed.

Pike nodded. "More than happy to give you the lead."

THERE WERE VEHICLES IN THE parking lot of the Savannah train station, but none of them were Reed's Corolla. He must have parked it somewhere and took public transit to get here. Since we expected that Reed would be armed, his being in a public place—especially one with so few security measures—carried the risk of civilian casualties, despite our best efforts to avoid them.

"Officer Mullen confirmed that Reed bought a

ticket." Pike's voice dropped lower. "And that train's expected any minute now. I have plainclothes officers clearing out civilians as quietly and as inconspicuously as possible. I'm also having an officer make sure the train doesn't allow its passengers to disembark until we get this under control."

Jack started walking toward the building, Pike keeping pace next to him and the rest of us trailing slightly behind.

We were about fifteen feet from the front doors when Jack asked, "Do we know exactly where Reed is inside?"

"He's at the doors for the loading platform," Pike responded.

"No doubt anxious to get out of here," I said.

Pike glanced at me. "He's wearing a blue baseball cap."

First ditching his Corolla and second an attempt at a disguise—a poor one, too, because it gave us something to look for.

The sound of a train horn blared through the station. We were running out of time.

Jack stopped about five feet from the doors and addressed Paige and Zach. "You guys go around back to the platform. We'll go in the front."

Paige and Zach ran off to follow Jack's directions, and Jack, Pike, and I went in the front doors. If Reed spotted us—and that would be easy enough to do given the three-inch-high acronyms on our vests— he'd either make a run for it or fight. My gut told me that, if cornered, he'd opt for the latter. I just hoped that Jack was more prepared now than he had been at the Havens'.

Civilians were moving past us to head out the front door. The officers were doing a great job keeping them calm and moving, silencing the mob mentality and the inclination to panic when law enforcement took over.

None of us had our guns drawn yet, but we were ready to do so at the slightest sign of provocation. The difference between life and death was often the fraction of a second, and we had to make every moment count.

Jack's episode at the Havens' struck me with intensity, and my hands became clammy. If Paige hadn't stepped in…

"I see him," I said. "Straight ahead."

At the back of the station facing the tracks was a wall of glass, and people were unloading from the stopped train.

"I thought your officers had it under control," Jack snarled as we all started into a jog.

People were coming through the doors next to where Reed was standing by himself. The officers must have managed to clear the other people waiting for the same train, but we were left with another problem. Reed was getting harder to keep an eye on, and there was more potential for causalities.

An announcement came over the loudspeakers. "Train seventy-seven is now boarding on track one."

"We can't let him get on!" Jack was in a full run

now, and so was I.

Pike was hurrying off in the direction of the front desk. He had to get the doors to the train closed.

Reed looked over his shoulder before stepping through the door to the platform and spotted us.

"He's coming through the back," Jack said over the comms to Paige and Zach. "Get him."

We kept running, the intention being to direct the rabbit right into the trap. But Reed had his own game in mind. He grabbed a woman by the arm and yanked her against his chest. He put a gun to her temple.

"Stand down. Hostage situation," Jack communicated.

Paige and Zach were just outside the glass. Reed spotted them and started working his way back inside the station. There was nowhere else for him to go. The train doors were now closed.

Civilians were scurrying around now, screaming and pushing to the front, but they were like a tidal wave that rushed over us and then was gone, leaving silence and a feeling of devastation.

Pike was back, and he and the plainclothes officers, Jack, Paige, Zach, and I all had our guns trained on Reed.

"Let her go," Jack told him.

"You come near me and I'll shoot her, I swear!" Sweat was beading on Reed's forehead, and he was sniffling.

"Let her go, and we can talk," Jack said.

"If I let her go, you'll shoot me!"

"She has nothing to do with this. Look at her. She's terrified."

The thirtysomething woman was trim and swallowed by Reed's six-foot frame and barrel chest. Tears were streaming down her bright-red cheeks and her chest was heaving. She looked like she was on the verge of having a panic attack or possibly something worse.

I glanced at Jack and blinked deliberately to let him know that I was going to move in. I took a few slow steps toward Reed. My gun was still drawn but not at the ready. It was time to become his ally. "Come on, Wayne. I know you don't want to go prison. Help us figure some things out."

Reed's eyes were bulging, and the woman was heaving for breath.

"Pl….ease." She struggled to get out a single word.

I looked at her and hoped that she received my silent promise. I would get her out of this.

"Wayne, I'm going to put my weapon away," I said.

"What the hell are you doing?" Jack's voice came through my earpiece.

I holstered my weapon and put both my hands up. "See? I'm unarmed. Just let her go."

Reed's eyes darted to all the other guns trained on him, ready to take the shot when they had the perfect alignment. But Reed kept the woman's head in front of his own, only peeking around it. Taking a shot was too risky.

"Lower your weapons," I said, directing the

comment through the comms while keeping my gaze on Reed.

Reed's shoulders relaxed. My colleagues had followed my direction.

"Now, let her go," I said.

"What's to say you still won't shoot me?"

"You have my word." I took a few more steps toward him. Adrenaline was helping me focus, keeping my heart rate calm.

"Please," the woman cried, turning her head the little bit she could to see Reed behind her.

"She's not involved in this," I reminded him, pushing yet dancing the tightrope.

Reed lowered the gun, and he released the woman. She took two steps and fell to the floor.

Crap!

She needed to move. Now.

I held up one hand to him and wormed in closer. I extended a hand to the woman while splitting my attention between her and Reed.

The woman was on one knee now, her other leg bent to get up. There was a flicker in Reed's eyes, and he raised his gun. It was aimed at me.

I let the woman go and reached for my holster.

The bullet hit him between the eyes, and he crashed to the floor. But I hadn't yet pulled the trigger.

I turned and saw smoke coming from Jack's gun, and he was hurrying toward me.

I let myself slide to the floor beside the woman. I'd almost died twice today.

I needed a big fucking drink.

Jack towered over me. "What's this, sitting down on the job?"

I glared up at him. "Just glad you found the courage to pull the trigger."

He smirked and held out his hand for me to take. I got to my feet and looked at my boss. Oh yeah, he was messed up, just like I was. Like we all were, really, in one way or another. But he had come through for me. He had saved my life, and for that, I owed him. Scratch that, I owed Jack a lot more than that. For a man who had rubbed me so wrong at the beginning, a drill sergeant who expected nothing but perfection from his team, he had become a mentor and friend.

"Thanks," I said.

He smiled and patted me on the back. "Anytime, Kid."

For some reason, hearing him call me *kid* now didn't feel like salt on a wound the way it normally did. I actually sensed some respect and affection for me in there. Guess I'd worked my magic on him over the last couple of years, too.

CHAPTER

49

WE'D SOLVED THE CASE, and some lab results hadn't even made it back to us, including the evidence sent to the private laboratory. That ought to please the higher-ups. But the findings would likely strengthen our case when they did come through. Although, if any of it pointed to Joshua Haven, well, he'd already paid the ultimate price.

At least we'd stopped the bad guys, but it would still be awhile yet before all the victims' families would get closure. But at least it was in progress.

Wayne Reed's photo had been shown to Tanya Lewis by local law enforcement, and she'd recognized him. So much for Wayne just taking an active role years in the past. Elijah had been taken three months ago. His body was yet to be identified, but I had a feeling that it was just a matter of time before either the X-rays or DNA confirmed that he was among the remains.

It turned out that Stanley had pictures on his laptop of Esther Pearson's body, and they looked eerily familiar to the crime scene photos. That meant one thing: whoever had taken the pictures had either killed her or watched. And while we'd pegged a thirteen-year-old Joshua as the killer, we might never really know for sure. People lied all the time. Maybe Stanley knew about Joshua longer than he'd claimed to, maybe he was involved in the actual torture and murder. The problem with being human and not a greater being was that all we had to go by was the evidence. Not to say that Stanley wouldn't be tried for Esther's murder, but he could always claim the photos had been sent to him by someone else. Hopefully, justice would prevail regardless.

We also found out where Patty had gotten all her money and it wasn't a pretty discovery. Her father, who was a powerful man and senator, had abused Patty most of her life and when she had Joshua, he'd taken liberties with his grandson. Patty must have threatened to expose her father because there was a large sum of money put into her bank account just before she'd moved to Savannah and regular amounts were deposited every other month.

The team was clearing out the conference room at the precinct when Lieutenant Pike and another man came in.

"I just wanted to say hello and introduce myself," the man said. "I'm Detective Hawkins."

This was the detective who we'd only met through the initial investigative reports. He was also the one who had recently lost his unborn child. I was the first to hold out my hand to him. "I'm Brandon

Fisher." I wanted to speak words of sympathy, but something wouldn't let me. I hoped he received the unspoken message, though.

The rest of the team introduced themselves to him, as well.

"Sorry for your loss, Detective," Paige said.

Hawkins's eyes glazed over. "I appreciate it."

"Paige, I want to give you an update on the missing kid, Colin West," Pike said. "The case has been reopened."

She grinned. "Good news to go home with. I hope you find out what happened to him."

"Well, we'll do our best."

I was listening to their conversation, but my gaze kept drifting back to Hawkins. The pain coming from him was palpable, and I remembered that feeling all too well. Old memories churned to the forefront, and I excused myself, stepped out into the hall, and headed for the bullpen.

I was alone again. Or at least I would be when I got home. An empty house and an empty love life. But I didn't want a love life. I didn't deserve one. I had a career I loved, and I made a difference by doing the job. That was more than some people ever got. Sulking over a ruined marriage and child I'd lost years ago didn't serve any purpose. And what would have happened to him or her now that Deb and I had divorced? I was on the road so much I'd have been a horrible father, just as I had been a crappy husband and a bad boyfriend.

"Hey, are you all right?" It was Paige.

I'd been so deep in thought, I hadn't realized that I was standing in front of the coffeemaker until I'd heard her voice. I turned to her. "Hey."

She plucked a couple of disposable cups from the stack and filled them with coffee. "You still like it black with two sugars?"

"I do."

God, she was so beautiful. Why did life have to be so complicated? Why did I have to be so complicated? But I couldn't just admit to loving her and let a relationship grow between us. First, I couldn't commit, and second, the job deserved our undivided attention.

She tore open two sugar packets, added them to one cup, and handed it to me. "Oh, you'll want this." She handed me a stirrer.

"Thanks, Paige."

"Don't mention it." She licked the leftover sugar from her fingers and took a sip of her black coffee. "Blegh. This stuff is—"

"Caffeine," I said. I was too tired to care about the delivery system.

She laughed. "Yes, it is that."

The sound of her laughter was sweet to my ears. But I had to let all my feelings for her go. It wouldn't work for so many reasons, and we'd revisited those reasons too many times since I'd come on board with the BAU just over two years ago. Not that it would matter if we left our jobs now anyway because Paige was in a relationship with another man.

"You never answered my question," she said.

I'd forgotten she'd asked one. "Which was?"

"How are you doing?"

"Right." I smiled. "I'm fine."

She put her hand on my arm. "It's me you're talking to."

I stopped all movement, my gaze tracing up her arm, to her face, to her eyes. The ones that were so familiar and full of love for me. I took a deep, heaving breath. "Like I said, I'm fine. I broke up with Becky." The last sentence had just come out, and I had no idea why. And had I broken up with her or was it the other way around? I couldn't remember now.

"Oh. I'm sorry to hear that." She sounded sincere, but I also detected a wisp of hope in her voice. But maybe that was my imagination.

"No, it's fine. It wasn't going to last anyway."

Her eyes narrowed slightly. "Right, because you can't commit to a relationship," she said in a light, teasing manner.

"You got my number." I winked at her. "Speaking of relationships, how are things with Sam?"

She laughed. "You really want to know?"

I bobbed my head side to side and grinned. "I wouldn't have asked otherwise."

"Right. You don't even care for the guy."

"That's putting it nicely."

Since you called me out, I may as well be honest.

"Hey." She smirked and pointed a finger at me.

"I'm telling the truth now, and I get penalized for it?" I smiled at her.

Her mouth fell in a straight line. "Honestly, I'm

not sure if it's going to last, either. He's pretty mad at me because our Valentine's Day plans were canceled. We haven't talked since Tuesday."

"He's such a girl."

She narrowed her eyes at me again. "You know me, though. I've never had a serious relationship before. Maybe I give up on them too easily."

I nodded. She normally kept her affairs brief and never gave her heart away. I had been an exception she'd wanted to make.

"Sam wasn't happy that I was here and not back home," she continued. "He was going to fly out to Virginia and spend Valentine's Day with me."

"Aw, how cute." I was trying here. I really was.

She shoved my arm. "Okay, now you're making me sick."

I laughed and wished I could just wrap my arm around her and pull her to me. She had a way of making me feel calm and complete.

Paige's eyes went serious. "Are you going to make up with Becky?"

"Am I?" Her question had me taking pause. "I don't think so."

"Why not?"

"Are you making up with Sam?" I tossed back.

She shrugged. "We'll see."

"You're considering it? You're a better person than me, then." Of course, I'd known that much about Paige for a long time.

"I hardly think that."

"Becky couldn't accept that I missed out on our

plans because of this investigation. But she knows what I do for a living. If she can't accept that, then—"

"Why bother?" she interjected.

"Yeah."

"I thought you two got along quite well, though."

"We do. Even outside the bedroom." I added the latter with a smile to try to lighten the conversation, to protect my emotions.

"In that case, maybe it's worth trying to save. At least I think so. Did you call her before you left town?"

I shook my head. "Nope."

"Ah. Same for me. I forgot to let Sam know until we were already here."

"I didn't remember at all until she'd left three voice mails for me."

Paige grimaced. "Oh."

"Yeah, and she wasn't too happy when we finally did connect."

"Did you really expect she would be?"

"Kind of."

"So you expect her to drop things for you and understand? But don't you realize that you're coming across to her like you don't think about or consider her? To make matters worse, it was one of the most romantic evenings of the year. You should be begging her to forgive you." She laughed off her last sentence, but I could tell she was being serious.

"What's so funny?" Jack asked as he walked up with Zach.

"Long story." Not that I'd found what Paige had

said funny—at all—but it had me thinking.

Jack put a hand on my shoulder. "Good thing we got a long flight home, then, isn't it, Kid?"

The three of them were smiling at me, and eventually, I returned it.

Maybe all wasn't lost in the romance department. Or even in the game of life, for that matter.

CHAPTER

50

The government jet landed in Virginia a little before midnight, and the cool temperature hit me immediately. I shrugged into my coat and said my good-byes to the team. I could head straight home, but there was something I needed to do first, even if it meant making a small drive.

The porch light came on and shone right in my eyes. I held up a hand to block it. The door cracked open and then it flung out wide.

"What are you doing here?" Becky's arms were crossed, and she was wearing a robe that covered her pajamas.

Maybe my coming here was a mistake. Just thinking that made my feet shuffle back.

She sighed. "You woke me up, Brandon. What is it?"

It was time to speak up, to lay it all out there. What exactly was I laying out there, though? God, the last time I'd laid it all out there, it had ended with my wife filing for divorce.

"The case I was working on in Savannah, it's closed now." My words dissipated into white puffs of fog.

"Good for you." Her steely gaze was hardened on me.

"Listen." I took a step toward her and put my hand on her elbow. "You've got to be freezing. Let's—"

"I'm fine, Brandon." She pulled away from me. "Talk."

I swallowed. "I missed you. I'm sorry I messed up Valentine's Day."

She didn't say anything. She just stood there looking at me.

"Please say something." I barely managed to get the sentence out. I'd put my heart out there— Or had I? Friends can miss other friends, right? But Becky was more to me than a friend. Or at least I hoped she would be.

I took a deep breath. "I've been doing a lot of thinking and—"

"I have been, too, Brandon." She blinked slowly and turned away. "I think we made the right decision. You don't want anything serious. I kind of do." The pain in her eyes when they met mine cut at my heart.

"I guess I messed up a lot more than one day."

Forget disappointment, heartbreak was definitely creeping in. But if my job taught me anything, it was that life was short and it certainly didn't always go the way we'd planned. But there are times when we have a say, when we can make a choice to stand up for what we believe in, when we can decide to take what we want or forever regret it.

"I love you, Becky." The words came out, and instantly I felt my bachelorhood slipping away, but it was too late to reel them back in. Besides, I didn't want to.

Becky was just looking at me, her eyes scanning mine.

"Please...say something."

Her eyes filled with tears, and she licked her lips.

"I know I've told you before that I don't want anything serious, that I just want to keep this—us—casual. But that's not the truth anymore. I missed you this week, Becky, and not like I would miss a pet or a friend."

"Okay..." She gave me a small smirk.

Progress.

"I missed you because you've started to become a part of me," I went on. "We are good together. I should have called you before I left town."

She didn't say anything for a few more seconds, and then she threw her arms around me. I hugged her tightly until she broke from the embrace.

"Are you sure this is what you want?" she asked. "For us to be dating officially?"

"Exclusive, actually." I wasn't seeing anyone else anyhow, and the truth was, I didn't need anyone but Becky.

Her eyes widened. "Wow. Exclusive? Who are

you?" She squinted. "Am I dreaming?"

"I don't know. If you were dreaming, would you feel this?" I captured her mouth with mine and backed her into the house, closing the door behind us. I would take her upstairs and make love to her because she was the one who made things all right, even when they weren't. She was the one who helped wash away the horrible things I'd witnessed and gave everything in my life more purpose.

ACKNOWLEDGMENTS

A lot of people have helped me along my writing journey. My husband, George, has been a rock and strong supporter from the beginning. He believes in me, and I have fun talking "murder" with him. I thank him for always being there and can't imagine life without him by my side.

I also thank my contacts in law enforcement for their selfless devotion to helping me get the police procedure and forensics right. Whether you've been following my work, or this book is the first of mine you've read, this is of great importance to me, and I am forever grateful.

A special thank-you goes out to Yvonne Bradley, who served as a forensic consultant for me on this book, and tirelessly answered my many questions and shared her expertise.

I'd also be remiss not to mention my editor, Danielle Poiesz, and her team, whose commitment to excellence and unwavering dedication has helped me to not only polish this book but has pushed me to grow in the craft.

Catch the next book in the Brandon Fisher FBI series!

Sign up at the weblink listed below
to be notified when new Brandon Fisher titles are
available for pre-order:

CarolynArnold.net/BFupdates

By joining this newsletter, you will also receive
exclusive first looks at the following:

Updates pertaining to upcoming releases in the
series, such as cover reveals, book descriptions,
and firm release dates

Sneak peeks of teasers and special content

Behind-the-Tape™ insights that give you an inside
look at Carolyn's research and creative process

Read on for an exciting preview
of Carolyn Arnold's exciting action
adventure series featuring Matthew
Connor

City of Gold

REPUBLIC OF INDIA

THE SOUND OF HIS THUMPING heartbeat was only dulled by the screeching monkeys that were performing aerial acrobatics in the tree canopy overhead. Their rhythmic swinging from one vine to the next urged his steps forward but not with the same convincing nature as did the bullets whizzing by his head.

Matthew glanced behind at his friends and was nearly met with a bullet between the eyes. He crouched low, an arm instinctively shooting up as if he'd drop faster with it atop his head. The round of shots hit a nearby tree, and splintering bark rained down on him.

"Hurry!" he called out, as he peered at his companions.

"What do you think we're—" Cal lost his footing, tripping over an extended root, his arms flailing as he tried to regain his balance.

Robyn, who was a few steps ahead of Cal, held out a hand, her pace slowing as she helped steady him.

"Pick it up, Garcia!" Matthew didn't miss her

glare before he turned back around. He hurdled through the rainforest, leaping over some branches while dipping under others, parting dangling vines as he went, as if they were beaded curtains.

His lungs burned, and his muscles were on fire. One quick glance up, and the monkeys spurred him on again. Not that he needed more than the cries of the men who were chasing him. The voices were getting louder, too—growing closer.

Robyn caught up to Matthew. "What happened to natives with poison darts?"

"The modern-day savage packs an AK-47 and body armor."

Several reports sounded. Another burst of ammunition splayed around them.

"If we get out of this alive, you owe me a drink." Her smile oddly contrasted their situation.

"I'll buy you each two," Matthew promised.

Cal ran, holding the GPS out in front of him, his arm swaying up and down, and Matthew wasn't sure how he read it with the motion.

"Where do you expect to take us, Cal? We're in the middle of a damn jungle," Robyn said.

"Round here. Go right," Cal shouted.

Another deafening shot rang out and came close to hitting Matthew.

"You don't have to tell me twice." Matthew ramped up his speed, self-preservation at the top of his list while the idol secured in his backpack slipped down in priority.

Most of their pursuers were yelling in Hindi, but

one voice came through in English. He was clearly the one giving directions, and from his accent, Matthew guessed he was American, possibly from one of the northern states.

"I have to stop…and…breathe." Robyn held a hand to her chest.

"We stop and we're dead. Keep moving." Cal reached for her arm and yanked.

Matthew slowed his pace slightly. "Robyn, you could always get on Cal's back."

"What?" Cal lowered the arm that was holding the GPS.

She angled her head toward Matthew. "If you think I'm going to get up there like some child, you are sorely mistaken."

Matthew laughed but stopped abruptly, his body following suit and coming to a quick halt. He was teetering on the edge of a cliff that was several stories high, looking straight down into a violent pool of rushing water. He lifted his gaze to an upstream waterfall that fed into the basin.

Cal caught Matthew's backpack just in time and pulled him back to solid ground.

The rush of adrenaline made Matthew dizzy. He bent over, braced his hands on his knees, and tucked his head between his legs. He'd just come way too close to never reaching his twenty-ninth birthday.

Robyn punched Cal in the shoulder. "Go right, eh? Good directions, wiseass. Maybe next time we'll just keep going straight."

"Sure, blame the black guy," Cal said.

More bullets fired over the empty space of the gorge.

"What do we do now?" Cal asked.

Matthew forced himself to straighten to a stand. He hadn't brought them all the way here to die. He'd come to retrieve a priceless artifact, and by all means, it was going to get back to Canada. He pulled off his sack, quickly assessed the condition of the zippers, and shrugged it back on. He tightened the straps, looking quickly at Cal and then at Robyn. One stood to each side of him. He had to act before he lost the courage. He put his arms out behind them.

Robyn's eyes widened. "What are you doing, Matt? You can't honestly be thinking of—"

Matthew wasn't a religious man, but he was praying for them on the way down.

CHAPTER

1

TORONTO, CANADA
ONE MONTH LATER…

DRENCHED IN SWEAT, CAL MYERS gripped the sheets and bolted upright, his body heaving, his lungs hungry for oxygen. The scream that had woken him was his own.

"Cal?" Sophie's hand touched his shoulder, and he sprang out of the bed. She rolled over to face him. "Another nightmare?"

That was one way of putting it. He'd been running and dodging bullets one minute, and the next thing he knew, the ground had disappeared from under him and he was falling, falling, falling. Just when it had seemed bottomless, there was the raging river with its white caps and jagged rocks dotting its surface.

"Maybe you should take a break from all these adventures." Her words were soft, thoughtful.

His gaze met hers. Sophie Jones was his girlfriend of five years. Given their similar personalities and restless natures, it was hard to believe they'd managed to stay monogamous for that long. They had yet to commit to living together or the big M-word, but she grounded him—her words, not his—and she was the one who gave his life any semblance of normalcy. Besides their long-term relationship, nothing else fit within the confines of an ordinary existence. He blamed—and thanked— Matthew Connor for that.

Sophie patted the mattress. "Come back to bed, baby."

The alarm clock on the dresser read 5:15. He had no reason to be up this early, but getting back to sleep was going to be impossible. His imagination would only continue to replay the dream.

"You went through a lot in India," she said. "I'm sure that Matthew would understand if you took some time off."

He refused to acknowledge her line of reasoning. Before Matthew, his life had been anything but exciting. While it was true that Cal had explored the world, writing travel pieces and photographing some of the most popular landmarks didn't hold a flame to treasure hunting and being shot at and— What was wrong with him? Why did he crave the element of danger? It wasn't healthy. If anything, his recurring nightmare confirmed that. Some time off might do him good.

He slipped back into bed, and Sophie snuggled against him. She traced her fingertips over his chest, her touch working to dull the flashbacks.

"Was it the same dream you've been having lately?"

He swallowed, trying to keep the calm she was compelling him toward. "Yeah, the one where the ground just disappears."

"I didn't think the ground disappeared from under you in India," she teased gently.

She was trying to make him smile, even for a second, and he loved her for that, but he didn't want to remember what had truly happened. Was it possible he had a touch of PTSD?

"Close enough," he said. "I still can't believe he pushed us over the edge like that."

She reached for his hand and gave it a small squeeze. "But all of you survived and you're fine."

"If you consider constantly having vivid flashbacks and nightmares *fine*."

"They will pass in time."

He exhaled loudly. "It's almost been a month."

"Hardly enough time to recoup from an experience like that."

"You make it all sound so positive."

Sophie laughed and flicked his nipple.

"Hey!" He squeezed her hand and then rubbed where her nimble fingertip had grazed.

"It's your life, you know," she said, becoming serious again. "It's up to you what you do with it."

Cal thought back on his life before Matthew. He had survived on a paycheck-to-paycheck basis and was deep in debt with student loans. He couldn't afford a car and he'd lived in a low-rent building where the landlord tracked the comings and goings of any visitors he had.

In addition to material freedom, Matthew provided Cal with adventure and satisfied his lust for action. It was more stimulating not knowing what each day had in store. If given the option between a calm and peaceful existence and a fight for survival laced with adrenaline, his choice would easily be the latter.

He glanced at the clock again: 5:20.

"I'm getting up, babe." He kissed her forehead and maneuvered his arm out from under her.

Sophie let out a moan. "It's so early."

"Yes, but *you* can go back to sleep."

"What are you going to do?"

"Don't worry about me."

Sophie sat up, putting her back against the headboard. "That's the problem. I do." Her face contorted in a way he was very familiar with. Her left eyebrow was jacked up, and her eyes held a deep intensity. If that wasn't enough to give away her agitation, she tousled her short, dark dreads before crossing her arms.

"There's nothing to worry about. You just said I'm fine."

"I was trying to make you feel better, but people were shooting at you and you jumped off a cliff—"

"I was actually push—"

"There you go," she interrupted as she unfolded her arms and kneaded the comforter. "Either way, things are out of your control when you…" She rolled her hand, searching for the right words.

He knew what she was doing because she didn't like the term *treasure hunting* and did her best to avoid it. Even the Indiana Jones movies were not her thing, and while she supported Cal in his "outings" or "adventures," she far from encouraged them.

"Gather historic objects," she finally said. "I know it makes you happy, for the most part anyway. I just don't like seeing you having nightmares and waking up in the wee hours."

It was his turn to laugh. "Wee hours? I would think that applies to two or three or—"

"You're missing the point." She threw the comforter off her and got out of bed, then gathered her clothes from the floor and tossed them onto the mattress.

"And what point is that?" They rarely fought, but when they did, they tended to revolve around his expeditions and treasure hunting.

She pulled her sweater over her head. "You might be in danger, you know. What if the men from India tracked you back to Toronto? They could know where you live."

He raised an eyebrow at her. "Now you sound like you've been watching too many movies."

"Do I?" She plucked her skirt from the bed and pulled it on.

Faced with the direct, two-worded question, his inclination was to back down. It was packed with fervor, and paired with her tone, it had the potential to set the room ablaze.

"Even Matthew operates under an alias," she continued. "If it's not because of risk, then why would he do that?"

"You know why."

"Uh-huh. His father, the mayor? You're still buying that? He's a twenty-eight-year-old man who can't be straightforward enough with his own father to let him know what he does for a living. Although I'm not sure how much of a living it provides when you put your lives at stake to do it."

"Why are you being like this?" It wasn't like they were married, or even living together for that matter. She had no right to tell him how to live his life. No one had permission to do that.

"Are you sure you want to know?" she snapped.

"I asked, didn't I?" He put his hands on his hips and realized he was standing there in his boxers. The lack of clothing somehow seemed to take away his power. He put on the pair of jeans that had been lying at his feet.

"All right, well, here it is. And so help me God, if you snicker or make fun of what I'm about to say, it's over, Cal. Do you hear me?"

And they were back to this. While he liked to believe that what they had was the real deal, whenever it came to verbal blows, her strike was always an uppercut to the jaw. She always pulled out the "I guess we're over" and "We had a good run" crap. At least they didn't fight often.

"Do you promise?" Her question was accompanied by a glare.

"I promise."

"I feel like someone's watching us."

He had made a promise not to jest about what she had to say. Hearing her voice her fear made him want to scoff, though. Was she serious?

He cleared his throat. "Why do you think that?"

"Don't patronize me, Cal Myers." She pointed a finger at him. "I see it written all over your face."

"Come on, baby. I just didn't expect you to say that, that's all." He found his legs taking him to her now. He reached for her arm, but she pulled it out of reach.

"Have you been listening to me at all? And you promised not to make fun of what I was going to say."

He held up his hands. "I'm not making fun. I swear."

She tilted her head to the left and studied his face. "Fine. You gonna listen?"

He nodded. The option was either that or hitting up a florist at some point during the day. Hell, he might end up doing that anyway.

"When we were out last night, I kept seeing this one guy. Whenever I'd look in his direction, he'd turn away really quickly."

Cal sensed her energy and saw it in the softness her features took on and in the way her eyes changed. She was afraid.

"You have nothing to worry about." He attempted to touch her again. This time she allowed it.

"Can you promise that? Because I don't think you

can. I didn't like the way this guy looked."

"And how was that?"

She gazed into his eyes. "Like Liam Neeson."

"Liam Neeson?"

"Yeah, you know, the actor? *Taken, Clash of the Titans, The A-Team*?"

He dismissed her with a wave. "I know who he is. I would like to know what you have against him." Her face fell, and he felt like a heel for causing that reaction. "I'm sorry. It's just I've been hunting treasure for two years now. I'm still alive. I'm not going to lie and say that it's the safest profession."

"If you did, I wouldn't buy it anyway."

"So? Liam? What made you suspicious of him?"

"You said that when you were in India, the person commanding all those men who were chasing you spoke English and was likely from North America."

Now he regretted having said anything to her about the trip. "Yeah, but that could describe a lot of people, Sophie."

"I'll give you that. It's just… What if he tracked you down? I don't want you to go tonight."

Tonight was the exhibit opening and gala to celebrate the Pandu statue they had recovered in India. He wanted to be there. He couldn't believe she was asking him to sit it out. "You what?"

"It's just that… I don't think you should go. Something's going to happen."

"And you're psychic now?" He put up with her feelings, her hunches, her suspicions, but if she was starting to foresee the future, it might be time to give her the "We had a good run" speech himself. And mean it.

She shook her head. "Of course not."

He let out the breath he had been holding. He'd grown accustomed to having her around.

"I just *know* that he was watching us and trying to act as if he wasn't," she went on. "I can feel it. He left the restaurant at the same time we did. When we were waiting at the curb for the valet to bring your car around, he was standing there and he lit up a cigarette." She stopped talking, but he sensed there was more.

"And?" he prodded.

"When we were pulling away, I saw him get into a black SUV."

The laugh erupted on its own.

She narrowed her eyes at him, and he could almost feel the daggers landing in his skin. "That's it, I'm outta here," she clipped. "I have a busy day ahead of me. Houses don't sell themselves."

He reached for her hand, but she swatted him away and kept moving.

"Babe, are you sure you haven't watched too many movies?" he called after her.

"Shove it, Cal."

The door slammed behind her.

Cal wanted to punch a wall. His fist was balled and ready, but somehow, he had mustered the control not to go through with it. Self-preservation, maybe. Instead, he drew back the blind and watched her drive off. He was about to retreat from the window when he saw a dark-colored Escalade parked on the other side of the street. And a man was silhouetted behind the wheel.

Also available from
International Bestselling Author
Carolyn Arnold

CITY OF GOLD
Book 1 in the Matthew Connor Adventure Series

Finding the Inca's lost City of Gold would be the discovery of a lifetime. But failing could mean her death...

Archaeologist Matthew Connor and his friends Cal and Robyn are finally home after a dangerous retrieval expedition in India. While they succeeded in obtaining the priceless Pandu artifact they sought, it almost cost them their lives. Still, Matthew is ready for the next adventure. Yet when new intel surfaces indicating the possible location of the legendary City of Gold, Matthew is hesitant to embark on the quest.

Not only is the evidence questionable but it means looking for the lost city of Paititi far away from where other explorers have concentrated their efforts. As appealing as making the discovery would be, it's just too risky. But when Cal's girlfriend, Sophie, is abducted by Matthew's old nemesis who is dead-set on acquiring the Pandu statue, Matthew may be forced into action. Saving Sophie's life means either breaking into the Royal Ontario Museum to steal the relic or offering up something no one in his or her right mind can refuse—the City of Gold.

Now Matthew and his two closest friends have to find a city and a treasure that have been lost for centuries. And they only have seven days to do it. As they race against the clock, they quickly discover that the streets they seek aren't actually paved with gold, but with blood.

Available from popular book retailers or at CarolynArnold.net

CAROLYN ARNOLD is an international bestselling and award-winning author, as well as a speaker, teacher, and inspirational mentor. She has four continuing fiction series—Detective Madison Knight, Brandon Fisher FBI, McKinley Mysteries, and Matthew Connor Adventures—and has written nearly thirty books. Her genre diversity offers her readers everything from cozy to hard-boiled mysteries, and thrillers to action adventures.

Both her female detective and FBI profiler series have been praised by those in law enforcement as being accurate and entertaining, leading her to adopt the trademark: POLICE PROCEDURALS RESPECTED BY LAW ENFORCEMENT™.

Carolyn was born in a small town and enjoys spending time outdoors, but she also loves the lights of a big city. Grounded by her roots and lifted by her dreams, her overactive imagination insists that she tell her stories. Her intention is to touch the hearts of millions with her books, to entertain, inspire, and empower.

She currently lives just west of Toronto with her husband and beagle and is a member of Crime Writers of Canada and Sisters in Crime.

CONNECT ONLINE
Carolynarnold.net
Facebook.com/AuthorCarolynArnold
Twitter.com/Carolyn_Arnold

And don't forget to sign up for her newsletter for up-to-date information on release and special offers at CarolynArnold.net/Newsletters.

CPSIA information can be obtained
at www.ICGtesting.com
Printed in the USA
BVHW031815060220
571668BV00001B/60